THE LOST SOUL

Gabriella Pierce

Canvas

Constable & Robinson Ltd
55–56 Russell Square
London WC1B 4HP
www.constablerobinson.com

First published in the US by William Morrow,
an imprint of HarperCollins Publishers US, New York, 2013

First published in the UK by Canvas,
an imprint of Constable & Robinson Ltd., 2013

A copy of the British Library Cataloguing in Publication
Data is available from the British Library

ISBN 978-1-78033-947-4 (paperback)
ISBN 978-1-78033-948-1 (ebook)

Printed and bound in the UK

1 3 5 7 9 10 8 6 4 2

Chapter One

HER FIRST THOUGHT was that the flame was beautiful. Brighter than bright against the dark, dusty air, it seemed like a living thing. Jane wanted to touch it, hold it in her hand, feel its intentions against her skin. But as she leaned forward, a dark, heavy shape beside her shifted, then jerked, then seemed to grow impossibly large. She didn't see the sharp, flashing hooves until one of them glanced across her side, knocking the wind out of her.

Billy? The gentle old horse, her only real friend in this cold, unwelcoming place, had become completely transformed by rage and fear. Air returned to her lungs

1

in a painful rush, and she let out a choked sob. Billy's eyes rolled toward her in panic and he shied again, twisting on his tether and lashing out angrily with his hooves at the wall behind him.

She opened her mouth to calm him down – animals had always listened to her better even than to their own masters – but then she realized what he saw. In the few seconds she had been dazed from his kick, her tongue of flame had blossomed into a small tree, and it was still growing. *Too fast. Far too fast.* It reached out to her with hungry hands, spitting a furious heat into the air of the barn. Somewhere behind its shower of sparks, Billy let out a frightened, high-pitched scream, and Jane felt a matching one tear its way out of her own throat. The far walls were catching fire, and she felt the skin on her legs redden and blister as the tendrils of flame crept across the rough planks of the floor.

There had been a door, she remembered dimly. She had come inside, out of the bald daylight and into the dark privacy of the barn to think about her secret. If she had walked in, couldn't she walk back out again? Jane shrank back from the pressing flames, her fingers scraping against the unfinished wood of the wall. She felt her way along it, ignoring the prickling in her fingers and palms as splinters detached and stuck to them. She could pull those out later, but she knew from her last home that fire gave no second chances. She heard a scream, low pitched, a man's, from deep inside the barn. Mr. Waller. Had he been milking the cows on the other side? She couldn't remember now. Faces danced before her in the shifting gold-and-red glow. Her new parents, her new sisters, her new start – as unreal now as if she had only ever dreamed it all.

Then her fingers found a beam of wood that stood out from the rest. She held her breath, her singed lungs straining in surprise. Beyond the beam was empty space. Closing her eyes, she thought the only prayer she knew and rolled her body forward. Cool, fresh air caressed her skin, though she could still feel the menacing oven of the barn breathing onto her neck.

Calloused hands grabbed her by the shoulder, and she blinked her eyes open, bleary from the soot stuck to their lashes. Mrs. Waller was staring down at her, her face contorted in rage. 'Where's John?' she shouted, gripping Jane's shirt collar and yanking her off the ground. 'Annette, you stupid thing, tell me – is he still inside?' Jane could sense more than see other people approaching from the house. 'Tom, check the other side; forget the horse and look for your father. Lucy, run next door and get help.' She turned back to Jane, her deep-set blue eyes boring into hers. She raised her hand, and it moved down in slow motion, knocking Jane onto the ground as it connected with her face. Hot fire shot through her cheek and seemed to settle inside her skull. 'Devil girl,' Mrs. Waller cried. 'We should have never taken you in. You may have just killed my husband.'

★ ★ ★

3

Jane's eyes flew open with a start. She blinked in confusion at the rectangle of orange light above her, struggling for a moment to remember who and where she was. Jane Boyle, her brain volunteered eventually. Lying in bed, staring up at the skylight, in the apartment off Washington Square Park.

Staring at the orange city haze, she felt a brief longing for the open sky in her dream, for a place where streetlights didn't crowd out the billions of stars. *But those places don't have Saks or Magnolia Bakery cupcakes, so . . .* They had painful histories and haunting secrets instead: hers, and Annette Doran's as well, if her recent nightmares were to be believed. Jane had been having these strange dreams ever since her showdown with Annette a week ago . . . dreams that seemed suspiciously like Annette's memories. But the dreams couldn't be real, could they?

Jane blinked the sleep out of her eyes and sat up in bed. Annette Doran had spent most of her life in the British foster-care system as Anne Locksley, an amnesiac who was plagued by mysterious fires. It wasn't until Jane had intervened that Annette learned she was actually the long-lost daughter of one of the richest families in New York . . . and the last in a long line of incredibly powerful witches. Jane had set out to reunite Annette with her mother, Lynne Doran, who also happened to be Jane's former mother-in-law – and her mortal enemy. Jane thought that by doing Lynne this service, she'd be safe from her magical wrath.

But Jane was horribly mistaken. By the time she learned

that Lynne's plans for her daughter were far more sinister than she could ever have imagined, Lynne had convinced the girl that Jane was the enemy. Annette had attacked before Jane could clear things up, her uncontrolled magic burning down the top three floors of the Dorans' Park Avenue mansion as she had burned down many buildings before.

Jane glanced up at the skylight; it was too early for signs of daylight, but she felt certain she wouldn't be able to fall asleep again before it really was morning. She swung her legs over the side of her bed, testing her balance on the edge of the white rug. Her right leg had been pinned under a billiard table during the struggle with Annette and still felt deeply sore. She poked at its bandage, trying to remember the last time she had applied a new poultice.

She eased herself out of bed and padded toward the kitchen, wishing Dee were here to whip up one of her signature breakfast spreads. The two friends had shared this apartment for a brief time, but Jane knew it wasn't safe for Dee to be around her right now. She'd insisted that Dee stay with the Montague witches, the closest thing Jane had to magical allies. Now she was completely alone in the apartment – and she was sick of hiding.

Coffee. A shower and a massive mug of coffee, she decided. It was a start. Next on the agenda was cornering Annette Doran, and making sure she knew just what type of witch her mother really was.

Chapter Two

SEVEN HOURS AND an unwise amount of caffeine later, Jane squinted resentfully at the pale spring sun. As far as she could tell it had gone from inching torturously toward its highest point to refusing to move at all, and her watch seemed equally reluctant to move. She lowered her eyes and pressed her oversized sunglasses more securely onto the bridge of her nose. The banded wooden doors of Park Avenue Presbyterian seemed to be smirking at her.

'Open,' she whispered fiercely, twisting her right foot uncomfortably in its sensible-but-still-painful kitten heel. The heavy double doors began to swing forward, and Jane flinched, hoping she hadn't sent out her magic without realizing it. But then a stocky, impeccably dressed man stepped out, turning back to help an elderly woman in Chanel across the threshold. 'Finally,' Jane muttered, watching the trickle of congregants intently.

Since the spectacularly destructive end of Annette Doran's welcome-home party the weekend before, her mother had been doing nonstop damage control. For Lynne Doran, socialite extraordinaire, that meant appearing in public − flawlessly turned out − as often as possible, in a wide variety of PR-friendly activities. Jane had even found a photo of her and Annette at an ASPCA adoption event, holding an undeniably photogenic puppy up to their smiling faces. Jane suspected that the pair would be conspicuously attending church as well, and so she had staked out a position in the shadows of an alley across the street, hoping to catch a glimpse of them.

A tall woman with dirty-blond hair stepped through the double doors and Jane inhaled sharply, but upon closer inspection the stranger was at least ten years older than Annette. *Not that Lynne would have let her out of the house in espadrilles, anyway.* A breeze curled around the side of the building she was leaning against, but to Jane it felt hot and angry, like the air in her dream from the night before.

Jane knew it was dangerous to get near Annette, and especially to try to reason with her, but this seemed like her only hope. If she could just make Annette hear the truth − the whole truth − she stood a chance at rescuing her from Lynne's clutches. Right now, Annette believed that Jane's family had been plotting against her for her whole life. And while it was true that Jane's own grandmother had helped abduct four-year-old Annette and erase her memory of her childhood, she only did so to keep her safe from Lynne. Jane's grandmother had known all along what Jane had only recently discovered: that the person known as Lynne Doran was actually Hasina, one of the world's original witches. She had survived over the millennia by taking over the bodies of her female relatives, leapfrogging from one generation to the next each time her current shell grew old. 'Lynne Doran' had been so anxious to reunite with her long-lost daughter not because she missed her, but because she needed a new body to inhabit. Now Jane had to somehow convey all this to Annette and convince her that she needed to get to safety. Malcolm, Annette's older brother and Jane's ex-husband, was already in hiding from his psychotic mother; Jane knew he would be eager for Annette to join him.

When Annette finally appeared in the doorway of the church, Lynne was stuck to her side as firmly as ever. The women made a striking pair. Their colouring was different and Annette's frame was a bit more solid than her willowy mother's, but the way they carried themselves in their demure Sunday suits marked them unmistakably as family. *Financially and genetically blessed family,* Jane thought ruefully, pressing herself back a little into the narrow alley. Fellow churchgoers flocked about the two women like butterflies around rare, impressive flowers, and Lynne greeted all of them with gracious nods and calibrated smiles. Annette carefully mimicked her mother's gestures and expressions, though she seemed a little uncomfortable to Jane's skeptical eye.

Finally, Lynne reached discreetly into her purse, no doubt sending a text message to summon their driver. *I thought they'd leave on foot.* They were only a few blocks from the mansion, and it hadn't occurred to Jane that they might be going somewhere else after the service. Park Avenue was wide, with a tree-lined divider down the centre that would shield her somewhat from view, but she hesitated. Was it worth the risk to step out into the open and hail a cab?

As she wavered, a strong arm grabbed her from behind and pulled her backward into the shadows. When the grip on her arm released suddenly, she stumbled for a few steps, her injured leg buckling underneath her, and fell to the ground. Jane threw her hands up instinctively to protect her face and felt the magic in her blood spring up, whipping the debris around her into a brief, frenzied tornado.

But instead of falling back to the concrete, the debris paused in midair, then parted abruptly to slam against the brick walls on either side. An older woman stood there in the silence, looking at Jane. She was all grey hair, cold pewter eyes, and sharp angles, and Jane felt a certain fleeting satisfaction at the sight of the thick white bandage peeking out beneath the sleeve of her cardigan. Annette's fire had at least gotten a piece of one of her aunts, Jane thought grimly. It was Cora McCarroll, she was almost sure, and not Cora's grumpier, more taciturn twin. Jane pulled her magic into a steady, more orderly shape around her body.

'You shouldn't be here,' Cora snarled, and Jane felt the static charge of her magic pressing angrily against Jane's own.

'You're blocking the way out,' Jane said between clenched teeth, rubbing at her aching leg and sending a tendril of magic to explore the shadows of the alley behind her. In a moment it found something solid but not too heavy. She held her breath and launched it forward.

Cora waved, almost contemptuously, as the garbage can that Jane had lobbed at her glanced off one of the brick walls with an empty, useless clang. 'There's more than one way for you to leave here,' she snarled, and the static charge pressed closer, taking on a sharper, more hostile feel.

Jane pushed back against it blindly. Malcolm and her gran had both told her that she was an extremely powerful witch, but the fact remained that she hadn't learned about her magic until very recently. Against a witch like Cora, who had been spell-casting for decades, raw power only mattered so much. 'You told Lynne that you wanted to be left alone,' Cora continued, almost conversationally. 'You didn't mention that you intended to keep sticking your nose where it didn't belong. I can't imagine what you're still doing in this hemisphere, but if you knew what was best for you, you'd stay away.'

'You didn't mind me being around when you thought you could use me,' Jane pointed out.

Cora laughed sharply. 'You had something we needed. But not anymore. We have Annette now, and *she* doesn't need some stalker following her around and filling her head with paranoid nonsense. She is heir to something more important than you could possibly understand, and your interference is entirely unwelcome.'

What they had needed was magic, and Lynne's blood. Jane had one of the two, and Lynne had manoeuvred her into marrying her son in the hope that the couple would produce a daughter who had both. Jane had run away on her wedding day, after learning the awful truth about her in-laws. It wasn't until she discovered Annette – who, of course, fit the bill perfectly – that she realized returning Lynne's long-lost daughter could gain her her own freedom. 'You guys really are just the picture of a close, loving family,' she spat back. 'I suppose Annette should consider herself lucky.'

Cora's thin lips twisted upward in a ghostly approximation of a smile. 'You have no idea,' the witch purred, her pewter eyes half closing in what Jane could only call rapture. Her mouth fell open in shock. Cora McCarroll *knew* what Annette's body was intended for, and she thought it was an *honour*.

The edge of the older woman's magic grew softer for a moment, and Jane instinctively pushed outward against it, clearing a little more breathing space around herself. Cora took a step back and frowned. 'This is a family matter,' she snapped, pulling the edges of her magic and her cardigan closer to her body. 'You're out, so stay out.' She spun dramatically and stormed out of the alley, leaving little eddies of trash and newspaper spinning around in her wake.

Jane made no move to follow; she was sure that Lynne had already whisked Annette away to their next photo op. Instead she found a clear space on the concrete ground and leaned her back against the cold brick wall, closing her eyes and trying to trace the currents of her magic as it returned to her body. Jane had put a lot of work into learning to harness and control her power during the previous few months, and knowing that she had held off Cora so steadily and still had some reserves left brought a grim, tired smile to her lips.

'*Family,*' she murmured thoughtfully, turning the word over in her mouth. Technically, witches were all one big family: they could all trace their ancestry back to one of the legendary Ambika's seven daughters. In the more modern sense, Jane was out of the family . . . but that didn't mean Annette was entirely without loving, concerned relatives.

Jane snapped her faux-lizard wristlet open and slid her cell phone out. The screen flared to life, displaying what she had self-consciously been looking at over and over throughout the previous week: the last of the fake 'junk' emails that Malcolm had sent her, so that she would know how to contact him. She scrolled to the bottom and tapped the number tacked on to the end of the email.

The line beeped in a measured, foreign-sounding way, and Jane waited patiently. Finally she heard what sounded like a voicemail tone, followed by an expectant, staticky silence.

'It's me,' she said shortly. 'I wanted to wait until I could tell you that everything was safe again. It mostly is – for you, I mean. But Annette's alive, and she's in danger, and I don't really know where to go from here. Malcolm, I think it's time for you to come home.'

She cut off the call and slid the phone back into her purse as she stood up, brushing dust off her clothes and stepping out of the alley.

Chapter Three

THE LOWELL HOTEL had changed since Jane had stayed there. She paused across the street from the stately building, taking in the three upper floors whose windows were dark and cracked. She took a deep breath and crossed the street, heading for the hotel's gold-rimmed doors. Inside, the smartly dressed staff looked oddly subdued, and a steady stream of workers in heavy-duty breathing masks passed through the marble-floored lobby.

Jane peered through her oversized sunglasses, inexplicably nervous that the woman at the front desk would recognize her. *I'm wearing a different face and body,* she reminded herself; the last time she was here, she had been Ella Medeiros, an heiress of vague origins. She had performed a complex spell to change her appearance and hidden under a new identity to protect herself from Lynne Doran. Crossing the lobby as quickly and quietly as possible, Jane headed straight for the bar, breathing an audible sigh of relief when she saw that the one person she had been hoping to see was still right where he belonged.

'My enemy,' André Dalcaşcu rasped, his Romanian accent thicker than she remembered. He raised a cut-crystal tumbler full of dark amber liquid toward her in a toast, but as he did Jane realized that even he was different: his half-mocking smile, which had become so familiar over the past month, seemed somehow skewed.

Jane pulled off her sunglasses, blinking as her eyes adjusted to the softer lighting of the lobby bar. Now she was close enough to see the long, angry scar running along André's right cheek, curling toward the corner of his mouth. It added a perverse hint of mystery to his already-handsome face, and Jane had a feeling that once it faded it would look positively rakish. At the moment, though, it still looked painful. She felt the impulse to reach out and stroke his damaged skin.

Instead she took another minute to collect herself, glancing around for André's sister, Katrin, as she arranged her Badgley Mischka hobo bag on one of the empty armchairs. The chain of its strap slithered down the red leather with a small sigh, and Jane echoed it as she sank into a second chair. 'You were hunting me,' she reminded him. He caught her staring at his scar, and she tried not to blush. 'Annette did that to you,' she said softly.

'She came up to my suite — my former suite,' he confirmed, his words coming a little more slowly and carefully than Jane remembered. He winced a little. 'She was already angry that I had helped you. Katrin was there, but Anne—' He shuddered, and shook his head.

'Annette's much stronger than Katrin,' she finished.

André's thick lips twitched. 'We tried everything to convince her that we were only trying to protect her, to do what was best . . .'

The Dalcaşcus were one of the less powerful magical families, and in order to survive, they had always been opportunistic. Many years ago, André and Katrin's parents had helped Gran whisk Annette away from Lynne and put her in hiding overseas, hoping to end Hasina's unnaturally long life — and her reign of power — by taking away her last healthy, young female blood relative. Once Annette was safely contained in British foster care, the Dalcaşcus sent André and Katrin, then just children themselves, to keep track of her, posing as her closest — and eventually her only — friends. Their attention had meant everything to the lonely young woman, although hers had meant significantly less to them. To the Dalcaşcus, Annette was a time bomb, a hostage, and a deep, dark secret all rolled into one. They had only kept her alive to secure Celine Boyle's continued cooperation. But they hadn't bothered to make sure Annette was *happy:* as long as she had a pulse and didn't run into any Dorans on the street, the Dalcaşcus had fulfilled their side of the bargain, as far as they were concerned. 'She didn't believe you,' Jane interpreted when he fell silent, and André sighed in agreement.

'Katrin lifted the block from my mind, so that she could see,' he began. Witches could read minds, including those of the men in magical families – the males carried magical blood, but wielded no power of their own. Most witches protected their male kin with spells that blocked others from learning their family secrets. 'I wanted her to know that she was in danger, and that we wanted to help her. But she saw . . . everything.' His black eyes closed, this time from pain that had nothing to do with his burns.

'Annette saw that your parents and my grandmother stole her from Lynne when she was little,' Jane filled in, a bitter note creeping into her voice. 'She saw that she was only an obligation to you, never a friend. She saw that you knew where her family was all along, and that you could have protected her from all those terrible fires if you had really wanted to. She figured out that she was only ever a chess piece to everyone.'

André nodded. 'We tried so hard to protect her from Hasina, and now look where she is.'

'I'm still trying to protect Annette,' Jane admitted. 'I want to stop Hasina from taking over her body. The spell takes a month to cast; there's still time to stop her from completing the transfer. But there's so much I don't know about Hasina, and how her magic works. I need all the help I can get. Yours and Katrin's. Where is she, anyway?'

'My sister has recently discovered the health club,' he replied, with a small twinkle in his black eyes. 'The poor rowing machine may never recover. So that's what you're here for, then – recruiting?'

'Look, no one's asking you to go in on matching sweatshirts,' she told him peevishly. The Romanian siblings were lifelong mercenaries. As Ella Medeiros, her interests and Andre's had lined up for a short while – in more ways than one – but, as she found out, he had been hunting Jane Boyle all the while. 'But your family has invested a lot – a *lot* – in trying to keep Hasina from inhabiting a new body. And the last time she saw you, Annette did a nasty number on the side of your face and took out a few floors of this hotel as collateral damage. I'm not asking you to be altruistic; I'm *telling* you that we're on the same side. Whether we like it or not.'

'You've made that claim before,' he said mischievously, and Jane vividly recalled the feel of his hands on the smooth skin of her thighs. *No,* she reminded herself strictly. *Ella's thighs.*

She cleared her throat, ducking her head to hide how flustered she suddenly felt, but she was sure André's keen black eyes didn't miss a thing. She snapped her head back up. 'You know, I'm not that great with fire – yet.' She saw André flinch ever so slightly, and studiously ignored it. 'But my friends would probably say that I just need some practice. I could go back over you limb by limb – you appreciate that kind of attention to detail, as I recall – and get all that skin Annette missed.'

André stared at her for a long moment, and Jane tried to remember if she had ever seen him speechless before. She had no intention of torturing him for information, of course; the thought alone made her feel light-headed. But she didn't want to fall into some 'nice and therefore harmless' category in his mind, either. He was still looking at her carefully when Katrin stepped into view. Her sharp angles and long, flat planes looked somehow less dangerous in workout gear than they had in cocktail attire, but the look on her face was unmistakably deadly. Something flashed at the edge of Jane's vision – the glitter of glass, headed in her direction.

'Stop it,' Jane snapped as her own magic sprang into immediate action.

In less than a heartbeat, Katrin was pinned down in a free armchair, the jagged edge of a shattered champagne flute pressed to her windpipe. The rest of the glasses fell to the floor, as lifeless as they had been before. Jane glanced around cautiously, but there was no one else in the dimly lit bar to notice what had just transpired.

'I come in peace,' she told Katrin more levelly, 'and your brother and I were managing just fine. You can stay if you want, but you'll have to behave yourself.'

Katrin nodded carefully, so as not to cut herself on the glass, and Jane let it fall to the floor with a pretty tinkling sound.

André watched her with amusement for a few seconds, then flicked his eyes back to Jane. 'Lynne didn't have the full measure of you,' he said approvingly, and the skin on the back of her neck crawled a little.

Lynne had once told Jane that she reminded her of herself when she had been younger, and Malcolm's father had echoed the same sentiment. *Is this what being a witch means? Getting pushed and pursued and tricked and trapped until everything really is kill or be killed?* Of course, she reasoned to herself, back when Lynne had been Jane's age, she had only been Lynne. Doubtless Hasina's daughters were born with a bit of a mean streak, and being raised by their immortal ancestress couldn't help. But if Lynne had stayed Lynne, she would have at least had a chance to grow into the sort of woman Jane hoped to be. *Just like Annette deserves,* she thought fervently. *That's the whole point: to give her the chance to be who she is.*

'Anne is a mess,' André told her bluntly, and Jane blinked rapidly at him. She waited, sensing that he was ready to tell her some, if not all, of what he knew. 'She was always an angry girl. She would latch on to people, build them up in her mind as her saviors, and then they would do something to upset her and she would act as if they had deliberately tricked her into loving them just so that they could let her down. I know you don't think much of our guardianship of her' – he twisted a wry smile at his sister, who huffed and looked away – 'but considering how long we managed to be in her life without setting the little pyromaniac off, I make no apologies.'

20

'She had no control over that,' Jane protested, the heat and fear of her recent dreams pressing in on her again. There was a charred, ashy quality to the air in the lobby that she hadn't noticed at first, but now it was all she could taste. She brushed a few strands of blond hair off her face. 'Don't you understand how magic works, when no one's taught you to use it?'

As if to punctuate her plaintive question, the lights in the bar area flared to brightness, and the clerks behind the main desk looked up curiously. Jane swallowed against the dryness of her throat, searching out her stray tendrils of power and containing them, and the lighting returned to normal. As a child, secluded in the French countryside with her austere, reclusive grandmother, Jane had always thought she was simply cursed when it came to electronics. It was only when she became aware of her magical abilities that she learned lights and computers responded to the flares in her magic — and the real reason Gran had fought to keep her hidden away from the world all those years.

'You understand,' Katrin purred in her clipped English. 'We know your grandmother told you nothing. But tell me, did the lights go off when you were reading a book, or had a song stuck in your head, or even when you stubbed your toe?' Jane started to answer, but Katrin cut her off. 'No. Your magic got loose when you were angry, or frightened . . . when you were out of control. Our Anne was plagued by fires in every home because she was *extremely* out of control.'

'She was a *child*,' Jane argued, but Katrin's words had effectively sown doubt. Jane had caused plenty of electrical trouble growing up, but the damage was minor: radio static, burned-out bulbs, constant computer restarts. The real light shows hadn't happened until her life had been turned completely upside down. *How angry did Annette have to be for the fire to trap a family of four inside their house?* Jane wondered with a sudden all-over shudder. Her next fire was a month later, and even more fatal. Annette hadn't been starting small fires in wastebaskets or making the room uncomfortably hot: she had set off major blazes as a child and was still doing it now.

'She's all grown up,' André replied softly. 'But that makes it easier, doesn't it? That she's so unstable?'

Jane frowned, uncertain of what he meant. His olive-skinned fingers caressed the cut crystal of his tumbler in a thoroughly distracting way. 'Easier – how?'

Katrin clicked her tongue impatiently. 'Because my brother thinks that you'll feel bad about killing Anne, no matter how much better it will make things for all of us. Hasina has plagued witches for far too long, as you know from personal experience. But he' – she jerked a bony thumb toward André – 'says that *still* wouldn't be enough for you, if Anne wasn't a danger in her own right, as well.' She rolled her eyes in profoundly expressive disgust.

Killing her? Had it really come to that? Gran's help had been contingent on André and Katrin's parents keeping Annette alive, and Jane had no intention of striking any other kind of deal. 'I want to banish Hasina,' she corrected. 'Or if I can't, then force her into some kind of truce or something where she agrees that her current life will be her last. I don't want to kill anyone – the whole point of this is that I'm trying to *save* Annette.'

The Romanian siblings looked at each other meaningfully, then back at Jane. 'Hasina won't honor a truce,' André told her. He held up one hand to prevent Jane from interrupting him and leaned forward. 'You say you don't know enough about her, so I'm telling you, all right? She's lived too long to really be human anymore. Humans act with one eye on the grave, but it's been thousands of years since Hasina has seen her own lurking in front of her. We're specks to her, mayflies who live and die in a day. She has no equals, so she will never keep her word.' He shrugged, his muscular shoulders rising and falling. 'Banish her if you can, but if you miss your chance, it will be gone. She'll stalk us, and you, and all our children and grandchildren, if you live long enough to have those. She kills witches, you know. That's why there are so few of you left these days. Whether she does it for fun, or to eliminate rivals, or some inhuman reason of her own, no one knows. All we know is that, with her, there can be no truces, no deals, no peace.'

Jane sighed. Deep down she had felt that Hasina wouldn't be open to any kind of compromise, but it made her task that much harder. 'So, banishing. Do you have any idea how I can do that?'

Katrin snorted, fishing an energy bar out of her gym tote and tearing the cellophane viciously. 'Kill her vessel, and her sons for good measure. We'll handle the two of them if you want, but that's the best offer you'll get here, *Baroness*.'

'We're done here,' Jane snapped, standing abruptly. She slung her hobo bag over her right shoulder, glancing around to make sure there was nothing she had missed. 'I'll find a way to get rid of Hasina on my own.' She took a moment to stare each Dalcaşcu in the eyes until both looked away from her steady gaze. 'I am going to do whatever I can to protect Annette. But let's be perfectly clear about this: her brothers – both of them – are under my protection. Touch either one and Hasina won't be your biggest problem anymore.'

She spun toward the door and strode out, but not before catching the ghost of a smile on André's face.

Chapter Four

B Y THE TIME Jane returned to Washington Square Park, her right leg was throbbing again, and her head felt nearly as wretched. As she climbed the stairs to her apartment, she wondered for the thousandth time if she was insane for turning down the Montagues' offer to stay with them at their Upper East Side brownstone. A little company would be nice right about now. But she knew that wherever she went, danger followed, and beyond that, she wasn't quite sure where they fit into all this — stopping Hasina was good for the whole magical community, but just how involved should the Montagues really be?

'So my fortress of solitude it is,' she muttered to herself, fishing around in her hobo bag for her Christofle key chain. A sound from the other side of the door caught her attention, and she froze. Dee still had a key of her own, but she hadn't been back to the apartment since she went to stay uptown.

Jane felt for her magic, which was as tired and out of sorts as the rest of her. She struggled in vain for a moment to bring it into some semblance of order, but it slipped away maddeningly, dancing around the edges of her control. *Screw it,* she decided abruptly, jamming her key into the lock. Anyone who tried to sneak up on her was in for a nasty surprise of their own.

'Hello?' she demanded, slamming the door shut behind her. 'I know you're here.' There was a pause, and then a distinct clang as something fell in the kitchen. She sighed in relief. *Dee.* Cooking up something delicious, she hoped.

'In a minute,' a familiar voice rumbled – but it wasn't Dee's. 'I don't want your omelette to burn.'

Jane ran into the galley kitchen so fast that her feet barely seemed to touch the floor. *Malcolm.* He stood over the stove, a broad smile on his handsome, tanned face.

'Forget the omelette.' She grabbed his arm and dragged him into the living room. 'I'm just glad you're okay.'

'You're the boss,' he said, sinking down into the buttery leather couch beside her. 'I can't cook anyway,' he added, spreading his hands helplessly.

'I know that,' she agreed, wrinkling her nose at the distinct smell of burnt eggs. 'It was a nice thought.'

His eyes focused on hers. 'You called, and I came,' he said simply. 'Bearing gifts.' He held up a small wooden box, pieced together from at least half a dozen different woods that came together to form a five-pointed star on the lid. Although there was a clear break to indicate where it should open, it seemed to be sealed shut.

Jane reached out curiously. A spark ran through her hand and up her arm when she took the box, and she jumped a little. 'It's beautiful,' she breathed, although she knew without needing to be told that it was more than just a pretty object.

'It's a spirit box,' he explained, his dark, liquid eyes watching hers carefully. 'It's for people who have . . . lost someone. The more you are near it, the more the spirits that follow you will infuse the box. It'll carry their intentions, and their love for you, and it's a way of keeping them with you. At least, that's what the witch who traded it to me said.' He frowned, looking uncertain. 'She *was* a real witch, for whatever it's worth.'

'She was telling the truth,' Jane murmured, closing her hands more tightly around the box. 'I can feel it.' She inhaled deeply, then forced herself to set the box down on the driftwood coffee table. As powerful as its presence was already, she could only imagine how difficult it would be to let it go once it had started to 'feel' like Gran . . . and maybe a bit like the parents she had lost, when she was too young to even remember. 'Where did you get it?'

'Ecuador,' he said shortly, glancing at the box and then away again. 'I kept hoping to see you around every corner. It's been so long.' His hand reached out as if of its own accord to brush a stray lock of hair from her face. Without thinking, she flinched, and his hand quickly dropped back down.

'It's been so long,' she repeated apologetically. He nodded in understanding, and instead reached out to pick up the spirit box.

'I hope it's all right,' he offered, gesturing toward it. 'I know it can never replace, or make up for, what I've taken from you. It was just something I thought you should have.'

'Thank you,' she replied automatically, her mind spinning. Malcolm and Jane's relationship had been complicated from the start. Lynne had manipulated her son into killing Jane's grandmother, who had long ago placed a protective spell on Jane to hide her from other witches who would seek her power. When Gran died and the spell was broken, Malcolm tracked Jane down in Paris, sweeping her up in a whirlwind romance that culminated with their wedding just months later. It was all a lie – at least at first. But then Malcolm fell in love with Jane for real. He risked his life to tell her the truth, and to try to help her get out of the city and away from his mother's clutches. Even when she decided to stay behind and hide in plain sight as Ella Medeiros, he had proven incredibly loyal, leaving everything behind and skipping from country to country alone so that the contents of his mind couldn't be used against her. Still, he'd been wrapped around his mother's evil finger for thirty-two years before Jane even met him. *He* might well believe that he had changed, but if it came down to Jane or Lynne, which version of Malcolm would he turn out to be? 'Tell me about the last two months,' she suggested finally.

Seeming to sense her mood as he had so many times before, Malcolm shifted easily into storytelling mode. He had started in Europe, where he had set up most of the safe houses that he intended to share with her. But after only a couple of weeks he had started feeling the pursuit closing in, seeing familiar shadows around every corner.

'Those were probably Dalcaşcus,' Jane supplied helpfully, guessing that Malcolm would recognize the surname of his mother's shifty so-called allies.

'That makes sense.' He frowned slightly. 'Mom always said the Romanians were only good for mercenaries.'

Not that good, Jane thought, frowning a little herself as she thought of all the ways André and his sister, Katrin, had betrayed Lynne. Malcolm went on to tell her how he had stowed away on a series of cruise ships and wound up in South America. His prep-school Spanish was more hindrance than help there, but the money from his safe houses smoothed over the worst of his communication troubles. He had gotten comfortable enough to start asking hard questions: about himself, his mother, and magic in general, although of course there was only so much he could learn when he had to conceal his reasons for wanting to know.

As Malcolm went on with his narrative, he played idly with the spirit box. The sight of it in his hand suddenly reminded her of the horrible moment when she had entered his memories and seen him kill Gran, and she shuddered. He glanced up in concern, but she didn't know what to say, so instead she just took the box from him and set it gently back down. She had been prepared to trust Malcolm, but if he was hiding anything from her, then maybe she was being just as naïve about him as she had been from the start.

'And the whole time, you never told anyone who you really were or why you were asking?' she prompted. She gathered some exploratory magic and sent it out through her eyes, wondering if she would even be able to see enough of his thoughts to make sense of. 'Never,' he told her firmly, his eyes wide and unflinching. 'I would never have risked putting your life in danger.'

Jane nodded. She knew for sure that he really believed what he was saying: his entire being throbbed with sincerity. *I don't even have to read his mind,* she realized, feeling the magical electricity swirl and eddy in the space between them, drawing them toward each other like a river of tiny magnets. *I just know him.* After a fairy-tale courtship, unsettling engagement, and disastrous marriage, she finally understood Malcolm Doran.

'It had been so long without any real news of what was happening up here, whether you were okay. I was going crazy, not knowing. And then the stories in the papers changed,' he went on. 'Suddenly I was a drug addict who'd kidnapped you and possibly killed the family driver.'

'I actually did that part,' Jane said in a rush, realizing just how much they had missed in the time they had been apart. She quickly sketched the scene in the alley when Yuri, Lynne's driver and personal hit man, had come for her. She shuddered at the memory of the vile things she had seen in his mind after he had lost control and attacked: Lynne had been covering up her pet thug's dirty little secrets for years. 'He started choking Dee,' she finished, 'and I couldn't get there in time. But he had a tire iron, and I had magic, and . . .'

She spread her hands helplessly. Even to defend an innocent woman from a certified sociopath, killing wasn't something she could easily shrug off. She knew that she had done her best under the circumstances, but it was impossible not to wonder about the 'what–ifs.' With a little more control of her power, she might have just knocked him out . . . but what was done was done. Hot tears stung behind her eyes, and she blinked hard.

Gran didn't tell me enough, she thought bitterly for what felt like the thousandth time. *She died before I even knew what to ask.*

Malcolm's hand inched over to cover hers, and the

warmth from it spread quickly up toward her heart. It was the first time since discovering Malcolm's role in Gran's death that Jane had been able to long for both of them at once. A hot tear escaped from her eye to roll slowly down one cheek. Malcolm looked for a moment as if he might lean in to kiss it away, but he hesitated, then brushed it from her skin with one gentle, calloused finger instead. 'I promise you: if Yuri attacked you, it was you or him. The same goes for . . . Dee, you said?'

'A friend,' Jane explained wryly, sniffling a little. 'She helped make our wedding cake.'

Malcolm swiveled his head toward the door, then back. 'She's the one I met in front of the house, right? On the day of the ceremony?'

Jane laughed out loud at the memory. Dee, knowing that it was too dangerous to attend a wedding full of witches with so many readable secrets in her head, had stopped by early in the day to drop off a couple of 'wedding cookies.' For Jane, that had been the only perfect part of Manhattan's so-called wedding of the century – that, and the knowledge that soon she and Malcolm would vanish into anonymous safety. Unfortunately, both the sweets and that hope had been all too fleeting.

'She cooks, too,' she told Malcolm more soberly. 'In fact, after she had to leave the bakery, she went to work for a catering start-up that was run by Katrin Dalcaşcu.'

Malcolm blinked rapidly, trying to absorb that piece of news. Jane explained how Katrin had seen her with

Dee, then lost track of Jane when she transformed into Ella. So Katrin had gotten close to Dee while her brother, André, explored other possible leads . . . not realizing that Jane herself was by his side for most of it. She politely glossed over most of those details, although the rigidity of Malcolm's neck and shoulders told her that she probably wasn't being quite as discreet as she'd hoped. *So I killed a guy and slept with the enemy for a while,* she thought crabbily. *Like he's never done anything he regretted?*

The hardest part, it turned out, was telling him about Annette. Malcolm, who had always felt responsible for his little sister's supposed death — guilt that his mother had encouraged and used to manipulate him — hung raptly on every word of her story. He barely breathed from Jane's initial, accidental vision of 'Anne Locksley's' apartment to their fiery showdown in the Dorans' billiard room. To her surprise, and relief, he didn't question a word of it, even when she got to the part about his mother's true nature.

'I'd heard things, growing up,' he admitted. 'And once I was in hiding, I realized that I needed to know everything I could about who was hunting me — especially if you were going to join me some day.' Jane was almost sure that he was blushing a little. 'I followed every occult trail I could, listened to every so-called witch. Most of what they had to say was nonsense, of course, and most of the rest was useless. But now and then there were hints about the woman whose name is on my mother's wall, and I kept my head down and listened. It was never really clear, but it was enough to know that – well, I'm not exactly surprised to hear that Annette's in danger.' He lowered his chin a little so that their eyes were level. 'I don't owe my mother anything anymore. Whether she even is my mother, or not, or sort of or maybe – whoever is driving that body has been using me for years. This Hasina person is entirely on her own side, as far as I can tell.' His eyes bored into hers. 'And I'm on yours.'

'I know,' Jane blurted before she could overthink it. Malcolm squeezed her hand a little harder, and a wave of heat coursed through her body. 'I'm glad you're here,' she added impulsively.

'I missed you,' Malcolm said gently, the corners of his mouth twitching toward a smile. 'I would have stayed away for the rest of my life if you hadn't called me, no matter what the papers said. Nothing else ever would have made me sure enough to risk it, to risk you.' He lowered his eyes, but his fingers wove their way between hers. 'If there's one thing I know – and there really might only be the one – it's how to be loyal.'

Jane stretched forward and kissed him lightly on the forehead, feeling the old familiar current crackling between them. 'You'll have plenty of chances coming up to prove that,' she promised. 'But for what it's worth: I already believe it.'

Chapter Five

THE MONTAGUES' STATELY Upper East Side brownstone looked even more pleasant than Jane remembered. Its inhabitants were similarly inviting – at least until they saw Malcolm standing behind her on the doorstep.

'He's here to help,' she announced quickly. Malcolm Doran and Harris Montague had taken a particularly active role in the rivalry between their two families, and there was no love lost between them. Jane had struggled with her magically enhanced crush on the redheaded Harris ever since they first met through his sister, Maeve, her first real friend in New York. But now that he was dating Dee, Jane had firmly pushed those feelings aside.

'Then he is welcome in my house,' said a voice from somewhere behind Harris's tall, lean frame. He stepped back with automatic deference, leaving Jane to gaze into a pair of bright, lively green eyes.

'I'm Emer,' their tiny, frail-looking owner said, smiling warmly. 'You'd be Jane – shame on you for running out before we could meet the last time you were here. But you've returned with another charming guest, so you're both forgiven and invited in for tea.'

Jane heard Harris sputtering at the word *charming* as she passed him, but he clearly had no intention of arguing with Emer. *His grandmother, and Maeve's,* she reasoned. The elderly woman moved with a stately authority, as befitted the matriarch of a family of witches. Jane couldn't resist mentally comparing her to Lynne Doran as they all settled onto candy-ribbon-striped couches in the sitting room. Both women had an air of unspoken command, and a ramrod-straight posture, noticeable in spite of the almost comical difference in their heights. But the similarities only made Emer's warmth more apparent, and Jane felt an immediate, instinctive trust in her that she had never felt toward her mother-in-law.

'Harris, darling, fix us a pot of tea,' Emer suggested mildly, and he headed for a swinging door that presumably led toward the kitchen.

'I'll help,' Dee offered huskily, smiling first toward

36

Malcolm and then, pointedly, at Jane before turning toward the same door.

'I'd rather you stay,' Emer countered in the same gentle tone, and Dee stopped midstride. 'Something tells me that Jane has returned to us on witch business,' the elderly woman explained. 'And while you may not have the bloodline, Diana, you know more about the craft than many who do.' She inclined her white-haired head toward Maeve, who looked like she wanted to sink into the couch and disappear.

Maeve had always resented her magical heritage and tried to keep it as far from her life as possible – until she met Jane. Once she saw that her new friend knew absolutely nothing about her abilities or the dangers of the Dorans, Maeve tried to warn her, only to be hit by a taxi courtesy of Lynne when she realized that Maeve was a threat. To Jane's surprise, Maeve had begun studying magic during her rehab. And even more surprisingly, it turned out that she did have a small spark of magic after all – despite the fact that Maeve's gift had passed to her through her father, which was almost always a magical dead end.

Dee, by contrast, had no magic of her own, but she had been fascinated by it long before she even knew that it was real. She had proven an enormous help when Jane was first attempting to understand and use her power. Dee sat back down obediently beside Maeve, discreetly pressing one of the girl's thin, pale hands with her own for a moment. 'Is there any chance you've come here with good news?' she asked lightly, arching a thick black eyebrow at Jane.

'Malcolm's back,' Jane offered with a forced smile.

'Good news for me,' Emer chimed in, beaming sincerely, and Jane felt her own expression soften. 'Handsome young men in my sitting room are always welcome.'

Maeve rolled her copper eyes, although she couldn't suppress a smile of her own. 'You must be happy your sister is alive,' she said to Malcolm.

'I'm very glad about that,' he admitted, 'but from what Jane tells me it's not entirely good news.'

Emer nodded crisply. 'Hasina is still alive. I wouldn't have thought such a thing was possible, but frankly it explains quite a bit. I'm sorry to say, young man, that our families have not traditionally been friends, but I never imagined it was because of our affinity to death.'

'It's sort of the family specialty,' Maeve explained when she saw Jane's quizzical expression. 'Séances, speeding the dead, calming angry ghosts.'

'A calling that would, of course, make us the natural enemies of a witch who repeatedly escaped her own death,' Emer added, as Harris swung open the door to the kitchen with one hand and balanced a cherrywood tray in the other. A fine curl of steam wafted up from a fragile-looking teapot covered in hand-painted yellow pansies. When he brought the tray carefully over to the sofa, Jane gratefully accepted a matching porcelain cup full of warm golden-green liquid. It smelled sweet and astringent at once, and Jane sipped it so eagerly that she immediately burned the tip of her tongue.

'I've been told that Hasina kills witches,' she blurted out. 'My, um, source didn't know why, but it sounded like a long-standing, routine thing. He said that's why there are so few of us left today.'

'"He"?' Harris repeated sharply, taking an armchair across from his grandmother and jerking his pointed chin in Malcolm's direction. 'As in *him*? Because, as reliable sources go . . .'

'It was André Dalcaşcu,' Jane admitted, staring into her tea to avoid the tense current swirling around the sitting room. 'I saw him yesterday.'

'Speaking of "reliable sources,"' Malcolm added pointedly, raising his dark–gold eyebrows in surprise.

Jane grimaced internally. Fortunately, Emer spoke again, covering the silence.

'I'd always been told that the Dorans were rather predatory,' she mused. 'We wouldn't have known, I suppose, if it was the same predator wearing different faces.'

'That was all he said?' Maeve asked skeptically, dropping a cube of sugar into her tea and sniffing at it. She wrinkled her nose, squeezing its dusting of freckles together, and reached for another cube. 'Nothing about how often, or how she picks them, or whether she even *has* a reason?'

'I know that all I'm bringing to the table are puzzle pieces,' Jane admitted frankly. 'But then Malcolm showed

39

up, and he had some pieces. Which made me realize: it could be helpful for us to all sit down and figure out what, exactly, we know. About Hasina, and how she jumps bodies, and everything.'

Harris stirred and looked like he might speak, but to Jane's relief Dee jumped in ahead of him. 'I've spent the last week and a half digging into research. I looked up all the antiaging and resurrection spells that I could find, but most of them seem sketchy at best.'

'They don't work,' Emer agreed firmly. 'Those are for charlatans, and the desperate.'

'That figures,' Jane admitted wryly. 'But I think that this spell is something a little more . . . unique. Gran's diary suggested that Hasina discovered this spell on her own, not that she learned it from anyone else. And I highly doubt she would have allowed her invention to make it into books. Gran said it took a month to prepare and was very difficult – and very dangerous.'

Harris chuckled, running a hand through his close-cropped reddish curls. 'So that's that. The limit of what we know. Good meeting, though.' His sister shot him a stern glare, and he flushed a little.

'A twenty-eight-day spell,' Emer mused, as if she hadn't heard him. 'That's what "a month" would mean to any witch. A precise time frame like that usually means a ritual of some kind on each day. She'll be using blood, and there might be some darker things. Sacrifices?'

'Wouldn't there have to be?' Maeve asked. 'To balance

the scales, or whatever? You can't make new life out of nothing, not even with magic.'

'But she isn't, really,' Jane countered thoughtfully. 'There's no new life; if anything, there's less of it. And maybe the body she leaves *is* a sort of a sacrifice. What happens to those bodies, anyway?' she asked suddenly, turning to Malcolm, who looked taken aback.

'I don't . . . know,' he mused. 'I tried to learn more about my family during my time away, but I guess I haven't wanted to think about that part too much. Hasina doesn't completely push the person out, from what I understand; she shares the body, two souls crammed into one. She's driving, but the other person is still there somewhere, not controlling, but maybe sometimes influencing. Or maybe not even that.'

Emer frowned. 'A soul with no body of its own, but stuck inside of one anyway.' She shuddered and clasped her hands together tightly. 'It's an abomination, not meant to be. That soul would be badly damaged from the start, then fade over time to almost nothing.'

Malcolm swallowed, and Jane felt a wave of pity for him. They were, after all, talking about his mother – and his sister, if they didn't find a way to stop it. 'A tarot reader in Cuenca told me that the host is just a collection of habits, a ghost in the back of her own head. I'm not sure there would even be enough of her left to take her own body back even if Hasina left it voluntarily. Dementia runs pretty thick in my family – among the women, anyway. I never thought to question that before, but it makes sense that it would be the former vessels, left by Hasina and with too little life in them to really come back.'

Jane slid her hand across the smooth fabric of the couch to squeeze his. 'Maybe we could inoculate Annette somehow,' she suggested, 'and make it impossible for Hasina to get in. Or if we could just convince her to *leave* . . . but so far Lynne hasn't left her alone for a second that I've been able to see.'

'It might not matter,' Dee told her. Her husky voice was reassuring. 'Hasina will have to cross some distance no matter what, to get into her new body. Surely she's marked her target by now, so I don't think the actual amount of distance would be much of an obstacle when the time comes.'

'Not *much* of one,' Emer murmured, glancing meaning-fully at her granddaughter. Maeve looked as confused as Jane felt, though, and so the older woman pressed on. 'But physical distance is still relevant, because she'll have to go airborne. There's no other way.'

'She's saying it's not a body switch,' Maeve explained to the others. 'Everything in the world takes up some kind of space, even Hasina's soul. She has to move from one body to the other in order to take it over, which means she has to be out of both bodies for, like, half a second.' She paused, looking pensive. 'It's a point of vulnerability, maybe.'

'A vulnerable half second?' Harris scoffed. 'So we could

kidnap Lynne and tie her up in our kitchen, and she could still jump bodies when we inevitably blink?'

'No, she couldn't,' Maeve replied, glancing at her grandmother for approval. Emer nodded for her to go on, her own green eyes glowing with pride. 'It's a difficult and dangerous spell with an exact time limit. The precise moment of the body-switch has already been determined; it was set in stone the moment she started the spell. Which she probably did as soon as she heard that Annette was still alive, so we can narrow it down to one specific evening.'

Jane flashed back to the moment she had told Lynne, during their tête-à-tête in Central Park, that she had found Annette. Lynne had breathed all her magic into her silver athame and handed it over to Jane in exchange for Annette's whereabouts, vowing to never come after her again. But Lynne had probably rushed straight back home to set the spell in motion, while Jane went off in the other direction thinking that all her problems were over.

'André wanted me to kill Annette,' she said quietly. 'He thinks it's the only way to make us all safe.' She glanced up, looking at each face for a long moment before moving on to the next. 'I want you all to be safe. I don't know if I'll be able to fight Hasina once she's in Annette's body, with all her magic and a whole new life ahead of her. But there's a week and a half left to prevent that from ever even happening, so now is the time to stop her. I dragged that poor girl into this mess, and if we can give her a way out, I want — I *need* — to try.'

'Of course you do,' Dee assured her quickly. 'And we'll all help.' She shot a meaningful glare at Harris, who looked like he was biting his tongue.

'Thank you all,' Malcolm told them sincerely. 'I know that my family has done nothing to earn your goodwill, so it means a lot to me that you'd even consider helping my sister. I hope that once Hasina is banished from our lives, we can be friends – or at least, not such enemies.' He shot Emer a smile that would have melted marble, and even Harris looked moved.

Jane glanced between them approvingly. *It's a start.*

Chapter Six

JANE PAUSED FOR a moment on the front steps of the brownstone to gather herself. The emotion and energy bottled up during the meeting had practically shoved her out the door. It was only once she was outside, breathing the fresh spring air, that she was able to slow down and make sure that Malcolm had kept up with her. But of course he was right on her heels, the sunlight picking up golden glints in the thick waves of his hair.

Jane's smile was both automatic and sincere. After more than a week of her near-desperate need for solitude, she felt strange spending so much time with Malcolm. It was, after all, the first time they had really been alone together since they said goodbye just after their wedding barely a month ago. But as confusing as it was to have him so near, it also felt inexplicably normal. 'Where are we going?' she asked him curiously; her own plans for the rest of the day weren't even half formed, and she wondered what he might have in mind.

'We're going where you've gone every day so far,' he told her, sliding his elbow deftly under her hand, which seemed to have been waiting for it. 'As soon as you got off the couch you were on your way to check up on my sister.'

I am, Jane realized. 'I feel so responsible for her,' she admitted, then noticed that Malcolm had begun gently steering her down the street. 'Wait,' she urged, pulling him instead toward a diner on the corner. 'It's a bad idea for either of us to lurk around looking for her; it's a terrible idea for *both* of us to do it. I've got it on good authority that your family doesn't exactly appreciate my interest in Annette.'

He resisted for a brief moment, then nodded and stepped ahead of her to politely open the door of the diner. 'Excellent point,' he conceded as she passed him. 'Let's take a break and strategize. Besides, I've been in the mood for blueberry pancakes ever since I got back.'

'Dee makes pretty good ones,' Jane remembered fondly, sliding into a green-vinyl-covered booth.

'Dee makes pretty good everything,' Malcolm agreed easily, 'but I have a feeling her version of "blueberry pancakes" would be crêpes with blueberry compote. I respect the artistry, but sometimes you just want the kind made from a mix.'

Jane opened her mouth in surprise. 'This is an American thing,' she guessed, and was rewarded with an embarrassed grin.

'You're trying some,' he countered, and proceeded to order what sounded like enough food for six people.

When the waiter had gone, Jane set her elbows on the table and twisted her hands together. 'The last time I saw her, your sister tried to kill me,' she pointed out, deciding to be blunt. 'I'm not exactly sure what she might do if we run into each other on the street.'

'I want to say "I'm sure she would hear you out,"' Malcolm told her carefully, 'but I guess I don't know her that well anymore.'

Jane felt suddenly guilty. She hadn't really considered how complicated Malcolm's feelings must be until now. Annette was back, was in mortal danger, and had nearly killed the woman he loved. It was a lot to take in, especially since he hadn't even been able to see her yet.

The waiter set down a stack of syrup-drenched pancakes between them, and their mutual reverie was broken.

'I read something on the plane that I thought was interesting,' Malcolm said, once a third of the pancakes were gone and three more plates of deliciously fried and greasy food had arrived.

Jane tried to look as encouraging and curious as possible

with her mouth full of bacon. Reading her expression, Malcolm pulled a few pieces of magazine print from his back pocket, unfolding them and sliding them across the table toward her. Leaning closer, Jane realized that she was looking at a six-page *National Enquirer* spread about the fire at 665 Park Avenue.

'All the other coverage I'd seen said "no serious injuries," which is great,' Malcolm explained, 'but they all also said that the most damage was to the top two floors . . . and the attic.'

In a flash, Jane understood. Malcolm's younger brother, Charles, had lived his entire life hidden in the mansion's attic. He was the result of a very late pregnancy that Lynne had risked in a desperate attempt to replace her lost daughter. She had held it together – barely – with so much magic that the child suffered severe, and permanent, mental damage. But even more disappointing was the fact that after all that, the child was a boy. Having spent most of her pregnancy on bed rest, supposedly grieving her lost daughter, Lynne was able to easily keep Charles's existence secret from the world.

While Jane had been living at 665 Park during her engagement to Malcolm, Charles had snuck out of his attic apartment a few times and come looking for her, responding to the same magical attraction that had caused so many problems for Jane. It scared her half to death. But when Lynne locked them in the attic together, trying to make Charles rape and impregnate her, Jane managed to break through the confusion of his mind and communicate with the lonely boy underneath. She had felt a certain affection for Charles since then, although it was, naturally, a wary one. He had helped her again when she went looking for some of Annette's things to use in a spell, and was the only one to see through her Ella disguise, which had perversely made her like him a little more.

And it didn't even occur to me until now to wonder what happened to him in the fire. Jane bit her lip and followed Malcolm's pointing index finger to a large sidebar on the last page of the article. ' "Rumors of Homeless-Squatter Discovery Persist in Spite of Denials," ' Jane read aloud, then frowned in confusion. 'Huh?'

'Just read,' Malcolm encouraged, and she did.

Although there was no proof and no confirmation from the authorities and not even any nameable sources, the paper asserted that a homeless man had been secretly living in the mansion, unnoticed by even its inhabitants until the fire had forced him to leave. 'It's a big house,' one person had been quoted as saying — anonymously, though Jane couldn't see much harm in such an obvious observation. *But of course you can't be too careful, when risking Lynne's wrath.* The 'mystery man' had allegedly been confronted by one of the mansion's staff members, and no one could account for his movements after that, so Jane concluded that he must have been led back inside and confined again before (almost) anyone had a chance to wonder what he was doing there. At least he hadn't been harmed in the fire.

'That's a relief,' she said out loud, and Malcolm cocked a skeptical dark-gold eyebrow her way. 'I mean it,' she assured him. 'He's as much a victim of your mother as you and Annette.'

A long pause settled between them, and Jane knew that they couldn't avoid coming back to the heart of the matter for long. 'I need to see her either way,' Malcolm began in a decent impression of idle conversation. *Of course he does,* Jane knew. After twenty years, seeing Annette's photo in the tabloids would hardly satisfy him.

'And I need to try to warn her again,' Jane mused. 'She was so angry that night; Lynne saw me coming and told her half truths to wind her up. But she will have had some time to cool down now. Maybe she even heard a little of what I was trying to tell her. Maybe she'll be curious.'

Malcolm pursed his lips thoughtfully. 'Or else she's in a very tense and vulnerable place right now and she'll kill us both on sight.'

'Yes, or else that,' Jane agreed miserably. She was prepared to take some risks to help undo the mess she'd made by bringing Annette here. But how was she supposed to decide what to do when there was no way of knowing how risky any given action even was?

'Maybe . . .' Malcolm pushed some hash browns around his mostly empty plate with his fork. 'Maybe we should do a little surveillance before jumping right in. I'd like to give her the benefit of the doubt,' he added quickly, 'but it's more important right now to tread carefully than to prove I'm a loyal brother. I promised I would do anything to keep you safe, for one thing, and I'm not eager to be burned to a crisp, myself.'

'Surveillance, then,' Jane agreed with a wry smile, thinking of her own surveillance outside the church just days before. 'Do you happen to have a pair of binoculars with you? Or maybe a high-powered telescope, so we can keep a really safe distance?'

'I had to travel pretty light these last few weeks,' he admitted. 'But on my way back into town I did manage to pick up a witch.' He lifted his dark eyes to gaze pointedly into hers, and she blushed automatically.

Oh, right. Magic. When Jane had needed to infiltrate the Doran family in order to search their mansion, she'd used a complicated spell to turn into 'Ella' for exactly twenty-eight days. But for staying incognito while tailing Annette for an afternoon, the glamours she had practiced with Dee would suffice. Annette hadn't even really seen either of them in person – when she knew Malcolm he was twelve, and Jane was Ella. *She will have seen plenty of photos, but still. A few minor tweaks should do it.*

When he saw the comprehension and agreement dawn on her face, Malcolm grinned and signaled for the check.

'Have I converted you to diner food yet?' he asked cheerfully.

Jane did her best to match his light tone, although her

full stomach was already beginning to twist with nerves. 'It was delicious,' she managed. 'And you may never tell Dee I said that.'

Malcolm glanced around conspiratorially. 'Your secret is safe with me. Speaking of which . . .' He gestured at the high walls of the booth on three sides of them, and the mostly empty diner.

Jane's gaze followed his gaze: no one seemed to be paying the slightest bit of attention to them. 'This is as good a time as any,' she agreed crisply. She folded her hands on the table in front of her, concentrating on the shapes they made against the white Formica. Then her mind's eye slipped a little deeper, seeing the blood that ran below her pale skin and the glow of the magic that pulsed through her veins. She let herself slip into it, flexing her magic like a muscle, feeling it grow stronger.

Her gaze traveled up Malcolm's black polo shirt, hesitating just for a moment where it opened to show the hint of his pulse beating next to his Adam's apple. Then she continued on, resting on his familiar, square jaw. Her breathing quickened as she sent little rivers of magic toward it, making it stretch and change until it was longer, more pointed. She narrowed his nose to match, although she couldn't bring herself to change a thing about his deep, liquid eyes. The hair, she decided instead, coaxing it straight and darkening it, making it grow until it brushed his shoulders.

When she had finished, she took an appraising look at

52

the whole picture. He was less handsome now, she had to admit, but that just meant that the experiment was a success: he didn't look like Malcolm anymore. She could recognize bits of his features if she looked long enough, but at most she would guess that he could be her onetime husband's third cousin.

Now me.

It was a little harder without being able to see what she was doing. She decided to make most of the changes to her coloring: chestnut-brown hair, darkening her grey eyes to match, and giving herself what she hoped was a spa-quality spray tan. She sent her magic experimentally groping toward her cheekbones just in case those changes weren't enough, drawing them upward to lengthen the lines of her face, but she felt horribly uncertain about the process. It was only an illusion, so she couldn't feel it. The alteration might have been minuscule, or she might have stretched herself into bad–plastic-surgery territory; there was no real way to know.

But Malcolm didn't recoil in horror, so she figured that she must have done reasonably well. *Actually . . . don't I look a little like that ex of his I met at Barneys that time?* She pushed that thought firmly aside and smiled with a confidence that she hoped she would start to feel again sometime soon.

'Let's go look for Annette,' she suggested, and together they slid out of their booth and headed for the street.

Chapter Seven

IT DIDN'T TAKE long to spot Annette leaving the Dorans' mansion, but as usual, she wasn't alone.

'Duck,' Malcolm hissed, turning his body away from the massive front door and using it to shield hers from view.

Jane peeked recklessly out from behind his arm in time to see Lynne Doran fold her tall body elegantly into a waiting town car. She wore a grey jacket with a mink collar that brought out some subtle highlights in her brown hair. Jane caught a glimpse of Annette's dirty-blond waves as the car pulled away.

She stepped out of Malcolm's grip and hailed a cab before she could lose her nerve. 'We don't look like ourselves,' she reminded him tersely as they slid into the backseat. 'We can just hang back and wait until they split up.'

Unfortunately, the mother and daughter didn't seem inclined to do any such thing. Jane had mostly been afraid that they were heading to brunch — a time-consuming activity, for one, not to mention that she couldn't stomach another bite after everything they'd eaten at the diner. But stalking the two Doran women as they examined every little thing at Bendel's was, she eventually decided, much, much worse.

'I think you need one of these,' Malcolm told her cheerfully, holding a retro powder puff up to Jane's cheek.

She sneezed before she could say anything, and a black-clad salesgirl glared. Chastened, Malcolm returned the puff to its box and stepped away. 'They're heading upstairs,' Jane murmured, turning away from the spiral staircase to examine a huge square studded with subtly different shades of Laura Mercier foundation. 'I have no idea if I'm a summer or an autumn right now,' she grumbled, counting the steps in her head until she guessed that Lynne and Annette must have reached the second floor.

'Is there any chance that there's less *stuff* up there?' Malcolm asked pessimistically, craning his neck to try to get a better look. His mother and sister had already spent nearly an hour on the first floor, seemingly examining every cosmetic in existence. The chattering crowd bouncing between one colourful display and the next had made it easy to stay unseen, but the energetic music was starting to give Jane a headache, and Malcolm was looking even more drawn than she felt.

'There's plenty,' Jane told him, although she suspected that he probably already knew that. 'But we're already all "dressed up," so we should stick it out if we can. Anyway, there's a salon in the building. They could still part ways.'

'Or they could be aiming for an entire day of mother-daughter bonding,' Malcolm pointed out grouchily. 'Hey, what would happen if I got this hair cut? Would mine get shorter by the same amount? Or would they even be able to cut it, since it's not—'

'Come on,' Jane interrupted. The staircase was clear, and she couldn't see Lynne or Annette anywhere. 'We don't want to lose them.'

She thought she heard Malcolm muttering behind her as she headed for the stairs, but she resolutely ignored him. *Spying isn't his thing,* she reminded herself charitably. *I wish it had never become mine, either.* Malcolm had given up an extraordinarily comfortable life for a dangerously uncertain one because he knew it was the right thing to do; she wasn't about to take him to task for not enjoying it enough.

The only ones enjoying this are those two, she thought grimly as a familiar chestnut coif came into view, bent close to a dark-blond one. Annette's apple-green Dior suit was a little mature for her age, Jane thought: she must be trying to mimic her mother's style. She was carefully settling an ornate jeweled comb in her tousled hair, and Lynne seemed so intent on helping her that for a moment Jane forgot to stay out of sight. Then Lynne's dark eyes swept her way, and Jane stiffened.

Before she could decide what to do, Malcolm stepped part of the way between them, holding up a sequin-studded Carnivale mask to Jane's stricken face. 'We're two hundred yards away,' he reminded her steadily, 'and you don't look like you.'

'She knew I was Ella,' Jane said in a whisper. 'I'm still not sure how.' She pulled him gently over to the store's remarkable front windows, remembering as she did that she had heard somewhere that they were Lalique. They were certainly lovely, although her attention as she pretended to examine and admire them was more than a little divided. *No matter how hard I try, Lynne will always have more experience at being a witch.* The comparison was so unfair that it was downright depressing. It was entirely possible that Charles had 'outed' her somehow when she had been disguised as Ella, or even that she had given herself away with some word or gesture. But she also had to consider the possibility that Hasina had used some spell that Jane would never live long enough to even hear about. *How could any witch hope to live a safe, quiet life until that ghoul is gone for good?*

Malcolm squeezed her arm, and she glanced up at him.

His face was a study in sympathy and concern. 'Can I help?' he asked softly.

'Just keep your eyes open,' she suggested with a tired half smile. Jane had never held a glamour in place for so long, let alone two glamours, and she was starting to feel the strain. For some reason – probably the simple fact that it wasn't a disguise of her own body – Malcolm's glamour was proving especially tricky, and Jane couldn't help worrying that she would let it slip. *But I'm glad he's here,* she thought gratefully. *He's making it almost . . . fun.*

Malcolm's dark eyes widened in surprise, and she whirled around to see what he was looking at. All she saw were the backs of his mother and sister, sorting through Loro Piana cashmere scarves. 'I've gotten dragged in here a few times,' Malcolm explained awkwardly. 'Isn't the third floor . . . lingerie? If they head up there, we may need a new plan.'

'But our old one is working out so well,' she joked, stepping back from the window and trying on a giant pair of Roberto Cavalli sunglasses for the hell of it. 'Let's not borrow trouble yet,' she counselled more seriously after a moment. 'I'm starting to wonder if today is just destined to be a loss.'

Malcolm pursed his lips thoughtfully. 'Is there likely to be a "good" day, though?' he asked. 'Won't my mother be doing everything she can to persuade Annette that this is some fabulous birthright she's won her way back to, just like we're going to try to convince her of the opposite?'

He was right, Jane had to admit. The fact that they had happened to follow the pair on yet another day of mother-daughter bonding probably had nothing to do with luck at all, good or bad. It would be smart for Lynne to keep her daughter as close and as happy as possible for the remainder of the twenty-eight days. Her life, after all, depended on a transfer with no glitches or interference. It would be careless to leave Annette to her own devices for the next week and a half . . . and Lynne was a woman with a keen eye for detail. 'She knows how badly Annette wants to be part of a family,' Jane grumbled, switching to a pair of Ray-Bans.

Malcolm nodded seriously, then adjusted the frames a little on Jane's nose. 'How do you convince someone that what she's wanted her whole life isn't all it's cracked up to be?' he wondered aloud.

Bitter experience is a pretty effective teacher, Jane thought ruefully, but unfortunately they didn't have the luxury of letting Annette make mistakes in order to learn from them. 'Malcolm,' she hissed suddenly, swiveling her head back and forth, 'do you see your mother anywhere?'

Annette's apple-green ensemble was still in view inside the luxury accessories section, but Lynne's demure, mink-topped grey jacket was nowhere in sight. Jane spun around, worried that Lynne had somehow snuck up behind their unsuspecting backs, but all she saw was Fifth Avenue traffic outside the stained-glass windows.

It's what we wanted, Jane almost said, but how long

would Lynne be gone? There was no way of knowing whether she was off to the salon for the afternoon or simply powdering her nose for a minute.

'You should go to her,' she said quickly. 'I'll back you up from here, but she's more likely to listen to you.' She reached up and waved her left hand across his face, releasing the magic that held his disguise together as she did. It was a bit complicated keeping her own in place at the same time – like separating a melody from its harmony in an unfamiliar song – but the feeling of relief afterward was so intense she had to close her eyes for a moment. 'Go,' she gasped, checking to make sure that Malcolm looked entirely like himself again. 'And hurry.'

Malcolm wrenched himself away from the window and crossed the store in a few long, eager strides. *Of course, he's been dying to see her,* Jane realized, feeling a little foolish. She'd been thinking of their afternoon in terms of a reconnaissance mission while he'd been painfully close to his long-lost sister the whole time.

Jane braced herself as Malcolm approached Annette, who was holding up an Hermès bangle thoughtfully. The curious look on her face turned to shock and then something approaching rapture, and Jane tried to make herself relax a little. Annette might be a bit of a hothead, but surely she wouldn't attack her own brother in a public place, even if he told her something she didn't want to hear.

Annette's face darkened, her square jaw setting. Jane balled her hands into fists, letting the magic that was holding up her glamour flow into the rest of the power that she held in reserve, ready to release it at a moment's notice. But no flames licked around the highly flammable cashmere; and Malcolm continued to speak earnestly, even fearlessly. Jane allowed herself to do a quick visual sweep of the store, checking for Lynne. She didn't see her anywhere, but considering how many tall, well-dressed, glossy-haired women were nearby, it was hard to be confident that they had enough time. 'Hurry,' she whispered again, wondering if there was some magical way to project her voice to his ear.

Out of the corner of her eye, she caught a glimpse of mink on the spiral staircase. In a near panic, Jane reached out with her hoarded power and pulled, tugging on Malcolm's arm as urgently as if she were standing there beside him. He swung around, surprise registering on his face, but when he saw Jane's expression he seemed to understand. He pulled a pen from his pocket, scribbled something hurriedly on a business card, and pressed it into Annette's hand before ducking his head and exiting back into the main part of the floor.

Jane swirled her magic around him as he did, darkening his hair and slimming his broad shoulders a little so that he would be harder to recognize from behind. She was nearly done before she realized that, as the one who was facing in Lynne's direction, she probably should have touched up her own disguise first. But by the time she had enough attention free to do so, Annette had crossed the floor to

61

meet her mother, steering her back toward the staircase. The two women began to climb again, chattering naturally, and then Malcolm wrapped his arms around Jane, enveloping her in his own spiced-champagne scent.

'Thank you,' he breathed into her hair. 'It's too soon to tell if she listened, but thank you for helping me try.'

Chapter Eight

A FEW HOURS LATER, after waking up from a much-needed nap, Jane wandered halfheartedly toward the kitchen. Without Dee's cheerful influence, though, nothing in it seemed especially palatable. She wandered out again, wondering where Malcolm had disappeared to. She didn't know if he was considerately trying to give her space, or if he felt like having a little space of his own, but the sudden tugging in her chest made her not care.

Slipping off her shoes, she padded down the hardwood hallway, encouraged to see that the bedroom door was open – but Malcolm wasn't in there, either. She half started toward the bathroom door, listening for the sound of a running shower, but then realized where he must be and stepped into the hallway instead. The door to the bedroom that she still thought of as Dee's was closed. But now Jane could sense the warmth of a live presence from the other side of it, as though she could hear Malcolm's heartbeat.

She entered before she thought to knock, and promptly blushed: Malcolm was extended along the floor's wide open space, stripped to the waist and glistening with sweat. She had caught him mid-push-up, and from the looks of things it wasn't his first or even his fifteenth. Never a small man to begin with, Malcolm had put on easily ten new pounds of muscle during his travels around the world. *Lots of calisthenics alone in his room,* she guessed, and then he saw her standing in the doorframe and she blushed harder.

'Sorry to interrupt,' she mumbled, stepping inside and closing the door behind her. Her palms suddenly felt slick with sweat, and it took her two tries to turn the enameled knob, but finally it clicked closed. When she turned around again, Malcolm was pulling a thin gray T-shirt over his head, and she felt a quick stab of disappointment.

'You seemed exhausted,' he told her, brushing a damp curl of dark-gold hair back from his forehead. 'And I didn't want to crowd you in your own home.'

'It's been a long couple of weeks,' she agreed non-committally, catching herself searching for the flat curve of pectoral muscle beneath his thin shirt. 'We're hurtling toward a deadline, and I can't make Annette contact you in time, or even figure out how to actually help her if she does.'

He smiled wanly and settled himself into a low white armchair. Jane, feeling uncomfortable about sitting on the bed without some sort of invitation, folded into a cross-legged position on the crocheted rug in the middle of the floor.

'We're underpowered.'

Malcolm didn't try to contradict or reassure her; he just nodded. 'How can I help?'

He leaned his upper body forward. His attention felt like radiating sunlight, and she closed her eyes for a second, basking in it. 'Help me think,' she requested, and he nodded.

They began with the nearest source of additional power: Lynne Doran's athame, which Jane had kept locked safely away in a bank vault ever since it had been handed over to her. Malcolm started out surprisingly neutral about it – technically it could be considered a part of his sister's inheritance, but under the circumstances that was a trivial concern. Annette had plenty of magic of her own, and Jane had bartered it from Lynne fair and square. Besides, to hear Malcolm tell it, magic was stolen fairly regularly, or mistakenly allowed to die with its owner; obtaining such a massive store of it was a rare gift that no witch could really expect. Still, he seemed reluctant to actually tell her to go remove it from the bank for their use, and Jane wondered if he shared her worries about the real nature of its power. *He certainly has reasons to distrust his mother's magic. Maybe his hesitation should mean even more than my own.*

'If nothing else, we could melt it down,' Malcolm suggested, as in sync with the direction of her thoughts as he frequently seemed to be. 'There's a spell – Emer would know. You melt it and then transform the silver into something else – mercury, usually, or zinc. Something that can't hold magic, and it dissipates.'

Jane considered this, but as troubling as the thought of having the athame around was, destroying it didn't seem much more appealing. 'I worry that we might need it someday,' she explained, spinning her plain silver ring idly around her finger. 'That it could be the key to saving Annette, or that we might need it . . . later.'

Worry lingered around Malcolm's eyes, but he didn't bother to ask what 'later' might mean – he had grown so much more serious in the last few months. When they had first met, his relaxed manner and easy charm had attracted her: she had wanted to share whatever life had made him so open and confident. *Of course, he didn't really have it so good even back then,* she reflected, but regardless, the change now was palpable. *He's grown up,* she decided finally. *Once he broke with his mother, he could start to become his own man.* And there was no denying that that new man was plenty attractive in his own right, albeit in a very different way from his former, lighthearted self.

'More witches would help,' Jane continued thoughtfully.

'Everyone keeps talking about how there aren't so many of them anymore, but obviously there are some, and plenty more than I've met.' Her mind's eye filled briefly with a button nose, spiky brown hair, and wide brown eyes, but that was a no-go. Dee's Wiccan group had all gone underground since Annette's party, and anyway Jane was pretty sure that her friend Brooke hadn't even known she was a witch before Jane's power had touched her own. *We need experienced witches, not a pack of untrained recruits.*

'I did meet a couple of them in my travels,' Malcolm mused, 'but none who I think would come all the way to New York just for the privilege of pissing off my mother. Most of them didn't have enough power to be much help, anyway, and the ones who do are the least likely to get involved.'

'André and Katrin are here, and they're already involved,' Jane reminded him nervously.

'You and André,' he said quietly. 'I wondered when you first mentioned him, if . . . while I was gone . . .' He lifted his hands, then let them fall helplessly in his lap.

Jane swallowed hard. 'We had a . . . relationship,' she confirmed, although she wasn't entirely sure that *relationship* was the correct word. They'd had a healthy amount of sex and an unhealthy amount of mutual deception. The fact that it ultimately added up to a sort of comfortable affection was serendipity – certainly it wasn't any kind of clever planning on Jane's part. 'It's over now; it ended when my disguise did.'

'They're power for hire – both of them,' Malcolm warned her, his voice thick with emotion. 'If my mother's bought them, they're hers. And even if their contract with her is up, they'll kill you the second it suits them, no matter what *relationship* you thought you had. The best thing you can do is just stay the hell away from hi – them.'

Way too late for that, Jane thought ruefully. 'Look,' she began in what she hoped was a soothing tone, 'I get that this must be upsetting for you. Especially knowing that they want us to kill your sister—'

Malcolm brushed that aside with an angry wave. 'Jane, I know damn well that Annie might not live through this mess – that none of us may live through it. I think I understand that better than you do, and it's sure as hell not why I'm angry.' He drew a shuddering breath deep into his broad rib cage, and let it out smoothly. 'The thought of that absolute creep so much as touching you . . .'

'You're *jealous*?' Jane blurted out.

Malcolm slid forward to kneel on the floor in front of her, his chair rebounding gently in response to his sudden absence. 'Yes,' he told her, so fervently that the force of the words made her shiver. 'I'm jealous that he kissed you, touched you, saw you sleeping. I'm jealous that he got to stand beside you and breathe the same air as you. I am in love with you, Jane, whether I have any right to be or not, and I will forever be jealous of anyone lucky enough to be in your life when I had to stay away.'

For a moment the world was perfectly still, and it was

filled entirely by Malcolm. The warm lamplight glinted off a million curves of dark-gold hair, and his face seemed to almost radiate it. There was no thought, no weighing of the pros and cons, no decision to make: there was nothing for her to do but kiss him, and so she did. Everything between them had changed, and so in a way it felt like a first kiss, but of course it wasn't that, really, and his lips fit to hers with the ease of long practice.

He hesitated for a moment after the kiss could have been complete, giving her the opportunity to gracefully break away, but that was the furthest thing from her mind, and she pursued him with her mouth, then her hands, then her body.

Her fingers found the hem of his thin T-shirt and sent it flying away from them. It landed with a whisper on an arm of the chair, dangling limply like a grey ghost. Apparently feeling that he had put enough of a good-faith effort into being restrained, Malcolm sent her own clothes sailing after his shirt piece by piece, pausing only to kiss the newly exposed bits of her flesh like a drowning man straining toward air.

Everywhere his mouth or hands went, Jane could feel tiny sparks of pleasure bursting in her bloodstream, as if some sort of electromagnetism were drawing them together. *Magic,* she thought wryly, *the best kind of chemistry there is*. But it felt different, somehow, from her dark, desperate connection with André or the shivery current that used to draw her toward Harris. *It's not all the same,* she realized. There had always been something between the two of them, but after everything that had happened, she had cynically assumed it was just good looks and the whisper of magic. And it was true that her blood knew Malcolm's — she could feel it whenever he was near — but now her body and her heart did as well, and the three combined into an attraction that couldn't be reduced to any kind of simple explanation.

The bed seemed impossibly complicated to reach, so instead she just hitched herself forward, using the waistband of his pants as leverage and conveniently pulling them off in the process. Malcolm wrapped strong arms around her waist, pulling her closer, and she wrapped her legs around his and slid herself onto him. For a moment they sat that way: locked together with their faces just millimeters apart, touching in nearly every possible way. Then Jane began to move, propelled by her thighs with eager support from Malcolm's arms, rocking along the length of him and back again until they both gasped together, stifling their cries with more kisses.

Finally, spent, Jane let her head fall onto his shoulder. Her hair spilled down over his muscular back, shining like molten silver in the lamplight. Disentangling carefully so as to stay as close together as possible, they rearranged their limbs just enough to fall asleep on the rug where they lay.

Chapter Nine

SUNLIGHT STREAMED THROUGH the damask curtains, but Jane knew immediately that that was not what had woken her up. A soft buzzing sounded somewhere off to her left. She jerked her body up to sitting and rocked onto her toes, trying to ignore the distraction of Malcolm's naked sleeping form as she attempted to take stock of where her clothes had landed the night before. The buzzing noise came again and she followed it across the room to where her bag lay underneath her crumpled Paige jeans and oversized Theory sweater. She fumbled inside with one hand and pulled on her sweater with the other, and somehow managed to flip open the rose-gold phone on the fourth ring while stepping out of Malcolm's room fully – if not at all neatly – dressed.

The Vertu phone – Ella's phone, she realized belatedly, wincing at her oversight. She hadn't been sure what to do with it once Ella didn't exist anymore. It was far too beautiful to just discard, but she had been letting all its calls go to voicemail and had intended to keep doing so indefinitely. The number on its screen was an unfamiliar one from the Manhattan area code; Jane guessed that she would hear André's voice on the other end of the line, growling with bad news. She took a last, longing glance toward Malcolm, but only one outstretched hand was visible from the hallway. 'Hello?' she said quietly, moving toward her own room for good measure. The rising sun hadn't reached the skylights yet, and the floorboards were chilly, but Jane consoled herself that at least they weren't creaking and giving her retreat away.

'Hello?' The voice on the other line was, she realized, definitely not André's. 'Ms. Me – um, Your Ladyship? Medeiros?'

Silly colonials still can't figure out titles, she thought with a lofty smirk, happy to ignore the fact that hers was entirely fictional. 'Yes,' she answered in a clipped approximation of Ella's confusing accent. Not wanting to run the risk of blowing her disguise by bumping into anyone from where she claimed to be from, Jane had given Ella a bizarrely varied background that would have taken far longer than her monthlong existence to unravel.

'This is Melanie Gabriel, calling from the Lowell Hotel,' the voice on the other line told her with renewed confidence. 'I'm calling to follow up with you regarding the recent fire incident here. I wanted to let you know that we've recovered a few undamaged articles from your suite. They're in storage at the moment, but I'd be happy to have them shipped to you absolutely anywhere that you would like. The shipping and the storage are complimentary, of course,' she added quickly, and Jane wondered how many threatened – or actual – lawsuits Melanie had had to field in the wake of the freak disaster.

'Thank you,' Jane replied, careful to keep her tone polite even as her mind was racing. *Undamaged articles.' Clothes? Shoes? Nail polish? Probably not nail polish*. Most of the items she had kept at the hotel were impersonal, trappings meant to shore up her disguise. But a few things meant a great deal more: a box that had been shipped to her all the way from her former desk mate in Paris, containing the last belongings she had of Gran's. She tried to imagine the glass paperweights dark with soot, or the reading glasses with their familiar grey plastic frames melted into an unfamiliar shape. Or the diary, with its cover burned off and the char chasing Gran from page to page. The image was chilling, even though she understood that the grandmother contained in the woman's journal was only a memory, not a living thing. Besides, if anything from the box had survived, something made of paper, cardboard, and fabric was unlikely to be it.

Still, Jane realized as she gave the address to Melanie, if anything of Gran's had made it through even semi-intact, it was one more link than she had had before. *Souvenirs would be nice, but what I could really use is Gran's advice.* Jane clutched the phone so hard that she barely noticed the beeping of the dead line. 'Right,' she mumbled out loud, flipping her phone closed and pushing open the door to her bedroom.

She closed the door behind her and stripped her worn, wrinkled clothes off again, tossing them carelessly onto the comforter. She tugged the thick terrycloth robe off the back of the door and trailed it along behind her on her way into her room's en-suite bathroom.

The steam and steady pressure from the shower's many jets lulled her into a relaxed enough state to start pulling her thoughts together, and she let them come without forcing them. First there was Malcolm, and she let her mind wander over every breath, touch, and smile from the night before. Then she put those memories gently aside; as important as the experience had been to her, she couldn't let it distract her from their goal.

Less than two weeks to go, she thought grimly, working bergamot-scented conditioner down to the tangled blond ends of her hair. She had notified Lynne of Annette's existence in the early evening, back when she had blithely believed that that would be the end of her troubles with the Dorans. That left just eleven days before Hasina's spell should be ready – eleven days to figure out how to stop her.

Jane longed to lay the problem at Gran's feet – even dead, she suspected, Celine Boyle would have a firm opinion. But although she had only half listened to Melanie Gabriel's explanations and apologies, she had retained the impression that it would take some time to get Ella's belongings out of storage and into the mail. And, of course, there was still no reason to think that Gran's diary would be among them. By the time that she had rinsed the last of the lather from her skin, Jane had managed to put the box carefully out of her mind. There was only time left to focus on the present, and at the moment there was only one person in the world she could imagine talking to about that. Jane shrugged haphazardly into her clothes, pulling her damp hair into a ponytail as she made a quick mental estimate of the time: Was it too early for a social call?

'You have to see this,' Dee said happily, leading Jane up a dizzying set of staircases to a nondescript metal door.

As Jane had suspected, moving in with the Montagues hadn't changed Dee's sleeping habits one bit. She sounded fully awake when she answered her cell phone, and by the time Jane made it uptown Dee looked like a well-rested woman who had already been awake for hours – which she most likely had been.

Dee paused a bit melodramatically before throwing open the door, but Jane could immediately appreciate why: the view was as stunning as it was unexpected.

The Montagues had made good use of the roof of their home, covering most of it in an idyllic garden. Trellises and vine-covered arches created one alcove after another, and wrought-iron benches and small statues peeked out from living walls of greenery. The air smelled of thick mulch and opening flowers, with the sharp, intense tang of a hundred different kinds of herbs. At the far end of the roof Jane spotted a far less witchy concession to modern living: a concrete patio surrounded an inset pool that glittered turquoise under the clear blue sky.

Dee kicked off her shoes and strode across the grass to a bench in the middle of the lush, wild garden. Jane happily followed suit.

'We've been talking it over,' Dee said with no preamble, stretching her long limbs like a cat.

Jane raised her eyebrows, surprised and encouraged that they had been working through things without her, as Dee went on. 'Emer thinks that, the farther away Annette is when the spell happens, the longer the window you'll have to interrupt it. It's probably just the difference between half a second and three seconds, but that's a big difference when you only have one shot, if you see what I mean. I know you're working on getting to Annette, so that's a solution in progress.' Jane started to interrupt, but Dee stared her down before tossing her black hair over her shoulders and continuing. 'Since the window will be so short no matter what, you'll also need to be physically in front of Lynne when it comes. There's no way you'll be able to interrupt her at the exact right second unless you can see it happen. She wouldn't do magic this major anywhere but her home, obviously, and we're working on a way to narrow it down so you're not stuck hunting her down through all eight floors. But, of course, you'll have to get in first.'

Jane straightened in surprise. 'The magic-proof door,' she blurted, her heart sinking. Her entry code couldn't possibly still be working, and doubtless Lynne had cancelled Malcolm's access as well. But without a valid code, the massive carved door and its antiwitchcraft enchantments posed a formidable barrier. If she couldn't stop the spell early, then she would need to stop it at the moment it happened, and the only way to do that was to be there – inside of 665 Park.

'We'll figure out the door,' Dee said confidently. 'At the end of the day, it's just a door.'

Jane nodded, wishing she felt as confident as Dee seemed. 'I slept with Malcolm last night,' she heard herself say, and Dee's expression went in about three directions at once.

'Is that good news?' Dee asked cautiously, but obviously couldn't bring herself to stay that way, because her wide mouth curved up into a massive grin. 'You said it like it's good news.'

77

'I think it is,' Jane admitted, feeling an answering smile tug at the corners of her own lips. 'It's complicated, though. Obviously.' When she and Malcolm had parted ways after their escape from the mansion, part of the reason had been that her feelings for him had changed. Learning that he killed her grandmother was something she'd been sure she would never be able to overcome. It wasn't enough to know how Lynne had manipulated him, how she had twisted his guilt over Annette into a lifetime of obedience. It wasn't even enough that he had defied her eventually and tried to protect Jane: atoning for his previous crimes couldn't erase them.

But since he had returned to her life, she explained to a raptly attentive Dee, Malcolm truly seemed like a changed man. He didn't just regret what he had done to harm her; he was someone who never could have done it. The old Malcolm would have acted differently in hindsight; the new one would act differently even without it.

'I think,' she finished awkwardly, blushing a little. She remembered belatedly that Malcolm's deception had cost Dee a lot, too: her apartment, her job, now her friends, and nearly her life more than once. 'Does that sound crazy?'

To her immense relief, however, Dee seemed far too preoccupied with Jane's feelings to harbour any resentments of her own. 'Do you *feel* crazy?' she asked skeptically. 'Jane, what you and Malcolm have been through isn't the way normal people live. It's not something you'll find a bunch of self-help books about, and it's not something that the usual rules can be applied to. If you can forgive him – if you can trust him – then don't resist just because it sounds crazy.' She frowned and picked at a chip in the pale polish on her fingernails, clearly choosing her next words very carefully. 'Even the best relationships aren't fairy tales,' she finished softly.

Jane pulled her feet up onto the seat of the bench, crossed her forearms over her raised knees and buried her face in them. *Harris.* Of course Dee was far too perceptive not to notice Jane's awkwardness and jealousy once her friends had paired off. 'I haven't always been the most selfless and supportive of friends when it came to yours,' she mumbled into her arms, and then nearly lost her balance as Dee shoved her sideways.

'Shut up,' she ordered in a friendly, almost cheerful tone, and Jane risked a peek out from under her hair. Dee didn't look angry or even upset, just thoughtful. 'You were what brought us together,' she explained, her voice a little throatier than usual. 'Helping you, caring about you, then missing you and worrying about you. I kept arguing that I should tell him you were still in New York after the wedding, but only because I knew you'd never let me.'

'I wanted to,' Jane admitted, resting a cheek on her forearm. A fat black ant moved purposefully across the bench between them, and she hitched her toes out of its way.

Dee shrugged philosophically. 'Things might have

79

been different between you, between us, whatever, if he'd known about you. I was sure they were going to be, after he found out. You should have heard him when he realized that he'd seen you that night at the Dorans' party and just walked out and left you there. I didn't think good society boys even knew half those words.'

Jane smiled in spite of herself, remembering her glimpses of him while she had been trying to get Annette alone, to warn her. 'I thought he had come to back me up,' she said. 'But then he recognized Katrin and went rushing off to save you.'

'I sort of hoped I would have to talk him into going back for you,' Dee confessed. She tilted her head down a little, away from the sun, and her eyes were hidden in pockets of shadow. 'You're like a sister to me, Jane, but it wasn't the easiest thing for me, knowing that you and he had a bond like that.'

'We don't,' Jane told her sincerely. Even if things didn't work out with her and Malcolm, she knew that she could never pursue Harris. Their moment had passed while she had been busy trying to save her own skin, and she felt certain that they wouldn't have another. 'I think he's great,' she admitted carefully, trying to make sure that she chose the right words. 'And the magic makes things a little . . . volatile, at times. But he grew up around that kind of weirdness, so I'm sure he knows how to ignore it, and I'm learning. I've felt several different kinds of magical chemistry now,' she pointed out, echoing her own thoughts from the night before, 'and it's no substitute for trust, understanding, and commitment. It's just the flash, and relationships are about substance. That's what makes for real bonds.'

'That's true,' Dee agreed amiably. Jane was impressed by her friend's serenity and was glad for it. 'However this thing between me and Harris started, it grew into something real. And I'm going to feel so much better about that now that you've actually said the words out loud, because it was too uncomfortable wondering how much drama was lurking below the surface.'

'None,' Jane promised, rolling her eyes. 'I probably should've just talked it out with you ages ago, but I had this insane idea that the whole thing might blow over without any of these awkward conversations.'

'Silly European,' Dee sighed loftily. 'Here in the New World, we understand that it's impossible to just quietly deal with conflict. We have to talk about *everything*.'

'I'm still trying to get the hang of you people,' Jane muttered darkly. 'I can't seem to blink without being accused of shutting people out.'

The ant's meandering trail was followed by a glossy brown beetle, and Dee flicked it gently away. 'I don't hear Malcolm complaining,' she remarked with a sly smile. Jane couldn't resist poking her in the side, and both girls dissolved into a fit of giggles. Then Dee cocked her head to the side, listening intently. 'I think I hear people moving downstairs,' she explained when she caught Jane's stare.

She hopped up onto her bare feet, holding out a hand to help Jane follow. 'I think it's time to get back to my *other* mission around here.'

'Making them all fat?' Jane guessed, brushing off the back of her slacks.

'Making *you* all fat,' Dee corrected happily, linking her arm through Jane's and tugging her cheerfully down toward the waking house.

Chapter Ten

B Y THE TIME they had climbed down through the brownstone's upper three floors, its inhabitants were awake and assembled in the kitchen, which was decorated in a chic but welcoming assortment of black-and-white patterns. Maeve blinked in surprise at the sight of Jane in their midst, then pulled two more dimpled white mugs down from their cabinet, filled each to the brim with coffee, and handed them over. Dee slid hers across the black marble counter toward the stove, strode quickly around to meet it on the other side, and had three frying pans set up on lit burners before Jane could blink.

'She spoils us so,' Emer murmured, smiling fondly first at Dee's back, then at Harris. 'I must have told her to relax a hundred times – we have meals delivered, you know – but she just . . .'

'I like it,' Dee insisted happily, pulling a fragrant, golden-brown coffee cake out of the oven and winking at Jane's astonished expression. 'It's a kind of meditation, especially when you wake up before everyone else. And it gives my hands something to do while I scheme.'

'Is that what I've been doing wrong?' Maeve wondered aloud, stirring a lump of sugar into her coffee. 'I've never actually set aside time to deliberately scheme.'

Jane leaned across the counter, admiring the bakery-perfect crumbly topping of the cake, and Dee playfully smacked her nose with a rubber spatula. 'Let it rest. There'll be plenty of food any second now.' She cracked one egg after another into one skillet while stirring some kind of thin batter in a glass bowl with her other hand. 'I was just updating Jane on all the problems she's going to have to solve in order to get to Hasina.'

Jane took a long sip of her coffee to combat the sudden gloom settling over them. 'You said you do death magic,' she said suddenly, turning to Emer, who nodded her white-curled head in agreement. 'I've been thinking . . . I would really like to talk to my gran, if there's a way to do that. You mentioned séances the other day, and I . . .' She held her empty hands up helplessly, and Dee dropped a slice of buttered sourdough toast into one of them.

Emer sighed noncommittally and sipped her coffee. 'Sometimes that is possible, though we usually have more traffic with souls than ghosts. The person, the "self" . . . it begins to fade with death, until only that pure soul is left, with no traces of its former life attached to it. The longer someone has been dead, the fewer living people who knew them, the less you have of what they've touched . . . the less of them you will be able to conjure.' Emer's vividly green eyes searched Jane's face. 'That wasn't what you wanted to hear.'

'It's not,' Jane admitted. She held up her left hand, with its plain silver band on the middle finger that had once belonged to her grandmother. 'I have this, but that's it.' She almost mentioned that Gran's diary might be coming from the Lowell Hotel, but hesitated. The diary had a magic all its own.

'I assume that its original owner is buried in France,' Emer mused, leaning forward a little in her white-painted chair, and Jane nodded. 'Pity. That ring's no good; I can see from here that it's been all mixed up with magic for decades. It confuses things. Having the body, though – well, that makes up for just about any other lack. With the bones . . .' She shivered, and a matching shiver seemed to run down Maeve's spine. 'If you're truly adept and you have someone's bones, you can call them back for real. Almost-soul, almost-body, and all the "self." You can command and compel them if you're strong enough. Most witches used to demand to be cremated,

85

to minimize the risk of being dragged from their graves by unscrupulous enemies. But of course, these days there aren't nearly as many witches who would even know what to do with a skeleton, so it's not as important as it once was.'

Jane thought guiltily of Gran in her casket, deep in the cold ground of Alsace. *But how was I supposed to know?* Gran had left her to figure out all these things for herself. She clenched her jaw in irritation. 'So I'm on my own, basically.'

'You have us,' Harris said. His voice was soft, but his tone was pointed, and Jane bit her lip.

'I do,' she agreed. 'And I appreciate that. It's just that now, with all these obstacles becoming clearer and clearer, I'm not sure what I think I'm doing taking on a thing like this. Six months ago I didn't even know that magic existed. Hasina is way out of my league – I can't even get through her front door.' Before any more self-pity could come pouring out of her mouth, she bit down on her toast, so hard that her teeth ached.

'A door is a door,' Maeve grumped, and Jane knew she and Dee had been discussing this problem at length. 'That one has some especially fancy tricks to keep it shut, but at the end of the day it's meant to be an opening that lets people into a building. We've got to be able to work with that.'

'I've never gotten through it without help,' Jane said, slumping into a black-and-white cushioned chair and resting her chin on her hands. 'I either had a code of my own, or a guest code for a special event, and I know those codes are deactivated by now.'

'But it *is* just a door.' Harris stabbed a stack of pancakes violently with a fork.

'Eggs Benedict for you, to start,' Dee declared, setting a beautifully full plate in front of Jane, who attacked it hungrily. She had suspected for a while now that performing magic burned extra calories, and that was as good an excuse as any to enjoy whatever Dee felt inspired to make. '"*Just* a door,"' the tall Wiccan repeated, practically dancing her way back to the stove. 'I wonder if we could learn from what Jane's already done.' She returned to the table with a platter of coffee-cake squares and passed it to Emer before sitting. 'When Lynne chased you and Malcolm out of the mansion, she had a shield up. She was magic-proofed, in a way . . . but you still used magic to get to her.'

Jane, caught with her mouth full of sweet, crumbly cake, hurried to swallow so that she could speak. 'I didn't exactly *get* her,' she mumbled. 'I used a tree.' She had pulled one down into the middle of traffic, causing a huge pileup. Lynne's magical protection had prevented her from being crushed by it, but in the confusion she had lost her hold on their taxi, allowing them to escape.

But Emer was nodding thoughtfully. 'You used magic on the things *around* her, because she herself was invulnerable. And it changed everything.'

She arched her thin white eyebrows at Jane, who understood that this was supposed to be the moment when she caught on, but she didn't really understand how that strategy translated to her current situation. *Do they want me to jam traffic until the Dorans come outside to see what's going on?*

Maeve, who obviously was not fooled in the slightest, snorted and pulled a paper napkin from the top of a stack on the table, unfolding it until Jane could see light filtering through. 'Grandma, spell it up,' she requested, and Emer squinted at the napkin intently. Her small frame seemed to grow somehow as she stared at it, her mouth forming silent words that Jane felt sure she should be able to hear somehow. Finally she leaned back and nodded at Maeve, who shot a glance at Jane. 'Check it out,' she ordered, shaking the napkin meaningfully. 'Try to tear it or burn it or something.'

'I'm not really in the mood for fire at the moment,' Jane admitted, but she dutifully breathed a little magic into her hands and sent it shooting at the napkin. Even though she understood what Emer had done, she still felt a genuine shock when absolutely nothing happened. It hung in Maeve's fine-boned hands, undamaged, and didn't even sway under the assault of Jane's magic. 'Okay,' she agreed, impressed. 'It's invulnerable.'

'To magic,' Dee corrected gently, and Maeve held the napkin toward her. Dee poked a French-manicured fingernail through it, and once again Jane felt a thoroughly inexplicable surprise as the paper tore.

'It's still just paper,' Harris explained, and to Jane's relief he sounded as though he was just putting it together himself. 'Just like the door is still just wood on hinges. You can't attack it yourself, but you could break it down if you find something heavy enough, and move it fast enough.'

'An SUV would probably do it,' Dee suggested archly, and Jane stuck her tongue out at her. 'Okay, too big; it might just bounce off all that stone around the door. Still, picking a battering ram is the easy part.' She hopped up from her chair, moving back toward the stove as if it were pulling her magnetically. 'Good ideas are best celebrated with bacon,' she explained over her shoulder, a satisfied smile playing on her wide mouth.

'Another tree might do it,' Jane mused, momentarily distracted when her fork clinked down on her empty plate. Harris slid another piece of coffee cake onto it with a mischievous smile, and she grinned back. She hadn't realized how much lingering awkwardness she had felt around him until Dee had pointed it out; and somehow, acknowledging it seemed to have broken the tension. She remembered how comfortable she felt around him when they had first met, before their chemistry had overshadowed their friendship, and broke off a forkful of cake happily. 'It took all my juice just to uproot the last one, though,' she admitted. 'I don't know if I could really *throw* something that heavy.'

'Last time you'd already done about sixteen impossible things before you even got to the tree,' Maeve pointed out reasonably. 'And besides, you were alone.'

Dee leaned over Jane's chair, scraping three perfectly crisp strips of bacon onto her plate. 'I may have forgotten to mention that part before,' she murmured near Jane's ear. 'We're your new coven.'

'You're my *what*?' Jane twisted to follow Dee's rapid progress away from the table. 'Are you bribing me with food so I'll completely ignore your personal safety?'

'You already agreed,' Harris told her complacently. 'We went through all this in my car a couple of weeks ago. You agreed to let us in and let us help, and now we're calling you on it.'

'A Circle is far more powerful than a witch, Jane, and more stable, too,' Emer added. 'If your objective is as important to you as it seems, then this would be a foolish thing to argue against.'

Jane opened her mouth, then closed it again. All her instincts told her that it was too dangerous to let anyone she cared about get onto Hasina's bad side, but Emer's words had the ring of truth. If she couldn't save Annette on her own, but might have a chance with her friends' help, then they would *all* be safer if she accepted their offer. *And wasn't I just talking with Malcolm about needing more power?* 'Okay,' she said. 'But if any of you takes some stupid risk and gets killed, I'm figuring out a way to bring you back so I can kill you again myself.'

Emer swallowed a bite of her sandwich and dabbed daintily at the corners of her mouth with Maeve's torn napkin. 'I'll make sure to get you some books that will help you get started with that,' she offered amiably, and Jane chuckled in spite of her renewed doubts.

'Thank you,' she said sincerely, then widened her smile to include the entire little group in the kitchen. 'Really; thank you.'

Chapter Eleven

I T TOOK NEARLY a week for Annette to contact Malcolm.
Jane was overcome with relief just to hear that she had
finally reached out to him – until she heard Annette's choice
of a meeting place.

'It's not exactly low profile,' Jane muttered, wrapping
her cherry-blossom scarf a little higher to cover part of her
chin as well as her neck.

'It is by my mother's standards,' Malcolm reassured
her, holding the door of the Ainsworth open to let Jane
through. 'There are television screens, for God's sake. I'm
amazed Annette even knows this place exists.'

Jane would have preferred something a little more dive-like, or better yet a dark alley or hidden park bench, but she knew that New Yorkers had a different scale for measuring privacy than the rest of the world. Nonetheless, she was comforted to find that the inside of the bar was dark and cozy and filled with chattering people who didn't pay the slightest bit of attention to the latest arrivals. The flat-screen televisions suspended from the ceiling projected a baseball game into every corner of the room. By the time she and Malcolm had slid onto the brown leather of one of the smaller booths, Jane, to her relief, felt more or less invisible.

'She told Mom that she was dying to go on one of those Statue of Liberty boats,' Malcolm told her absently, drumming his fingers on the table. 'It was smart, you know? Annette acted really enthusiastic, so Mom would have to break her heart, tag along, or let her go alone, and she really couldn't stand either of the first two choices.' He had already said essentially the same thing when Annette had first contacted him, and twice more in the cab on their way to the bar. Jane, feeling a wave of sympathy for the confusing muddle of emotions that he must be feeling, reached her hand out to cover his and help it to still.

'You should try the edamame burger,' a low voice purred, and Annette slid in next to Malcolm. Jane reflexively jerked her hand back, and Malcolm abruptly stopped his tapping. After a brief once-over of Jane's body that was uncannily reminiscent of Lynne, the girl added, 'They'll make it without the bun, if you ask.'

Jane bit back a retort. Starting off with sarcasm wasn't exactly the best approach to a compromise.

During the past week, Jane and the Montagues had done their best to guess the details of Hasina's body-switching spell. It would be crucial, Emer explained, to get Annette as far away from Lynne as possible. The distance wouldn't be enough to save her on its own, but it would buy Jane precious time to interfere and stop Hasina before she could transfer into her new body. That part was still the most uncertain of all their plotting – no one had figured out how they could accomplish the banishment in question.

Annette and Malcolm traded an awkward sidelong glance, and Jane suddenly felt that she was intruding on something private. She glanced around at the Lacoste-wearing strangers with their bright cocktails and expensive beers, wishing for a moment that she could join them. They looked so happy and *normal*, not at all like people staging an intervention to prevent the survival of a bloodthirsty immortal spirit. *Then again,* she thought wryly, *we probably don't look like that, either.*

Jane pretended to study a menu, trying to give the siblings enough distance so that they wouldn't feel crowded. Malcolm cleared his throat uncomfortably, then took a deep breath and began to explain the Dorans' true heritage to his sister.

'I can only imagine how hard this is to hear, after you've wondered about your birth mother for so long,' he finished. 'The family that you come from is a seriously screwed-up one, Annette, and you deserve so much better. But I'm here, and I'll always be here for you.'

'Did *she* tell you all this?' Annette asked when he paused, indicating Jane with her chin.

'She didn't have to.' Malcolm pressed gently on his sister's arm to turn her back toward him. 'There were clues all over the place. I heard hints and suspicions from a lot of people before I got back here and learned that Jane had put them all together. And I'm glad she did, because you've only just come back to me, and I don't want to lose you all over again.'

Jane felt her throat swelling a little at the emotion in his voice, but Annette's face could have been chiseled from flint. 'I'm sure it was an awfully long twenty years for *you*,' she snapped. 'Why don't you ask her about that, too?'

This again. Lynne's hold over her daughter was so strong, she had Annette convinced that Jane was responsible for everything that had gone wrong in her life – even things that had happened when Jane was barely a toddler. 'I didn't know,' Jane interrupted, then paused as a server passed perilously close to their table, balancing a tray laden with drinks. 'I didn't know that Gran had anything to do with your kidnapping until after I'd found you again,' she resumed in a lower voice. 'I didn't even know about magic at all until after Gran died. She never told me any of it.

I grew up a lot more like you than I think you realize, actually.'

She was aware as the last words were leaving her mouth that they were a bit of a risk, but Annette seemed interested rather than offended. 'Your magic . . . did things?'

'Not like yours,' Jane admitted, 'but yes. It happened a lot, and Gran would get upset and angry, and I wouldn't know why. She was always afraid. I understand her much better now, but it doesn't erase the things that happened, or how I felt for all those years. It doesn't undo the loneliness and confusion, and all that time I spent thinking I could never be part of the world.' She shook her head, trying to shake away the memories, but they clung to her like smoke. 'Maybe we don't get to be, really.'

'Our mother took nearly everything from Jane,' Malcolm added into the silence that followed. 'She's about to take everything from you. Think hard: Haven't you had any doubts these last few weeks?'

Annette pressed her full lips together, her jaw tensing a little into its familiar stubborn set. 'Has she encouraged you to make friends?' Jane prompted. 'Join any clubs or charity organizations? Look for a job or take classes or anything?'

When his sister didn't answer, Malcolm picked up Jane's line of questioning. 'I'm sure you've been doing a lot of "catching up" and "bonding,"' he guessed. 'Has she let you do that with anyone other than her?'

'Just because she doesn't want me hanging out with

traitors and kidnappers,' Annette started hotly, indicating first Malcolm and then Jane with her defiant glare, 'doesn't mean she's some kind of creepy body snatcher.'

'The fact that she's going to transfer her essence into you five nights from now, on the other hand . . .' Jane muttered, gripping the leather menu in her frustration. *I glossed over this part when I imagined our rescue plan,* she admitted to herself. Somehow she had let herself think that Annette would naturally see the truth – despite the fact that when she said the truth out loud, it sounded ludicrous, even to her.

The air around them seemed to grow perceptibly warmer, and Jane smelled something that reminded her of burning leaves. The candle on the table between them flared suddenly to life, its flame stretching to an impossible height. Annette's eyes had widened into bottomless black pits. Jane narrowed her own in response, focusing her energy on the flame, which flickered obediently down to a normal size.

'Here's the thing,' Malcolm hurried to interject, glancing nervously back and forth between the two witches. 'It's a spell with a deadline. We're trying to block it, but the farther away from her you are when it starts, the better our chances of success. If you could give us a heads-up about the exact timing of the spell, that would be a bonus, but the real problem is that if you're in the same room as her when it happens, the transfer will only take a split second. The most helpful thing would be if, five days from now, you leave town. Get as far as you can, so that we maximize our chances of intercepting her. Then you can come back in the morning, and if it turns out that we were wrong about everything, I promise to drop this whole thing forever.'

Annette hesitated and looked to Jane for confirmation, allowing the candle to extinguish in the cool afternoon air. 'We'd never ask you to hurt your mother,' Jane agreed. 'We're not trying to convince you to attack her out of the blue, or run away for good, or do anything else you can't take back. It's just one night. One night, and it will save your life.'

There was a long silence as Annette looked down and twisted her fingers together. 'For this spell you think she's going to do,' she said finally, so softly that Jane had to lean forward to hear, 'would she maybe need some of my hair?'

Malcolm gently pulled her hands apart and pressed one between his own. Emer and Dee had both speculated that Hasina would 'anchor' the spell to its intended victim, but the forewarning didn't stop a chill from running down Jane's spine anyway. She set her menu aside and began tracing the patterns of the table's wood grain with one fingertip.

'I want to leave now,' Annette whispered. 'I could get farther away if I went right now. That's what you want, isn't it?'

Malcolm's voice was steady, low, reassuring. 'There's no way she'd agree to you taking a trip now, with the deadline so close. And if you left without a word, she'd know you were onto her. She'd find you, for one thing, but first she'd take out Jane and all the other people who are trying to help us. There'd be no one left to stop her, and then you would be gone, for real. I know it's scary, but your best chance is to wait.'

'And you can't let her guess that anything is wrong,' Jane added, glancing back up when Annette remained silent. 'She thinks you believe that you two are rebuilding your family. It's the only reason you got out alone today, and it's the only way you'll avoid getting tied up for the next five days.'

'Literally,' Malcolm agreed, squeezing Annette's hand for emphasis. 'She's done that to both of us before; she wouldn't hesitate with someone she needs as badly as you. You have to make her trust you enough to let you move around freely until the moment comes when you can escape.'

'Is this the kind of thing you two had to do?' Annette asked plaintively. This time, when she tilted her face up to include Jane in the question, her eyes were soft and completely without resentment. 'Was there all this . . . horribleness, back before you ran away?'

Jane locked eyes with Malcolm for a moment, remembering how carefully they had planned their own escape from Lynne. It hadn't worked at all the way they'd intended, so it was impossible to be as naïvely optimistic this time as she had felt back then. But Annette already

99

looked miserable, and there was nothing to be gained from telling her the whole truth. 'It was a little like this,' she admitted, 'but we have much more outside help this time, and a better idea of what we're up against. It's still scary, and we still have to be really careful. But we are going to get you out of this.'

Malcolm nodded in emphatic agreement, and Annette managed a wan smile. Jane smiled back, and some of her imaginary hope began to feel real. *It's going to work,* she repeated to herself, and it sounded a little less implausible every time. *She's with us now, and it's going to work.*

Chapter Twelve

SPIRITS IN THE Montagues' brownstone had started to flag a little under the uncertainty of their planning, but the news that Jane and Malcolm had finally gotten Annette's cooperation brought new life to the little group. Jane herself felt absolutely elated for three whole days. But then the doubts started to creep back in, and by the morning of their planned attack she was thoroughly worried about the enormous task in front of her. It was all well and good to be able to get into the mansion, and great that Annette had agreed not to be in it, but there was still no way of knowing what might be waiting for them on the other side of that door.

Jane had every confidence that whatever Hasina needed for her spell *would* be there, of course. The mansion was Lynne's fortress; she wouldn't trust her preparations anywhere else. But there was no way to know for sure what form those things would take, or how they would be guarded. Dark magic required dark materials, and nightmares crept back into Jane's sleep, full of grinning skulls, pools of blood, and fire, always fire.

To compound her worries, the timing of their assault on the huge stone house was perilously uncertain. Annette had reported overhearing Lynne mention something about 'midnight' to her twin cousins, but Lynne's meeting with Jane in Central Park had been sometime midafternoon, which meant the spell could easily take place several hours earlier. Annette's information had divided their group and created a creeping sense of uncertainty. Jane had decided that the consequences of arriving late were worse than those of being too early, but she could tell that Malcolm, in particular, had serious reservations about her decision.

So when Malcolm approached her that morning, asking if he could help Annette get to safety instead of joining the assault on the Park Avenue house, she felt a distinct sense of relief. Her feelings for him were still wildly complicated, and she needed to focus on the monumental task at hand without that distraction. His place was with his sister, helping her get quickly and safely out of the house, while hers was here, making it safe for them both to eventually return.

Besides, the biggest advantage that Malcolm brought to the table was an intimate knowledge of his former home, the need for which had been eliminated thanks to Dee and Maeve's dedicated work. Playing with variations of the spell Jane once used to find Annette's old belongings, they had succeeded in tweaking it so that it would lead her to Hasina's spell ingredients instead. The modifications hadn't been easy – Harris lost half an eyebrow in the experimentation, and Maeve had spent an entire day unable to speak anything but Gaelic – but Dee guaranteed that this final spell would work. Annette needed Malcolm much more than they did at the moment.

Breaking in and finding the spell ingredients was only the first step. Once inside, they would have Lynne's creepy twin cousins to contend with – and Lynne herself, of course. Jane knew that even without her magic, Lynne Doran's slender, couture-clad form was still the scariest thing that would be waiting for them inside 665 Park Avenue.

Once we're past all that – Jane forced her brain to move on – *the end of the plan is solid, at least.* Emer had spent every moment of the last two weeks fashioning a wooden box. Though it looked, on the surface, almost nothing like the whimsical spirit box Malcolm had brought Jane, whenever she glanced at it out of the corner of her eye, she kept thinking it was hers. They were, after all, both designed to contain souls. When Hasina's spell forced her essence out of Lynne's body, Emer's box would trap her

103

before she could travel to Annette's. All they needed to do was make it to that one vital moment – if only the obstacles in their way didn't seem to multiply every time Jane counted them.

She tried to distract herself with a walk in the roof garden, meditation in the sauna, cup after cup of Emer's fascinating homemade herbal teas . . . but the bustling preparations of her friends chased her from room to room until she began to feel like a trapped animal. *I can't let them see me scared,* she thought: against all odds they had succeeded in making her vague, unlikely plan possible. It would be unfair and unkind to let her nerves take anything away from that remarkable accomplishment, especially now, when they were so close to putting their ideas into action. *So close to following me through an unbreachable door into a nest of angry witches and making them even angrier,* Jane's brain corrected. She pushed away from the breakfast bar, dropped her stoneware mug in the dishwasher, and all but ran out of the kitchen.

But the tension in the sitting room seemed to crackle almost audibly, giving Jane a stress headache from the moment she walked in.

'I don't even know what this does,' Harris exclaimed, picking up a waxed-paper bundle and then tossing it back onto the coffee table. There was a sudden, blinding flash and a small puff of smoke, and Dee and Maeve took shelter behind the striped couch.

'That was *supposed* to be edelweiss and a little basil,'

Emer called reprovingly from across the room, where she was occupied with a length of rope and a tiny silver knife.

'I punched it up a little,' Dee admitted, rolling her eyes and dusting her arms off theatrically. 'I'll go make some more.'

Harris watched her go, then turned his glittering green gaze to Jane. 'Where's the man of the hour?' he asked, with minimal sarcasm. 'I would have thought he'd be here by now.'

Jane took a deep breath. The Montagues had made so much progress in coming to accept Malcolm's presence here, but it was always clear that he wasn't really one of them. She hadn't yet told them that he wouldn't be joining them tonight. She knew it was cowardly, but she'd put off this discussion as long as possible, knowing it would break the town house's fragile sense of peace. 'He's not coming with us tonight,' she said slowly.

'He's with his sister,' Maeve guessed in the pause that Jane's discomfort left.

'She was really upset,' Jane confirmed, not quite looking at anyone in particular. Malcolm had read her a few of Annette's increasingly frantic text messages until she had to ask him to stop – Annette's panic was so intense that it began to feel contagious, and she needed a clear head right now. 'Apparently Lynne told her that there was some kind of supersecret family initiation tonight and she totally freaked out. Malcolm tried to calm her down, but

105

she begged him to pick her up at the house this afternoon and help her get out of the city.'

Emer nodded her approval, but Harris's voice sliced through the air like a knife. 'What did Malcolm tell her, exactly, to "calm her down"?' Jane frowned, not understanding why the phrase would sound so sinister to him, and after a moment he clarified. 'Did he tell her that we'd figured out how to break down the door? That we could find her mother – or at least, her tools – as soon as we got inside? That we know the earliest moment the spell could begin, because we have *Ella*'s call history? That Grandma knows how to trap Hasina between bodies?'

'In other words, "our entire plan,"' Dee translated from the doorway, twisting her tawny hands together.

Jane froze, her tongue feeling heavy and uncooperative. 'She was—'

'Scared,' Emer finished for her. 'Sending frightened messages.' Her voice was flat, and her face unreadable.

'She was,' Jane insisted, trying to fight off the new, squeaky note in her voice. She knew the truth – she had seen it on Annette's face just a few days ago. Of course Harris doubted Annette's sincerity. He hadn't seen the horror that slowly overtook her, the pure fear etched into her features as though with a knife. Jane wished she could explain in a way that would show him what she had seen. 'Look, I don't know for sure how much Malcolm told her about any of that, but he's with her right now. He'd tell us if anything had gone wrong.' Her last words met a resounding silence that reminded her of the breathless pause before thunder.

When the thunder came, it started off deceptively softly. 'Call it off,' Harris growled, then he turned to include the rest of the room. 'The whole thing is off, starting now.'

'We can't do that,' Maeve temporized, but Harris was still gaining steam.

'Jane. Can you reach him? He's in a car with Hasina's new body, so either he's in on it, or he's in danger. He has to pick one. Tell him that he drives his sister into an overpass this minute, or he's not setting foot in this house again.'

His grandmother cleared her throat warningly, clearly gearing up to remind him whose house this actually was, but Jane found her voice first.

'No one's calling anything off,' she insisted, wishing that she hadn't delayed this conversation to begin with.

Harris leaped to his feet. 'The hell we're not,' he shot back, his voice a low snarl. 'They're waiting for us. If you think any of us is going to follow you into the trap your boyfriend and his sister have set, you're absolutely insane.'

'Harris,' Dee murmured, her amber eyes flicking anxiously between him and Jane. 'Can we hear her out?'

He snapped his mouth angrily shut, crossed his arms across his triangular torso, and waited expectantly. *Thanks, Dee,* Jane thought silently at her friend, unsure how much of her own thought was sarcasm. 'It's not a trap,' she began, improvising wildly as she went. *'I think I*

107

love him' isn't going to be on anyone's top-ten list of convincing explanations. 'Malcolm's been totally up front about everything having to do with his family,' she began. 'He showed me his phone so I could see Annette's texts, and I . . . I checked it, okay?' She had felt an uncomfortable mix of embarrassment and vindication after scrolling through his messages and had hoped that ignoring it would make it go away. 'The very first contact he's made with any of them was when *we* asked him to reach out to his sister. There was nothing else; nothing that didn't belong.'

'That doesn't sound like a double cross,' Maeve agreed reasonably, laying a soothing hand on Harris's sleeve.

He shook her off with an irritated shrug. 'Or they just covered their tracks with, you know, magic,' he countered angrily, gesturing at the cluster of women in the room. 'Can any of you honestly rule that out?'

A charged silence filled the room. 'You could do it,' Dee murmured, her eyes downcast. When she lifted them, Jane could see how painful her indecision was for her. 'I'm not saying that they did,' she rushed to add. 'If you trust Malcolm, then I do, too. But it's not like it's a completely unreasonable point Harris is making, is all.'

'She married Malcolm Doran,' Harris exploded, and Dee flinched away from his side. He balled his hands into fists and closed his eyes. When he reopened them, he seemed to have mostly regained control of his emotions, but Jane could see the fear and anger still bubbling just below the surface. 'Am I really the only one who can see that Jane's opinion isn't the one we should trust when it comes to these people?'

'He's practically lived in our house for a week now,' Maeve pointed out.

Is that all? Jane wondered; it felt as though it had been much, much longer. In spite of her certainty that Malcolm had been truthful with them, a tendril of doubt snaked its way into her mind. He hadn't been back in New York for very much time at all.

'And he tried to help Jane,' Maeve pushed on. 'Even after seeing what happened to me when I tried.'

A heavy silence filled the room, and Jane felt herself losing the will to argue. She believed that she was right about Malcolm, but was that enough of a reason to keep endangering her friends? *I could have just left New York when I had the chance, and it wouldn't matter whose side Malcolm was on,* she thought miserably. *I could still leave, and they could go back to arguing about where to go for brunch and which Broadway opening to attend this weekend.*

But even as the thought passed through her mind, Jane knew it was a lie. *'She kills witches,'* she heard André say, as clearly as if he were sitting on the loveseat in their midst. *'No truces, no deals, no peace.'* Running away from Hasina wouldn't help anyone – she had gotten to Celine Boyle, after all, who had been about as isolated as it was possible to be. *She found her and sent Malcolm to kill her.*

'I trust him,' Jane breathed, and for a long moment Harris's green eyes remained locked with her own. *I trusted him before, too,* she didn't say, and she knew that everyone in the room was thinking the same thing. 'I trust him,' she repeated, this time more firmly, 'and I'm going to Park Avenue tonight, even if I have to go alone. You all know how much I hate putting you guys in any kind of danger, anyway,' she half joked, trying for a winning smile but fairly sure that it missed.

'Don't be silly, Jane.' Emer waved away her protests. She turned her attention squarely on Harris, who shifted a little uncomfortably under her clear green gaze. 'It would be an awful trap,' she explained in a clipped, concise tone. 'The spell is meant to happen tonight. If they know we're coming, then letting us get all the way into their own home would be absurd. All they would have to do is keep us away for a few hours and then deal with us when Hasina has her brand-new body. Using Malcolm to lure us *closer* would be thoroughly pointless.'

Harris looked like he wanted to argue, but no words came out. Jane knew that, no matter how strong his dislike of Malcolm, he was a fair-minded man. She sighed gratefully when he threw up his hands in defeat.

'All I had to do was out-logic you?' She tried to joke, although there was still a lingering edge to her voice.

Emer turned squarely toward Jane, and this time it was her turn to flinch. 'None of what I've said means that we're safe,' she reprimanded. 'Annette should never have been told the details of our plan. I understand how you feel for the girl, but it was a terrible risk, and it's put her life in worse jeopardy along with ours. We will all need to proceed very, very carefully tonight. Jane, you will prepare a message for Malcolm, ordering him to kill his sister immediately. If we are mistaken and the Dorans are ready for us after all, you must send it. I do hope that your trust in him is well placed, as he has now become our very last line of defense.'

It sounded like the meeting was adjourned. Most of the others made a decent show of returning to their preparations, but Harris lingered behind, his hands in his pockets. Jane could tell that everyone was watching them with faintly disguised interest. 'I'm sorry,' he murmured, and Jane could tell that he meant it. 'I know I haven't exactly been the guy's biggest fan, but your opinion of him is based on personal stuff as much as mine, and my family is staking their lives on it. I hope that you're right, you know.' His eyes glinted with sudden mischief. 'Hell, if it all works out right, maybe I'll even get to go to your next wedding.'

'Trust me,' she told him, keeping her voice perfectly steady. 'If I ever get married again – to anyone – I'm eloping.'

'I'm still doing the cake,' Dee shouted cheerfully from the kitchen. Seconds later she reappeared in the opening of the swinging door, arms full of bright-green branches with a baffling assortment of differently shaped leaves.

'Better have a food taster on hand.' Emer crossed to her in a few quick steps and pulled two of the branches out of

Dee's bundle, holding them as far away from the rest as her arm could reach. With the immediate danger out of the way, her tone became less tight and more playful. 'What have we said about "improving" spells, young lady? I was just starting to look forward to living through the night.'

'It'll enhance the juniper,' Dee protested, and the argument shifted her way. Jane watched with increasing amusement as her dark-haired friend fielded a storm of objections from the room's 'real' witches, defending her herb choices with a quick wit and an impressive breadth of scholarly support.

It was clear that the storm over Malcolm's plan had passed, and Jane hummed a bit to herself as she double-checked the little pouches that would make her magical 'eye shadow,' which Dee had given to her earlier that afternoon. The last one had been a rather strong gold color, but Dee had told her that this one should come out a shimmery pale pink, which could go with just about anything. Jane had chosen to pair it with a fashionable-yet-stealthy knit cap, jeans, and a thin black sweater she'd bought for 'Ella,' but which hugged her real curves surprisingly well.

She checked her Cartier tank watch (another Ella purchase, and one of her favourites), slid the pouches into her knapsack, relocated them to her pocket, and checked her watch again. Around her, the good-natured argument ranged from one corner of the great room to the other, getting further and further off topic as increasingly wild accusations and long-forgotten stories were tossed about as ammunition.

How can this group not succeed at whatever we set our minds to? Jane thought fondly. 'All right, everyone,' she said loudly, and the chatter stopped abruptly. 'Starting tonight, Hasina's done stealing bodies.' A single purpose filled the faces that turned toward her, and Jane had to suppress the urge to hug each of them. 'Now let's go put that bitch in the ground.'

Chapter Thirteen

A N UNSEASONABLY CHILLY wind blew through the open car window as Jane studied the front of the Dorans' house. Although the brass plate read '665,' the house squatted heavily between 664 and 668. *They could at least have left the right number, to warn people of what's really living there.* The eight stories of greenish-grey stone seemed to loom over the sidewalk. No lights shone from the windows, which looked like so many empty, soulless eyes, and Jane's heart beat a little faster.

Out of the corner of her eye she saw Emer and Maeve climb purposefully out the opposite door of Harris's electric-blue Mustang. Dee was still up front. Then she turned her attention inward, focusing all the power of her mind on the five shimmering powders in front of her. She poured four of them into the largest packet, which contained the fifth, and closed her eyes.

Mian an chroí an Hasina, she thought fiercely. *Mian an chroí an Hasina.* It wasn't enough to find any old thing belonging to Hasina, as it had been when she was looking for something of Annette's. Everything in the mansion – even the mansion itself, its walls and floors and ceilings – belonged to Hasina. The difference called for this incantation, rather than a simple name, and a tricky extra powder. *Mian an chroí an Hasina. Mian an chroí an Hasina. Mian an chroí an Hasina.* Jane was just glad that she was allowed to recite the words in her mind; even thinking the Gaelic made her feel as though she had a mouth full of marbles, and it had only gotten worse when Maeve wrote it down for her. She balled her hands into fists and pictured the malevolence behind Lynne's odd, lens-like eyes. *Mian an chroí an Hasina.* She recalled her own dreams and visions through Annette's eyes; wasn't that the view that Hasina wanted more than anything? Her spell would give it to her, and this would lead Jane to the spell. *Mian an chroí an Hasina.* She dipped her fingers into the mingled powders and smeared them liberally across her still-closed eyelids.

'She's ready,' Dee's husky voice murmured from the passenger seat, and Jane heard the leather protest a little as she twisted. 'Jane, they've got one.'

Jane heard some more rustling, and then something soft landed beside her in the backseat. She opened her eyes slowly, carefully, but the house looked the same. *It doesn't have to feel like anything to work,* she reminded herself dutifully.

The Montague witches stood on either side of one of the trees planted in the median. Its branches were starting to sway drunkenly. The women's bare arms glowed white-gold in the light from the streetlamps, and Jane realized that they, like Dee, had half instinctively removed jackets and sweaters before going to work. The night was cool, but she could already see sweat glistening on Maeve's smooth forehead.

Jane absently folded the red hoodie that Dee had tossed into the back, then slid out of the car. 'Stand back,' she warned Dee and Harris, who had quickly stood up as well, but she didn't have to watch them to know that they wouldn't go far, despite her warning. The other two melted back from the tree a bit, which started to sway even more dangerously until Jane's magic reached out to prop it up.

Her friends formed a loose half circle around the door to 665 Park. From her position in the centre, Jane looked around at them: they stood too far apart to hold hands, but she could almost see the lines of magic stretched taut between them, pulsing with energy. Then four pairs of eyes locked on her in unison, and with it came all the power they had been working to pull into their Circle.

Her knees buckled under the sheer force of it, and her head swam. She felt momentarily drunk, but the sharp boundaries of the Circle around her held her in place until she could bring the street back into focus. She could sense her own intentions reflected back at her from every side, herding her toward her target: the tree.

The others had loosened it for her, she could tell: its sprawl of roots was partly visible, still covered in rich black dirt. Its branches, full of perfect miniature leaves, continued to wave softly. The other trees on the median strip swayed as well, but when she looked closely it was obvious to Jane that her tree was responding to something other than the brisk wind. When she reached her magic out toward it again, she could feel its wrongness like a loose tooth in the back of her own mouth.

Then the tide of magic from the people around her swept her mind onward again, and she solidified the grip of the magic on the tree's rough trunk. She could almost feel its sap sliding beneath her skin. The wind moving through the leaves stirred her hair with the same touch. The power channeling through her was changing, and Jane changed with it: lifting and turning a burden that would have been far too heavy for one person alone. Five, though, could hold the tree suspended in thin air, and Jane marveled at the relative ease of it. Uprooting her first tree had taken nearly all her energy; this time she still had more than enough left to throw it.

An intangible change ran through the Circle, jumping

117

from nerve ending to nerve ending, tingling up through Jane's arms and into her brain. *Ready.* The thought was hers, but she heard Dee's voice in it as well, and Harris's more faintly, and a sort of rich vibration below that she knew must belong to the other two witches.

The tree held steady for a moment, shaking slightly from the pressure of magic on every side of it, and then it shot forward like an arrow. Jane felt her hair and sweater whip around her in its wake as she watched it crash resoundingly into the carved front door. The door splintered with a satisfying crunch, but the tree rebounded back into the empty air. Jane could see that the door was badly damaged, but she didn't dare look closer: even shared between them the tree was beginning to feel heavy. She focused all her attention on the tree and felt the answering magics of her Circle backing her up.

Again, she thought, or maybe they all thought it at once, and the tree surged forward a second time. It was almost imperceptibly slower, but still landed solidly enough to do the trick: the thick brass hinges let go with a high-pitched wail, and the door sagged brokenly inward.

Inward into the lions' den. Jane shivered at how hollow and thin her own thoughts suddenly sounded in her mind. *I'm alone again in here,* she realized with a feeling much like grief. She shook her head to clear it and tried to make herself step forward, to where Dee and the Montagues were approaching the gaping ruins of the carved wooden door. Their linked Circle had served its purpose, Jane knew, and there was a lot to do in the next few minutes, but she couldn't quite shake her lingering feeling of loneliness.

She moved up toward the doorway, and they moved instinctively to let her peer inside. The familiar gold-and-marble entryway was littered with dark splinters. Jane immediately saw the uniformed figure at the security desk to her left, and her magic flared up protectively – but it was only Gunther, and he was slumped over, unconscious. *Knocked out by the blast,* she thought charitably, although she knew the ancient doorman had probably been asleep before they even arrived at the mansion. Either way, he seemed to be breathing but not moving, so she decided to ignore him, stepping gingerly over the remains of the door and across the threshold.

Her flats clicked on the grey-veined white marble, and she heard more footfalls behind her as her friends filed in. 'You know what to do,' she whispered without turning around, and a quick flurry of activity followed. Harris and Dee swept past her together, bypassing the waiting elevator and the wide-mouthed marble staircase in favour of the humble wooden door that housed the back stairs. Without the benefit of Jane's magical eye shadow, they would do a cursory search of the lower floors. Jane felt sure, though, that the spell would be on one of the higher ones, so she had elected to start from the top and work her way down.

Maeve hurried into the gold-panelled elevator, her

brown eyes round and bright with excitement. Her grand-mother followed her halfway in, frowning and running her papery-skinned hands along the edge of its retracted door. Jane stepped carefully around Emer to join Maeve inside but kept her eyes anxiously trained on the older woman.

'I have it,' Emer declared proudly, and Jane let out a breath she hadn't even realized she'd been holding. Emer stood squarely in front of the open door and pulled a silky amulet bag out to rest on top of her blouse. She closed one hand around it, then pulled a small blue crystal out of her shoulder bag with the other. She kissed the crystal, or maybe whispered something to it, squeezed the amulet a little harder, and pressed the crystal to the elevator's control panel. The elevator whirred to life almost immediately.

'Go, Grandma, go,' Maeve whispered, and Jane could see a small smile on the old woman's lips as she began to whisper an incantation. Jane strained to make it out, but she couldn't hear any of the words. *Trade secrets,* she thought with a shrug; as long as they got where they were going, Emer could be as stealthy as she wanted.

Jane had never really doubted that Maeve's grandmother could get the elevator going without the usual electronic codes, but she still felt giddy relief at her success. If anything, the machine seemed to be rising even faster than usual. *Five . . . six . . . seven . . .* The elevator's last stop would be the atrium, one level below the hollow square of an attic that had once been Charles's home. *I wonder if they've repaired it enough to send him back there,* Jane thought, bouncing nervously from the ball of one foot to the other. *Or maybe he's wandering the halls full-time now.* It was a sobering thought, even in the midst of their successes so far. If the attic was still damaged badly enough by the fire, Charles might be anywhere – including right in the way of the couple moving up the stairs.

They'll be fine, she assured herself, gripping the edge of her wide belt so tightly that the soft leather left angry marks on her skin. Charles had no magic; even his unpredictable, sometimes-violent self would be no match for a resourceful Wiccan and an athletic young man.

She closed her eyes and drew her magic together. It was ready, waiting, eager to leap out from the tension-filled cage of her body. She soothed and corralled it, trying to remember all the possible attacks that the twins might use first. Then the floor lurched beneath her feet, and her eyes flew open. The delicate '8' above the door had lit up. *Already?* she thought, just as another part of her sighed *Finally.*

The doors slid effortlessly open, and Jane stepped past Emer into the atrium. It was a sooty, broken shadow of its former elegance, and for a moment André's scarred face swam in her vision. Not for long, however, because the atrium, for all its devastation, wasn't empty. *Of course they're in the first place we looked.* For a wild moment she wondered why she had even bothered with the pretence

121

of searching the mansion: part of her had known all along that the spell would only take place right here.

Belinda Helding and Cora McCarroll stood in the shadows to either side of the elevator – Jane couldn't tell which was which, but it didn't matter. Both wore lots of long, grey layers that melted almost seamlessly into their long grey hair, and their twin pairs of pewter eyes shone flatly in the low light. The other two figures were nothing but silhouettes against the floor-to-ceiling windows, but Jane knew them all the same. The tallest and thinnest, her sleek chestnut hair pulled back into a perfect twist, could only be Lynne. But it was the slightly fuller one with the curling tendrils of shoulder-length hair that held Jane's full attention.

'Hello, Jane,' Annette Doran purred, her voice as smooth and sharp as glass. 'Welcome home.'

Chapter Fourteen

THE INSIDE OF the elevator seemed to catch fire, and when Jane opened her mouth, it seared the air out of her lungs. She lunged forward and down, to where the air was cool and dark — a hand clutched at the back of her sweater, and she jerked instinctively farther forward away from its grasp. In just a few seconds she had become completely disoriented.

'Jane!' Maeve called desperately, and Jane realized too late that it was her hand she had pulled away from.

I went the wrong way, she realized. *I should have gone back into the elevator.* Instead, she was crouched on the floor, thoroughly disoriented and vulnerable.

'Jane!' a different voice called, its sound warped by another wave of strangely unreal heat. She couldn't even say for sure which direction the blast came from, but she did know that she couldn't stay where she was for long. *I'm right where Annette wanted me.* The shock of the girl's betrayal shook Jane every bit as much as the first blistering assault of her magic had. *Why didn't Malcolm tell us that she never met up with him this afternoon? When did this all go wrong?*

The room around her thickened unnaturally and the smell of smoke filled her nostrils, but this time Jane was ready to act. She clenched the magic in her blood like an invisible muscle and pushed, forcing it out through her skin and into the surrounding space. A bubble of air cleared, though she could see waves of distortion just outside it. Out there, she realized, the battle was already joined.

Maeve and her grandmother had retreated into opposite sides of the elevator, only visible in bits and flashes as they lobbed spells and amulet bags half blindly into the atrium. Lynne's twin cousins seemed to have their hands full blocking those attacks while trying to advance on the open door, and Jane could tell that they were still making steady progress. But she couldn't help the trapped witches just yet: Annette was heading across the soot-blackened floor toward Jane, and the buzz of magic around her was so strong that Jane could almost see it. An unfamiliar, metallic taste filled her mouth when she inhaled, and she tried to breathe mostly through her nose to avoid it.

The Dalcaşcus had been right all along: Annette was no innocent victim in need of rescue. She was an unstable, untrustworthy, vengeance-minded killer.

'You must have thought I'm hopelessly stupid,' Annette remarked. Her mother hadn't even bothered to step into the fray, Jane noticed. *And why should she? No magic of her own, and plenty of puppets to do her bidding.* 'Did you really think Mom wouldn't tell me all about my inheritance? Or that I'd let that jealous waste of a brother try to trick me out of it?'

'Malcolm,' Jane croaked, trying to force her parched and cracked throat to turn the word into a question.

'He's been jealous of me ever since that day he "lost" me on the beach,' Annette snarled, launching another wave of vicious heat into the air. 'And now he's trying to separate me from my family all over again. But this time I'm strong enough to fight back.'

For a fleeting moment, Jane wondered what Annette would be like if her grandmother and the Dalcaşcus had never interfered that day in the Hamptons. Would she have turned into a miniature Lynne – or would having Malcolm as a brother have helped make her a warmer, more caring person? Jane wanted to think the latter, but she had a feeling Annette would be . . . problematic, no matter how she'd grown up.

A faint glow near Lynne became visible against the dim

light filtering through the windows. Jane squinted at it as she upheld her magical shield, trying to see clearly. It was definitely inside the room with them. But Annette was still inching closer, and her nearness was searing the air and sucking it dry of moisture. *She's been learning,* Jane thought, coughing sickly.

She reached down through her veins again, trying to separate some magic from what was keeping the shield around her in place. It was confusing at first, like she was looking through two pairs of eyes at once. But she managed to grip some into a ball and hold it for a moment, ready to strike—

'I do wish you had told me what you had in mind, Annette,' Lynne said suddenly, and Jane held her magic back, momentarily distracted. 'Soon you'll be far too powerful to bother with these little revenge scenarios; you have nothing to prove to these insects. Be a dear and kill them so that we can get back to it.'

A bolt of energy darker than the half darkness around it glanced off the side of Jane's protective bubble, grazing her shoulder rather than hitting her squarely in the back. *Belinda,* she thought through gritted teeth. Her whole shoulder felt numb and heavy, and Annette had almost reached the edge of her shield. The heat was already intense, and Jane knew that she absolutely couldn't allow Annette to get inside her magical barrier. She felt for the edges of her shield and retracted it toward her body, pulling it into a dense sort of second skin.

'I would have thought that you had had enough of party-crashing, Jane,' Lynne went on in her deadly purr. 'Have you missed us so much that you simply couldn't stay away?'

'Shut up,' Jane grunted, forcing her magic out and forward in a solid wall. Annette stumbled backward, and Jane gulped a quick lungful of the relatively clear air.

Her vision seemed clearer as well, but the odd glowing near Lynne was as indistinct as it had been earlier. There was a large shadow moving in front of it, which Jane slowly realized was the lank hair and large, bowed shoulders of Charles Doran. He was pacing back and forth, agitated and nervous, in front of . . . *in front of what?* she wondered again. Nothing behind him seemed to provide a source of the unnatural light, which was vague and shimmering. Something about it nagged at the edges of Jane's mind, but by then Annette had regained her balance, and Jane turned back to her, fumbling for what remained of her magic.

'Mother's right, you know,' Annette hissed. 'In a few minutes I'll be too powerful to care whether Malcolm dies, or you live. You just had the bad luck – or bad planning – to show up while I still *do* care.'

A heavy crash sounded from somewhere behind her, and one of the twins screamed shrilly. *Pain? Fury? Triumph?* It was impossible to tell without taking her eyes off Annette and Lynne, and Jane was sure that if she did, it would be the end of her. She pressed the tattered remains of her magical shield together into an intense new knot just below her heart. Her skin felt naked and exposed, but there was no way around it: she couldn't attack *and* defend *and* keep an eye on whatever Charles and Lynne were hovering around by the far windows.

She jabbed outward with her power, thinking of snow and icicles and the wind off the mountain slopes in Saint-Croix-sur-Amaury as she did. She didn't have any particular reason to think that it would help, especially not enough to offset Annette's unnatural pyrotechnics, but the atrium chilled perceptibly and the tall girl seemed to almost shrink in on herself. A bright-green flare shot past from the elevator, and Jane saw a moment of intense pain on Annette's square-jawed face. She pressed her focus forward harder, feeling her flagging energy surge as Annette cringed back another step.

A shadow flickered behind Annette, and Jane barely ducked down in time as a heavy silver platter flew past the place where her head had been moments before. She was less quick with the stoneware pitcher that followed: it caught her squarely in the rib cage and knocked the breath out of her lungs in a single painful rush. The room whirled sickeningly, and she fell forward, managing to catch herself painfully on one knee. It took her a full, panicked second to figure out that she was facing entirely the wrong way, back toward the pitched battle for control of the elevator. Emer held the door almost closed, she and Maeve ducking out from behind its cover to fire spells at

Belinda and Cora. The twins' swirling grey forms were closing in, and they didn't look tired at all.

Flames ripped across Jane's still-numbed shoulder, setting her sweater ablaze and blackening the long ends of her hair. She tried to turn toward the assault, but then the pain came, cutting downward across her body and doubling her over. For a long moment she had no idea where Annette was, or Maeve, or even her own magic; she was alone in the middle of the floor with the fire and the pain. Then there was a stabbing in her lower back – not magic this time, but the point of a boot. Annette kicked her again, viciously, and Jane fell forward to curl in the fetal position as she tried to think of something, anything, to buy herself some time. Her magic was reduced to tattered shadows at the corner of her consciousness; she could barely feel it, much less control it.

Then in a strange, frozen moment of clarity she realized what was glowing at the far end of the room: Hasina's spell must be there, setting off the powder on Jane's eyelids. *And Lynne started lobbing spare parts at me when it looked like I might have an edge on her daughter.* Her mind flashed inexplicably to the moment twenty-eight days earlier, in Central Park, when Lynne's face had been filled with wonder at the knowledge that Annette was still alive. It was followed quickly by Annette's broken expression five days earlier, when she seemed to realize that her mother was her enemy. And then she saw Malcolm: the molten pools of his eyes, the thick waves of hair that glinted with gold lights, the way that one corner of his mouth tended to quirk upward in amusement – and she felt somehow stronger.

Jane rolled instinctively, feeling the air stir alongside her ribs as Annette tried to kick her again, but missed. Her vision felt blurred as she struggled to her feet, and it took her a moment to make sense of what she was seeing. The door to the back stairs was hanging open as two dark shapes darted inside one after the other. *The cavalry.* The hall lights glittered briefly off Dee's long black hair; Harris had already come through. Cora McCarroll fell to the burned floor, twitching and spasming – and Jane tore her attention back toward Annette, who was advancing warily, her dark eyes flickering from Jane's face to her hands and back again.

'I can't believe you ever thought we had anything in common,' she rasped, her low voice a strange, feminine echo of Malcolm's. 'You're nothing. I'm a part of *this*.'

Out of the corner of her eye, Jane saw Dee moving stealthily along the bank of floor-to-ceiling windows, circling them. Her hair danced wildly as she passed two panels that had been shattered in the fire. She wasn't sure what Dee was up to, but she did know that she didn't want the Dorans to notice her. ' "This" will be the last thing you ever do,' Jane retorted. 'But if you're feeling suicidal, go ahead. I can take out Hasina just as easily after she's wearing your skin. My mistake was thinking that you'd want someone to try to save it.'

Annette lunged at her in response, raking her arm with four sharp fingernails that left a fiery trail of magic behind them. Jane spun away just as a hoarse scream filled their end of the atrium, and something like fireworks erupted near the elevator in a shower of sparks and light. Jane whipped around to see Dee, her hands clutching that strange glowing light, bent precariously backward by the grip of Lynne's slim hand in her hair. *She went for the spell,* Jane realized with a surge of hope. They'd lost any hope of securing the house waiting for the perfect moment to destroy Hasina, but they could still destroy the spell components.

Out of the corner of her eye she saw Annette moving and spun back to meet her attack, but Annette seemed not to even see her anymore and was instead charging toward the struggling figures of her mother and Dee. Jane reached both hands out toward the running girl, forcing a focused jet of power through them with every molecule of her will. Annette stumbled and fell heavily to the floor, her ankles tangled in Jane's magic. Jane caught up to her quickly, placing her body squarely between Dee and Annette before the girl could regain her feet. She flexed her magical shield open again.

She was much more tired than she had been the first time, though, and she could feel thin spots and even gaps all over its wall. Behind it, Annette rose to her feet, a thin trail of blood sliding down her chin. Jane risked a quick glance back at Dee, who had broken away from Lynne.

When her eyes came back to Annette's face, though, there was something truly horrible about the girl's smile. Her mouth seemed to move, but Jane couldn't hear any words – she couldn't hear anything at all, she realized, though the thought seemed to come to her from a great distance. Annette's hands spread out wide, each one holding something that Jane couldn't see but somehow knew was sinister, and then she clapped them together and Jane's world spun sickly.

Everything went black.

Chapter Fifteen

SOUND FILTERED IN, and light — far too much light. Jane knew that some of the sounds were voices, but it seemed like an unreasonable amount of effort just now to remember what words were. Her head lolled back against something firm but pliant, and she hoped that she could stay there. She closed her eyes more tightly against the light and drifted.

Hours or seconds or no time at all later, Harris set her down on her feet, holding her firmly upright by the shoulders while shouting something at her. *We've done this before,* she managed to think, but something was different this time, and it was starting to bother her a little. Figures moved out of the ruined doorway; her eyes wouldn't focus that far away, but she could locate them by their hair. *Red, white. One, two.*

That was wrong, and something else was, too. She tried to ask Harris about it, but her mouth wouldn't make the right shapes. He wasn't paying attention, anyway: he fumbled with something out of her line of sight and then half lifted, half pushed her onto a cool leather seat. *A car,* she thought confidently, but her pride at remembering the right word was swallowed by her realization that she was in the wrong place.

'I . . . go there,' she managed as Harris slid into the driver's seat next to her. Her speech was getting more distinct, but she couldn't pull her muscles together to point exactly where she meant. She sort of waved, turning her body a little, just enough to catch a glimpse of Maeve moving the limp red hoodie out of the corner of her vision.

His jaw clenched violently as he started the car. The jaw worked back and forth for a moment, and Jane watched it, fascinated. 'We have to go,' he snapped. 'We couldn't – we had to get out.'

The car jumped forward, pressing Jane back against her seat. *No, not mine.* 'Dee,' she gasped. The hoodie; the hair; the tall figure bent backward in the atrium.

'She was pinned down all the way across the room, and we had to go,' Harris repeated, and now she could hear the brokenness in his voice. 'I got you, though,' he added.

134

There was no relief to the statement, no real emotion; nothing but the practical satisfaction of checking an item off a grocery list.

'Turn around,' Jane grunted, dragging herself upright with more effort than she thought it could possibly take. 'They'll think we've gone.' She reached gingerly inward, checking for magical damage to match the total collapse of her nervous system. The hum of her magic was faint, but to her relief it was there, and the pulse grew a little stronger as she followed it. Her power would come back, she knew, along with her coordination and the mental organization that was getting sharper by the minute. 'Turn *around*,' she insisted again, but he just kept driving.

'They know she's with us,' he said hollowly. 'They know we – they'll want to trade. Ransom her. We just had to get away, and they'll tell us what they want, and send her back.'

Jane stared at him. 'Harris,' she began softly, but stopped when she saw his knuckles go white around the steering wheel.

'We're too strong to attack as long as you're with us,' he explained. His manner was so patient and rational that she could almost taste the screaming panic underneath. 'They'll have to keep her, to trade.'

Jane's mind was clear, she realized finally: it was Harris who was still in the fog. 'We don't have anything they want,' she explained tiredly. His jaw kept working back and forth, but other than that she saw no sign that he

had even heard her. *Is that actually true?* she wondered
suddenly in the painful silence that followed. She did still
have one last thing of Lynne's: the ancient-looking silver
athame into which she had poured all her power. A few
generations' worth of accumulated magic wouldn't mean
much to a witch as long-lived as Hasina, but it might be
enough of a reason for her to keep Dee alive.

Jane reached across her body to hold the edge of the back
of her seat and struggled to turn herself partway around.
The red hoodie lay between the two women behind Harris
like a pool of blood. Still holding on carefully with her
right hand, Jane reached for the sweatshirt with her left.
She knew that they all must be aware of her actions, but
they made no move to help her, and Harris's eyes stayed
riveted on the road.

Her phone tumbled out of the folds of the hoodie as
she lifted it, and the screen flared briefly to life from the
movement. Its screen was cheerfully devoid of any alerts,
and she shuddered: Where was Malcolm now? Annette
had implied that he was still alive, but Jane's silent phone
suggested otherwise. She let it fall carelessly onto the seat.

'I'm going to try to see where she is,' she told the side
of Harris's immobile face, pulling the red hoodie onto her
lap.

She had done this magic twice before: once with a great
deal of preparation, and once with a great deal of energy.
She had neither this time, but it was some help that the
sort of detached trance-state she needed her mind to slip

into was familiar to her now. It helped even more that her grip on consciousness was already a little shaky. She clutched at the hoodie for a moment, then felt her grip relax as her inner self drifted loose from her body. *Show her to me,* she pleaded desperately, coaxing and cajoling any of her magic that would still respond to her, and aiming it toward the sweatshirt on her lap. *Let me see what she's seeing right now.* Dee's amber eyes filled her mind, then her long, calloused fingers, her hoarse, husky laugh. Her own body tugged back at her, tired and burned and needing her, but Dee couldn't afford to wait, so Jane yanked herself away harder.

With a final, sickening wrench she was free, and then she was trapped.

I'm not, she realized a second later. *She is.* Dee was seated on the blackened floor of the atrium, bound hand and foot, with her back pressed against one of its windows. The huge room seemed unnaturally quiet after the chaos that had raged there just minutes before. Charles was nowhere to be seen; Jane guessed that he had only been allowed in the atrium at all to lend his brute strength to the Dorans' fight. Now that it was over, only the most vital core of the family remained.

Annette, Cora, and Belinda were huddled in a close circle around something that bubbled and hissed, while Lynne paced behind them, glancing over their shoulders impatiently. *The spell,* Jane realized. *It must be almost ready.* The four of them had probably spent all the previous twenty-seven nights just like this, she realized; how foolish of her to imagine that Annette might ever believe the worst of the mother who had saved her from a life she hated. *Nothing like evil to really bond a family together.*

'Do you still like magic?' Lynne asked her suddenly. Jane tried to jump, but of course she couldn't: Lynne was speaking to Dee, not her. 'You're hardly the first witch-groupie to get stuck in the middle of this sort of thing, you know, but most have better sense than to go *looking* for death.' Her dark eyes were intent as they flicked back and forth from Dee to the sitting witches. 'A little slower,' she instructed, and across the half-dark room Jane saw Annette's dark-gold bob nod in acknowledgment. 'It should feel like your heartbeat controls it.'

Dee said nothing, and Jane wondered if she were restrained somehow from speaking, or simply afraid. *She has to be gagged,* Jane decided after a long pause; Dee would never have let a comment like that go without some kind of snappy response.

'It's a tremendous privilege for you to see this, of course.' Lynne turned back to Dee, apparently satisfied with whatever Annette was doing for the moment. 'It's normally quite the . . . family matter. But Jane is family, I suppose, and I expect she'll be along shortly.' She leaned down toward Dee's face, scanning it closely. 'Or are you there already, dear?'

I'm here, Jane thought fiercely, although she meant it more as a comfort to her friend than an answer to Lynne.

Neither of them could hear her, anyway, but it was the only thing she could do, so she thought it again. *Dee, I'm here with you.*

'It often happens this way.' Lynne sighed. 'I get quite attached to a body – they'll tell you I've outgrown caring about that sort of thing anymore, but it's not true. Family is a different matter: after the first seventy children or so, they stop being such a big deal. Most of them live such *short* lives, and the new ones don't even look like me anymore. It's been so long since I could recognize my features – my own, I mean – in any of them. But the skin I wear, the mind I live inside . . . I can actually become quite sentimental about that. I'll be sorry to see Lynne Doran go, but I'd be sorrier to see her live on after I've left her behind.' Jane shivered in her own mind, though Dee remained still and silent.

'It's the sort of thing that hangers-on like you can't even imagine.' The tall, chestnut-haired woman resumed her restless pacing. Jane saw Dee's legs shift suddenly, and guessed that she was trying to kick or maybe trip her as she passed by, but if Lynne even noticed the attempt, she didn't bother to respond. The bubbling thing between the seated witches gave off a pale, sickly gleam that illuminated the faces around it, which were glassy-eyed and drawn with exhaustion. Annette was frowning, her brow coated in a fine layer of sweat that glistened in the unnatural light.

I was trying to help *you, you psychotic bitch,* Jane thought furiously. *Dee's worth twenty of you, and she wanted to help you, too. If it meant getting her back now, I'd set you on fire and walk away without a second glance.*

A shudder ran through Lynne's thin body, and an answering one shook Annette so hard that Jane thought it must be rattling the girl's teeth. Lynne slipped a little glass vial from the pocket of her Chanel jacket and smiled wanly in the general direction of Dee. But her eyes seemed so far away that Jane doubted she really saw anything in the room anymore, except for the bubbling substance and her daughter's vacant face.

'Usually I let the spell be the judge,' she murmured, watching the small coven fixedly. 'It's deadly more often than it's not, thankfully; I never do enjoy watching my last shell wander around without a true owner. But you and your meddlesome friends have made it so that I can't participate in the ritual this time. Without it, there's no risk to this body at all, so I have to decide its fate all on my own.' Her eyes flicked toward Dee with a quick flash of irritation before locking back on Annette and her cousins. 'I hold you entirely responsible for how positively vile this will taste.' She unstoppered the vial and tipped its purplish contents into her mouth, grimacing as she swallowed. Another tremor ran along the length of her body, and the vial dropped, forgotten, to smash on the floor.

The sound it made was almost completely drowned out by a strange roaring, rushing noise that Jane realized must have been in her ears all along, steadily growing louder until it was impossible to ignore. She watched as one of

Lynne's perfectly manicured hands reached up to clutch briefly at her chest before she fell to the ground in front of Dee. Her body twitched a little every couple of seconds, her chest rising and falling in the shallowest of breaths, but her eyes rolled grotesquely and her lips had a tinge of blue underneath their customary peach lipstick.

Dee looked away from her, though, so Jane had to do the same. Annette was rising. Not standing: rising into the air as if in the grip of some huge, invisible hand. The twins remained on the ground, but whatever was holding Annette seemed to be affecting them, too: the small grey women looked even smaller and greyer, as if they were drying out somehow from the inside. Jane could see their skeletons beneath their skin, and then right through it. The bubbling thing between them grew bigger and brighter as they seemed to shrink in on themselves, and Jane realized that they were feeding themselves to it in some way that Dee's eyes couldn't perceive. One of them slumped forward as a ghostly green light began to radiate from Annette's eyes, mouth, nose, fingertips, from every bit of exposed skin that Jane could see. In another moment it was blinding, and the atrium lurched and spun into darkness as Dee turned away and shielded her eyes as best she could with her thick curtain of hair. *This was when we needed to be there,* Jane thought, and she would have clenched her fists if she could feel them. *We just needed ten minutes more, and Annette took them from us.*

141

When Dee turned back to the Circle, the unnatural light and the bubbling substance were gone, and Annette's feet were planted firmly on the charred floorboards. Dee barely had time to take in the three still, lifeless corpses around her before Annette turned her way, and Jane quailed inside her body: Annette's eyes had changed. They were still their same dark color, but even in the dimness of the ruined atrium, Jane could see that there was something different about them. *It's as if she's wearing contacts,* she thought, remembering where she had seen this before. Whatever used to make Lynne Doran's eyes so strange was looking at her now through Annette's.

'That's better,' Hasina purred through Annette's full-lipped mouth. Then she pressed it closed tightly, rolled her shoulders in their sockets, rose onto her tiptoes and settled back down again, with a contented smile that Jane had never seen her wear before. 'Now, I think Jane's seen enough, don't you? She can stop trying to interfere and "rescue" poor, helpless Annette. And I certainly don't want her to trouble herself with breaking in again to rescue *you*.' Her lips curved up cruelly. 'Believing in magic gets you nothing, you idiot wannabe witch. The only thing that matters is *having* it.'

She raised one hand and pointed, aiming a blood-red fingernail carefully at Dee's throat. Before she could scream or Jane could react at all, Annette slashed her hand sideways, the nail cutting through the air with a soft, dangerous hiss. There was pain, and there was something warm and thick spilling down the front of her shirt, and then the room spun and Jane was gone.

For a few heartbeats she was bodiless, frozen in absolute blackness with nowhere to go and nothing to move in order to get there. No mouth to scream through; no legs to kick; no heart to break into a million pieces.

Then she was back in the leather seat of Harris's electric-blue Mustang, Dee's red hoodie resting limply on her lap. Her hands tightened reflexively around the soft material, but it was cold and lifeless and no consolation at all. She bent down and buried her face in it, feeling hot tears begin to flow. Her body shook, then doubled over as she was racked with sobs.

In some dim corner of her brain she registered the feeling of the car slowing down, then drifting to the right. It came to a stop, and somewhere beside her she heard Harris begin to cry as well.

Chapter Sixteen

THE CAR'S HEADLIGHTS flashed over flat, well-fitted stones as Harris turned the car off the main road and onto a driveway. Jane blinked, trying to make sense of the indistinct shapes rising around them: a grouping of buildings silhouetted against the starry sky. Jane caught a quick glimpse of iron-bound wooden doors before they were replaced by a long row of wooden boxes on either side of a wide aisle. *A barn,* Jane thought hazily. *He drove us into a barn.*

'This is the family farm,' Maeve's voice said softly in the darkness, and Jane nodded, her foggy brain putting together that they had driven to the Montagues' compound in the Hamptons.

The stalls on the left were closed, but the doors of the ones on the right were all wide open. Jane could make out the darkened headlights of a car in each one, and so was unsurprised when Harris spun the wheel and turned into an empty stall about two-thirds of the way along the centre corridor. When she stepped gingerly out onto the concrete floor, Jane heard soft whinnies from one of the closed stalls on the other side of the aisle, and the sound of something heavy shifting around inside. *Half cars, half horses,* she thought. *How modern.*

They crossed the stone courtyard in silence, Maeve carrying Dee's hoodie like a fallen banner. Lights were on in the main house, and when she stepped inside, Jane stopped short. Pacing back and forth across the great room, looking for all the world like a caged lion with his tanned skin and dark-gold mane of hair, was Malcolm. She hadn't fully processed the fact of his presence when Harris stepped around her to rush at him.

She wanted to interfere, or at least protest, but the short walk from the car had already made her feel a little woozy, and all her body wanted to do was sag against the doorframe. Harris's attack caught Malcolm completely off guard and the two rolled off, out of her line of sight.

She heard running footsteps on the staircase somewhere overhead; no doubt more Montagues. Gritting her teeth, Jane pulled her aching body slowly upright, trying to ignore the way the room pitched and swayed as she moved.

'Back to your corners,' she said, her voice trembling. 'Harris, back off.'

She took a careful step forward and saw Malcolm's head lift to look at her as she did. But then Harris's hand swung up from somewhere below the couch and clipped him on the ear, and the two of them were off again. Jane tried halfheartedly to dig around for any magic left to her, but she knew it was futile. She had nothing left.

A light touch on the shoulder made her jump, and she turned to find a pair of worried brown eyes peering into hers. A regal woman with a cloud of red hair piled on top of her head was standing in front of her, partially blocking her view of a sullen-looking teenaged girl who practically vibrated in her eagerness to get closer to the action.

Jane inhaled, letting the air fill her lungs and expand her rib cage, and feeling the pain in her shoulder flare as the muscles in her torso moved. 'Hasina killed Dee,' she told the two newcomers shortly, guessing that they must be Emer's daughter and granddaughter, Charlotte and Leah. Dee had mentioned them once or twice. She would have preferred to break the news a little more gently, but assorted freckles and red hair kept swimming in front of her, and she had to communicate the key points quickly in case she was going to pass out again. 'Harris is trying to kill Malcolm, over there.' Her shoulder refused to respond to her instruction to gesture toward the floor of the great room, and she remembered belatedly that it had been injured somehow during the battle in the atrium.

'Well, that won't do,' Charlotte replied crisply and moved out of Jane's line of sight. After a few more thumps and a couple of barked orders, Harris stood, panting raggedly, beside his watchful sister. Malcolm, a few new scrapes and bruises decorating his handsome face, had moved to a corner near the fireplace, and finally the rest of the Montagues filtered into the centre of the room to join the pair of siblings there.

'I *just* got him patched up,' Leah exclaimed, stepping toward Malcolm to run a finger across the beginnings of a black eye. 'Harris, look what you've done!'

'What *I've* done?' Harris exploded, so viciously that even Maeve shrank away from him. 'He got her killed!'

'He nearly died, too,' Charlotte told him quietly, slipping over to rest a calming hand on his sleeve. 'That horrible sister never met him today; she sent some thugs to do it instead. It was only luck that we found him in time.' She frowned, deeply worried lines forming on her pale skin. 'I thought it best to get him out of the city immediately.'

Jane stepped forward tentatively to peer closer at Malcolm's wounds. *'In a few minutes I'll be too powerful to care whether Malcolm dies, or you live.'* Annette had wanted to punish him; Hasina would have just killed him. 'Found him?' she repeated absently, running a finger along a tear in Malcolm's sleeve.

147

'At your apartment,' he told her softly, and Leah heaved a dramatic sigh.

'When you didn't come back, we thought you might be regrouping at the apartment downtown,' she explained, her tone faintly accusatory. 'But the only one there was him. Looking much, much worse than now,' she added as an afterthought.

'They took my phone first thing,' Malcolm apologized, spreading his empty hands as if to demonstrate.

'Of course they did,' Harris snarled. 'You had a great excuse for staying out of the firefight tonight, and then these mysterious strangers conveniently prevented you from warning us that your own dear sister was there, waiting for us. Because you told her we were coming!'

Charlotte and Leah were adamant that Malcolm had been too gravely wounded for it to have been a smokescreen, which Harris insisted was exactly what Malcolm wanted them to think. It didn't help matters that their impressive healing skills had made it difficult for Harris or even Jane to see the extensive injuries that the women described. *And at the end of the day, it's the Montagues and the Dorans.* Even Emer seemed reluctant to stem Harris's vitriol, and Maeve was still too shaken by Dee's death to say much of anything at all.

'Enough of this,' Jane finally forced herself to say, and was pleased to note that her voice sounded almost strong. Every head in the room swiveled her way, and the arguing stopped.

'Jane, I didn't know anything about this,' Malcolm rumbled softly. She wanted to go to him, lean her head against his chest, and let him tell her that everything would be all right, but she couldn't. *It won't, anyway, no matter what he says.* 'Please let me make it up—'

'How?' Harris spat, the word twisting his handsome mouth into an ugly shape. 'You mean you want to buy your way out of this, just like everything else? How much is she worth to you?' Jane noticed that he hadn't said Dee's name since they'd left the mansion, and she understood. She was terrified, too, of the fresh pain that had come with the sound of it.

'He didn't mean it like that,' Leah insisted, trying to step toward her cousin, but Charlotte pulled her daughter back and held her close.

Didn't he? Jane wondered. The faces before her wavered a little in her vision, as if she were looking at them through uneven glass. She wished that she were still leaning against something solid. Harris's angry words of warning before they had gone to the Dorans' mansion came back to her vividly. *Can my judgment really be trusted where he's concerned?* She would never believe the worst of Malcolm, but was it possible that she'd been too eager to always believe the best?

'I'll do whatever you need, whatever you ask,' Malcolm answered simply, lifting his hands and then dropping them back helplessly to his sides. 'I know I can't undo what's happened, but my last offer cost one of you her life.

149

If it'll help you, you can have mine.' Harris looked grimly interested in that offer, but Emer turned away in obvious disgust.

'No one is dying,' Jane corrected him tiredly. 'Enough people have died.'

'Not quite enough,' Maeve muttered, softly but not so low that she couldn't be heard by everyone in the room.

'Hasina is alive,' Malcolm agreed. Jane thought that that was a rather generous interpretation of Maeve's remark under the circumstances, but she wasn't about to correct him, and Maeve didn't either. 'She's wearing my sister's face and she killed your friend. So let me kill her.'

An uneasy silence settled over the room, and glances flicked nervously between Malcolm and Jane. *André warned me to kill Annette from the beginning,* she remembered, and her stomach churned. *And even Emer had endorsed it as a last resort. If I had listened . . .* She had ignored every reason not to trust Annette. She had committed them to a dangerous plan that hinged on the reliability of an unstable stranger, and it had cost them so much more than she would ever have willingly paid. But even if killing Annette were the only answer now, could she really let Malcolm do it?

'I can get close to her in public,' Malcolm insisted urgently, and Jane saw interest on a few of the assembled faces. 'Some event, some party. To everyone there I would just be her brother; even if she saw me coming, she would have to try to stick it out. She cares about what people think more than anything,' he went on, picking up speed

150

in his enthusiasm. He was right about that, Jane knew: Hasina's desire for a huge society wedding between Jane and Malcolm had been the reason Jane was able to escape her the first time.

'You make it sound so easy,' she murmured, her mind spinning.

'I don't expect to get away with it.' He shrugged. 'It's not that hard to kill someone if you don't mind getting killed, yourself.'

'That's not what I meant,' she countered, stepping back, away from him. She swayed a little, but her legs held her. 'I thought you had changed.'

Malcolm opened his mouth to argue, but then closed it again. Confusion pulled his dark-gold eyebrows together tightly. He seemed completely at a loss.

'*You* think he was in on this with Annette?' Leah demanded, hands on her skinny hips and head cocked angrily. She tossed her perfectly straight strawberry-blond hair over her shoulder in a gleaming cascade.

'I don't,' Jane clarified quickly, glancing around the room to make eye contact with everyone. She didn't want them to have any doubts about her certainty that Malcolm was not on Annette's side. 'Can we have a minute?'

Emer, Charlotte, Leah, Maeve, and finally a very reluctant Harris filed slowly from the room. Jane waited until they were completely gone before she spoke again. 'You can't make everyone's problems go away by killing them,' she began, and Malcolm's dark eyes widened in surprise.

151

'This isn't – I don't know what you—'

Her heart broke for the pain written across his face, but she couldn't give in to it: her bad judgment where Malcolm was concerned had already cost Dee her life. 'You make a mistake, you think you can fix it just like that,' she went on when he sputtered to confused silence. 'You don't think about the consequences; you just want the mess to disappear so you can go back to your happy life and never feel bad again. I thought you had grown past that, but you haven't.'

'I have.' Malcolm's voice was low and throbbing with sincerity.

Jane closed her eyes, wanting to believe him but knowing that she couldn't trust anything she wanted so badly. When she opened them, he had crossed the room to stand just inches from her and was holding his arms out as if to gather her in. 'You can't stay here with them – with us,' she told him. His arms fell to his sides in defeat. 'I need you to leave. I know you want to be a part of this, and I thought you could, but you can't. And I can't let you try anymore. I can't lose any more people I love to your need for redemption. You'll have to find that somewhere else.'

She expected an argument, or at least a protest. But Malcolm simply stared into her eyes for a long minute, until he seemed to find something there that satisfied him. Then he leaned down and kissed her forehead gently, his warm lips lingering only a little longer than the gesture required, and turned to step out of the door of the farmhouse.

Jane swayed a little and rested her palm against the ivory wall for support. *He didn't even argue,* she thought dully. Did that mean that he knew she was right? Or that he thought she was too far wrong to even reason with?

She heard a soft rustling noise from the kitchen, and the muffled sound of a voice. She couldn't stand to go there, though; she knew she would never be able to walk into a kitchen again without feeling Dee's absence like a physical wound. She circled around the ground floor in the other direction instead: past a darkened sunroom, through an even darker formal dining room, to a staircase, where she removed her flats so as to make as little noise as possible.

Tomorrow, she knew, she would have to face the Montagues. She would have to talk with them about what had gone wrong and tell them what she had seen of Dee's last moments. She would have to decide what she wanted to do next. And she would have to do all of it while Harris's grief surrounded her like water that rose over her head. There would be no way to breathe without feeling it, just as there was already no way to breathe without feeling her own loss. She was in no hurry to see it mirrored on the faces of her friends.

Jane chose an empty bedroom at random, tugged her jeans off, and slipped underneath the white bedspread in just her sweater, realizing long after the fact that she must have lost her knit cap sometime during the evening's struggle. *Not mine to begin with, and not mine anymore,* she thought superstitiously. Objects that still belonged to a person could be used to locate them, as Jane had done with Dee's hoodie. In the magical world, it didn't pay to be sentimental about possessions.

One of them did still matter to her, though, now more than ever; and she sat up to dig around in her knapsack for the small wooden box that Malcolm had brought back from his travels. Gran's strong, work-roughened hands flashed briefly before her eyes, so quickly that she wasn't sure if it was magic or her own tired and confused brain. *How long before this begins to remind me of Dee?* she wondered bleakly, lying back down and curling her arms around the box's edges as though cradling a lover. *Would she even choose to hang around me, after all this?*

Her arm snaked out until it struck something warm and furry among the high piles of pillows, eliciting a soft meow of protest. A pair of green eyes gleamed out at her. *That's got to be the biggest cat I've ever seen,* Jane thought curiously, retreating politely to her own side of the bed while the cat's eyes closed sleepily again. It seemed willing enough to peacefully coexist, so she stayed put, allowing herself to feel just the tiniest bit warmed and soothed by its presence. It was a relief to have company that couldn't talk, especially considering how much talking she would have to do in the morning.

They'll be relieved that Malcolm is gone, at least. The thought caused the dull ache in her heart to harden into an angry knot; and she shoved her face into the pillowcase, trying to block out her own miserable thoughts.

She's dead. Dee's wide smile flashed before her eyes with such clarity that Jane almost thought she was in the room. Her eyes began to sting and burn. She heard the cat's heavy body shift restlessly beside her, but any sense of companionship had vanished. She was all alone in this, alone with her illusions and her tears. *It wasn't her fight, but I brought her in anyway. And now I can't even tell her I'm sorry.*

Chapter Seventeen

THE CAT HISSED, and Jane flipped over, startled out of her nightmare-filled sleep.

'Ow,' Maeve remarked crossly, setting a mug of tea on the white-painted dresser and sucking on the skin of her hand where some had spilled.

'Sorry,' Jane mumbled, although her contrary, sleep-deprived side wanted to point out that Maeve was the one who had walked into her room unannounced. She yanked her hair into a messy bun while the cat turned in a couple of huffy circles and plunked back down onto her legs.

Sunlight streamed onto a couple of deep-blue throw

rugs scattered across the white-painted floorboards. The bedspread and cushion on the rocking chair in the corner were white, but all their wood had been painted a rich, matching blue, which was echoed in the thin molding at the top of the walls. It was like she had slept inside of a piece of Delft china, though considerably more comfortable.

'Damn cat.' Maeve shrugged, picking up the mug again. 'His name is Maki, by the way. That was Leah's call, but she's also the one who chased him around the grounds every day trying to dress him up in little outfits until he turned into such a grump.' Maki's ears twitched, and the slim redhead hesitated briefly, but when the huge cat's eyes remained closed, she crossed the rest of the distance to hand the mug to Jane. 'Bael fruit,' she explained, 'and lemongrass and rhy – rhodiola?' She grimaced. 'Grandma made it; I don't really know.'

'Maybe it's poisoned,' Jane suggested hopefully as she took the tall, ivy-patterned mug from her friend's hands. She took a deep sip before Maeve could answer, earning herself a scalded tongue as well as a disapproving scowl.

Maeve sat on the bed, smoothing the quilted bedspread on either side of her with her palms. Maki, who was indeed the largest and fluffiest grey cat that Jane had ever seen, made a noise somewhere between a purr and a growl. 'Were you planning on hiding in here forever?'

Jane felt that the accusation was distinctly unfair, especially when there were so many fair ones readily available for use. She pulled her left wrist free of the covers and checked her watch. To her surprise, it was one o'clock. 'Oh,' she mumbled, then lay back down and stared at the ceiling. 'I'm still tired,' she said truthfully. She felt as if she could sleep all day and still not be strong enough to shower, dress, go downstairs. *And face them . . . no. Sleep is better.*

'I miss her, too,' Maeve said quietly. 'We all do. It's something we've been talking about, last night and this morning. It's something you could come downstairs and talk about, too.'

Because talking helps, Jane added bitterly in her own mind. *We can all share stories about how she helped us or recount jokes that she used to tell; we'll reminisce and pretend to ignore the fact that my colossal failure took her away from us.* Maeve seemed to read the answer on Jane's face, which at least saved her the trouble of having to speak out loud. Between the fighting and the profound draining of her magic, she felt like a giant bruise inside and out.

'She went after Lynne Doran with her bare hands,' Maeve murmured, and Jane clamped her eyes shut. 'It was crazy brave – I wish I'd been half as brave. Instead I was just hiding in the elevator with Grandma.' Her voice twisted bitterly at the end, and Jane, curious, opened her eyes. Unshed tears glittered in Maeve's. Jane took another, more cautious sip of her tea, unsure of what to say, but Maeve continued on without her help. 'My point is this: she went straight for Lynne. Even though Charles was lurking around her, even though she was by the spell

158

ingredients that everyone would be protecting with their lives, and even though it meant she was cut off from all of us by three pissed-off enemy witches.'

'I know all this,' Jane hummed into her mug. The tea was growing on her, but Maeve's company wasn't.

'Oh, good,' Maeve replied tartly, wiping her eyes with one sleeve, sniffling a little, and then shaking her shoulders resolutely. 'Then you know that, once Dee did that, she was dead no matter what any of us did.'

Like if none of us had led her to the slaughter in the first place? But Jane knew what Maeve wanted her to say, and she also suspected that the newly minted witch wouldn't leave until she'd said it. 'I hadn't thought about it like that,' she answered out loud, her own voice ringing false and hollow in her ears. 'I guess you're right.'

Maeve's eyes narrowed into hard copper slits, and Jane sighed. 'They got the better of us, Jane,' Maeve told her sharply. 'We can all have our opinions about how that happened – mine is that it was bad luck, by the way. We didn't know that Annette was a suicidal psychopath who was immune to reason, and Lynne did know it, is all. But my real point is that once we were in the atrium, Dee chose to make a really desperate play. The rest of us were hanging back and cautious, but not you, and not her. So you had one set of problems, and she had another – you both chose. She'd be livid if she knew you were up here sulking after she did something so incredibly badass.'

Her words rang true, but there was a hard, painful

place in Jane's heart that even true words couldn't touch. 'I know you want me to hang out in the kitchen and get all philosophical about tactics—'

'I *want* you to help plan your beloved friend's funeral,' Maeve snapped, 'but I'll settle for you getting up and taking a damn shower.'

Funeral. Jane's entire being quailed at the word. She had been too young to remember her parents' service, and Gran had kept their little family carefully separate from everyone else in their town. The first time that Jane had actually attended a funeral, it had been Gran's. *I wore that cheap black dress and Malcolm hovered over me, jumping to attend to every little thing so I didn't have to,* she recalled. She also remembered the glares and grumbling from her grandmother's neighbours, especially the creaky old man who had apparently seen Malcolm on his previous trip into town. But mostly, her impressions of the day were dark colours, salty tears, hushed voices, and the thick, sweet smell of incense in the stifling air. It had been a struggle from start to finish, and she had left as soon as it was decent to do so. *Or maybe a little bit before then, if you ask the neighbours. And that was before I even knew that I was the reason she'd been killed,* her brain noted viciously. With Dee, she had known the truth immediately. How much harder would it be to stand in front of a cold grave by herself, knowing that she was the reason for its having opened?

'It wasn't your fault,' Maeve said in a softer tone, and Jane found herself blinking back tears of her own.

'I know you have to say that,' she explained helplessly, and the first tear broke loose to roll down her face. It left a burning trail that reminded her of the fiery scratches left by Annette's fingernails.

'I don't *have* to say anything.' Maeve tossed her reddish curls imperiously, even managing a small smile, and Jane laughed a little in spite of herself. The laughter hurt.

'You have to start at the end to make it not my fault,' she pointed out. 'I dragged her into this, then let her be involved again after her first near-death experience, kept asking for her help, and finally came up with this brilliant plan: let's all risk our lives just to protect the enemy from herself. Because there's some huge difference between Hasina and the people who hang around her. Who *choose* to be on her side, even after being warned. We should all be willing to die for them, and by the way I just know that my former husband is totally going to fix it so it'll all go fine, because he's never let me down before.' She took a long swig of her tea and then set the mostly empty mug on the night table next to her spirit box.

'For what it's worth, I still trust Malcolm,' Maeve observed, and Jane frowned, caught off guard by the shift of topic.

I do, too, she thought, but she didn't say so. 'Well, you can all rest easy now because I made him leave, and—'

'You made him *what*?' Maeve nearly shrieked. 'Look, Jane. I know you've been in here beating yourself up about all the mistakes you've supposedly made and how

161

awful your judgment must be. But if you've sent away the one person who was completely, automatically, exclusively on your side, then I'm thinking of joining you. Your judgement sucks.'

Even more than her resentment at Maeve's efforts to cheer her up, Jane felt wounded by her sudden about-face. 'Good to know the rest of you have my back,' she grumbled.

'We love you.' Maeve sighed exasperatedly. 'We're on the same side as you, and you know it. But Malcolm is on *your* side, no matter which one that is. And I'm pretty sure you can tell the difference.'

Jane bit back a retort; the distinction actually did make sense to her. 'I don't know if I want him on my side,' she admitted instead, quietly. 'I also don't know if he's become the partner – I mean, the person – that I thought he could be, and that he wants so much to be. I don't know if he'll ever quite get there.'

'We'd been wondering about you two.' Maeve hesitated, then shrugged her frail-looking shoulders. 'You seemed to be getting along with him,' she finished tactfully.

I thought I was. Truth be told, the last couple of weeks with Malcolm seemed highly confusing viewed in the bright light of this afternoon. Jane had been so sure that she was getting to know him all over again or, rather, finding out that what she had thought she knew about him at the beginning was finally true. In other words: confusing. Their relationship hadn't been normal or simple since day one, but everything up to their wedding had been a lie. How could she ever make sense of their new, postannulment romance? 'Things with him were finally making sense . . . then,' she equivocated.

Maeve seemed to understand. 'That must have made it even worse once they didn't,' she guessed perceptively.

Jane bit her lip. 'I'm a horrible person. I'm talking about Malcolm the morning after . . . after . . .'

'It's complicated,' Maeve translated gently, sparing Jane the pain of finishing her sentence. It was difficult enough to talk about Dee in the heat of emotion, but to mention her death in normal conversation was like rubbing sandpaper across an open wound. 'Too much has happened for you to work through it all at once, especially by yourself. It's all getting mixed together, and that's just going to make you feel worse. So will you *please* stop behaving like a sulky hermit, because it's not helping anyone. Least of all you.'

Jane wriggled her way upright, casting a meaningful look at the mug on the spindly white-painted table beside her. 'If there's more of that,' she compromised, 'I might consider coming downstairs to get it. I'd even be willing to shower first.'

Maeve's face broke out in a mischievous grin, then relaxed into a sadder smile. 'I'll get some water boiling.'

Jane didn't need to be able to read her friend's mind to know what she was thinking as she spoke. Dee had been the only one in the house who could do anything much

163

more complex in the kitchen than boiling water. *And now she's gone.* That ache was almost unbearable . . . but only almost. However difficult it was, life had to go on.

Chapter Eighteen

L EAH MOVED SILENTLY around the marker driven into the earth, her beaten-copper sheet of hair glowing brilliantly against her black peasant top. To Jane's eye, her steps measured out a perfect circle. She sprinkled salt from a little leather pouch as she went, and it glittered prettily in the sunlight before disappearing into the grass. When she had completed one full turn, she repeated her path, this time pouring water in a thin, steady stream as she went.

Emer, wearing a voluminous green cloak over a classic navy sheath, cleared her throat and raised her arms. 'The Wheel turns,' she intoned. 'Our brave sister has set with the sun, and with it she will rise into a new day. Our hearts are dark without her, but we rejoice to know that she still walks in light. Her passage into the Summerlands was paid in blood, and today we gather to give her comfort and show her the way.'

The cadence of her words was soothing, almost like a lullaby. *Singing the dead to sleep,* Jane thought randomly, but of course Emer would say that the point was to help Dee to reawaken. *Just not as herself . . . and not with us.*

Emer's belief in a beautiful afterlife and eventual reincarnation seemed truly sincere to Jane. Although she had been deeply saddened by Dee's death, she often sounded almost envious that the girl would move on to the heavenly Summerlands of her childhood lore. Jane knew that she should try to take her cue from the elderly witch and find something to celebrate in Dee's passage, but she couldn't quite summon the right spirit. It would be a lovely ending to a too-short life, and certainly just what the young Wiccan deserved, but was that enough to make it real?

She could be lost, Jane thought anxiously, fidgeting a little. *Frightened and alone. Or she might just be . . . gone.*

Emer poured wine onto the ground from a glazed Provençal pitcher. She had told Jane that the absence of Dee's body wouldn't matter, that Dee herself was beyond things like physical distance now. The ritual was for her soul and for her mourners, and it would serve its purpose just as well even with nothing to bury.

166

But in spite of that reassurance, Jane couldn't help thinking about the fate of that body. It was so much of what made her Dee – her height, her calloused hands, her raven hair, the throat that produced her hoarse voice. *And now Annette has it.* Although they had all kept a close eye on the news since Dee's death, her body didn't seem to have been discovered. Realistically Jane knew that Annette had probably burned it to ashes, but it was hard to imagine such a fate befalling all that remained of her beloved friend.

She couldn't help but wonder how their cobbled-together Wiccan ritual compared with the triple funeral under way on the Upper East Side. High-society maven Lynne Doran, along with her twin cousins Belinda Helding and Cora McCarroll, had supposedly passed away in a tragic private-plane crash into the Atlantic Ocean. Jane had recognized Hasina's fingerprints all over the immaculate cover-up – she had even included a pilot in the wreckage. *Another innocent casualty of that monster.* The three women were being buried in a ceremony that rivaled those for heads of state, Jane had no doubt. Even though they had given their lives up voluntarily, unlike Dee who had had hers ripped violently away, they would be celebrated and praised by the entire city while Dee got nothing but a little marker in the grass. Jane had tried to contact everyone she knew from Dee's old life, before she got mixed up in the magic that ended up costing her everything – co-workers from her old job at the bakery, her Wiccan circle, her former roommates – but without any luck. The only

167

people mourning for Dee would be the ones who had grown close with her the most recently.

Maeve squeezed her hand gently, but on the far side of her Harris sat as still and cold as marble. Jane wished that he would just be angry at her, yell and curse and lose his temper. But he hadn't, and she had a feeling that he never would. *I miss her, too,* she thought at his stony profile. *It's something we could talk about, something that could even bring us a little closer together.* But his eyes stayed fixed on his grandmother and never so much as twitched Jane's way.

Emer bent with surprising flexibility and began carving runes into the earth on all four sides of the makeshift headstone they had erected. She spoke as she worked, spinning the story of Dee's life out into a beautiful, meaningful web, but Jane only half listened to the words. Instead she felt around the edges of the gaping, Dee-shaped hole in her heart, poking at it mentally and wincing at the fresh wave of pain it caused.

With Dee missing from the group, Malcolm's absence felt even more pronounced. Jane was sure that she'd been right to send him away – or as sure as she could be, at least. Still, his departure left Jane as the only non-family member on the Montagues' farm, and that was beginning to feel a little awkward. She wasn't sure that she even had a valid reason to stay, except that she didn't know where else to go.

Part of her longed to return to France and slip back into

her old life like a disguise, but she knew it wasn't realistic. Hasina was still at large and had plenty of reasons to want her dead. Even if Jane completely gave up on the idea of banishing her from Annette's body, Hasina had a nearly infinite amount of time to nurse her grudge and decide to strike. Going back to France would just endanger a bunch of people on a whole new continent. *Elodie, Antoine, Marjorie, that woman on the ground floor of my old building who used to wave me over to her window when I walked past and demand that I pick up a loaf of bread for her.* She had enough of the money she had withdrawn from Malcolm's escape account to rent a little studio in an outer borough for a while, and she knew that she probably should. She could even cast a fresh glamour on her passport and withdraw a bit more, and buy as much time as she needed to figure out her next move. But the idea of moving out – of moving anywhere – seemed too much like moving on for her to handle right now. It would be closing the last chapter of her life that had included Dee, and she wasn't ready, even if Dee's spirit was.

Gone, she thought blankly. How was that possible? Dee had been all heat and action and life. What could she be without that motion, that passionate energy? What would happen to the void she had left in their lives – would something else seep in to fill it, or would it collapse with a crash, dragging the rest of Jane's world behind it like a terrible black hole? *And if her soul moves on and forgets, and her body is lost somewhere, what has happened to the Dee we knew? Where will her memories go, and all the little quirks that made her a complete human being?*

Emer had talked about that one morning at the brownstone, Jane recalled. *'The longer someone has been dead . . . the fewer living people who knew them . . . the less you have of what they've touched . . .'* She had been listing the reasons why it would be nearly impossible to contact Celine Boyle, but of course the opposite of all those things was true about Dee. As soon as the realization hit her, Jane felt an almost unbearable longing at the idea. It was all she could do not to run out of the depressing Circle, across the lawn, and up to Harris's room to start rifling through Dee's things, looking for possessions to power the spell that would bring her back. *Only a shadow of her, and only for a little while,* Jane reminded herself, but her pulse raced all the same. *I could still tell her how sorry I am . . . and I could give him the chance to say a real goodbye.*

Jane balled her hands into fists, fighting the urge to tap her foot impatiently as the service wound on. Occasionally she heard sniffles or saw hands dab tears away, and she knew that she should be concentrating harder on helping to celebrate Dee and speed her along this last journey. But the simple fact was that she didn't want Dee to be gone – and maybe she didn't have to be, not completely.

Jane bent her head obediently for the final prayer, feeling an electric sort of rush as Emer opened the Circle that Leah had cast. *Have a safe journey home,* she wished wholeheartedly at Dee's soul, wherever it might be. Knowing how it had lived Dee's life, Jane was sure that it wouldn't stay at rest for very long before returning in search of a new one, and she smiled a little at the thought of Dee's spirit reincarnated in a body with decades of adventures in front of it.

I guess I am starting to believe a little, she admitted to herself. In spite of her distraction during the ritual, she felt lighter somehow, almost refreshed. It might not have been the fancy society funeral that had sent Lynne, Cora, and Belinda into their next lives, but the intimate little ceremony had surely done the job – and was more appropriate for Dee, anyway.

Their group straggled back toward the house one by one, each clearly lost in her or his own thoughts. But Jane saw Harris heading in the opposite direction, through the dunes toward the beach, and she followed him. When she caught up, he had kicked his loafers off and was standing barefoot in the sand, staring out over the gently rolling waves.

'Hi,' she started softly.

He turned slightly toward her, but his eyes stayed trained on the ocean. He didn't seem startled by her voice, and she suspected that he had heard her coming, or guessed that she would.

'I miss her, too, you know,' Jane told him, struggling to keep control of her voice as it threatened to break. 'I know there's nothing that can make this horrible thing right, but

I thought of something that could help. A little, anyway.'

Harris shifted onto the balls of his feet but didn't answer. After a long moment of waiting, Jane took another two steps forward, trying to edge into his line of sight. She might as well have been invisible for all the notice he gave her.

She sighed, wondering if she should just give up and go back inside. Finally, she cleared her throat. 'I thought we could talk to her,' she began, her voice growing steadier in her eagerness to share her idea. 'She hasn't been gone long; from what your grandmother said we should be able to—'

'Go back to the house, Jane.' Harris's tone was flat and cold, his entire body utterly still except for his lips.

He just doesn't understand yet, Jane told herself, smoothing down the goose bumps that had suddenly risen on her bare arms. The day was certainly warm enough, but a spontaneous cold front seemed to have moved in on their little patch of beach. 'It's what your family does, Harris,' she went on calmly, trying to pretend that he hadn't spoken. 'Her soul has moved on, but the part of her that remembers, the part that was her, lingers. We could say goodbye, tell her how much we love her; we could—'

'Go *away,* Jane.' Harris's mouth clamped shut. A muscle in his jaw twitched; he seemed to be struggling now to stay as still as he had been since she had arrived.

She felt her own jaw jut forward into a stubborn angle despite her best intentions. 'You really expect me to believe you have nothing to say to her?'

He turned his gaze toward her at last. She expected anger, but it was pain that she saw burning in the depths of his eyes. When he spoke again, however, his voice was icy. 'I can talk to her whenever I want without more witchcraft, and although it's none of your business, I happen to believe that she can hear me just as well. What you want is for *her* to talk to *you;* this is all about *your* need. And your needs aren't my problem.'

He went back to staring out over the water, leaving Jane openmouthed but speechless. After a frozen moment so strained that it felt like screaming in her ears, Jane turned on one heel and trudged slowly back to the house, leaving Harris barefoot on the sand.

Chapter Nineteen

WHEN JANE ENTERED the great room through its wide, glass-paned French doors, she heard voices from the formal dining room. There was soft speech, some crying, and the occasional burst of muted laughter. She wanted to join the storytelling and commiseration, but the sting of Harris's parting words made her feel stiff and awkward, and impossibly separate from the rest of the mourners.

She took a step forward, trying to convince herself that companionship was just what she needed, but her eye hesitated on a largish cardboard box next to the front door. It was addressed in loopy black marker to Ella Medeiros and bore a forwarding sticker that had redirected it from her Village apartment to the Montagues' brownstone and finally to the Hamptons. She drifted toward it as if in a dream. *I've lost so much,* she thought plaintively. *I stopped hoping to get any of it back.* She picked up the box, tucked it awkwardly under her arm, and circled back into the kitchen and then up the stairs. Whatever had survived Annette's fire at the Lowell Hotel, she needed to see it, even if it was nothing but a few shoes that would no longer fit her feet.

When she set the box down on her bed and began pulling at the tape, she smelled acrid soot almost immediately. *Whatever it is will be damaged,* she warned her racing heart. The smell grew stronger as she opened the box's flaps, but by then she had stopped caring.

The first thing her fingers found was the slick satin of the brick-red top that Ella had worn on André Dalcas,cu's private jet to London. She shook it out: it smelled like smoke, but there was no visible damage. The fabric seemed to almost glow from within against the cool blue-and-white background of the bedroom. *Too bad this will never work on me again,* Jane thought wryly; where Ella had been flat, Jane was all curves. Underneath was a dove-gray pair of suede ankle boots, too big for her real feet, and when she lifted them out of the box, an enameled pair of Van Cleef & Arpels earrings tumbled merrily out onto her quilt. *Those will still fit,* she thought, managing to savour the feeling for a full five seconds before her sorrow crowded it out of her mind again. She took that to mean that the box was a useful distraction. She missed Dee horribly, but if she spent every waking moment drowning in grief she might just curl into a ball and never get up again.

There was a pair of wide-framed sunglasses whose tortoiseshell frames were a little too melted to wear, an eyeliner brush that seemed unharmed, and a couple more bright, slinky articles of clothing with discreet singe marks here and there. A good tailor could probably fix most of them, Jane guessed, and made a mental note to repair what she could and donate it to charity.

At the bottom of the box her fingertips scraped more fabric, but this was rougher than any of Ella's clothing and seemed to be stretched over something flat and hard. Jane found its edges and lifted it gingerly, pushing the empty box aside as she did. In her hands was a book, covered in old-fashioned floral fabric. The edges of its pages were faintly yellowed by time, but the fire hadn't so much as touched it. Jane lifted it to her nostrils and inhaled curiously; even after being packed tightly in with all the other smoky items, the book smelled like dust and paper and nothing else. She shouldn't have been surprised that Gran's enchanted journal would come through a massive inferno unscathed. It must have been loaded with more protective spells than Jane could learn in a lifetime.

Deep down, Jane knew that Harris was right about her motives for wanting to communicate with Dee. The sense of peace that had settled into the Circle after Emer's funeral ritual should be honoured, not disturbed. Jane still felt a pressing need to pour her heart out to her friend, but Dee had more than earned her rest. It wouldn't be fair to inflict the problems of the living on her afterlife.

But the thing that lives in this book was never alive, and it isn't dead. It was a shadow of her gran, a memory that Celine Boyle's magic had turned into a sort of reference guide to the story of her life. It didn't have a peace to disturb, and as a bonus, Jane had never done anything to hurt it. The burden of her constant guilt seemed to get heavier with every wrong choice she made. Even just speaking with someone whom she hadn't harmed would be a very welcome relief.

Jane opened the book, flipping through the apparently blank pages while invisible writing played at the edges of her sight. Her magic prickled, responding to the journal's curious spell, and Jane sent it searching deep into the secrets of the paper. *Show me,* she thought at it, hearing the words both inside her mind and, somehow, inside the book. *Let me see who your owner was. Let me see the mark she left on you.*

Then she was falling, her own body somewhere far above and behind her. Images rushed by, too quickly to be anything but a blur of colour and light and movement. She knew to expect them this time and tried to watch, looking for familiar faces, but before she could recognize so much as a single frame of the slide show it was over. Jane was motionless in the dark, standing on nothing, face-to-face with the memory that looked identical to Gran.

'You again,' it observed in a tone so Gran-like that Jane didn't know whether to laugh or cry.

'Me again,' she agreed instead. The diary version of Gran had been the one who told Jane about Hasina in the first place. She had showed her the real Gran's pursuit of the witch she suspected of killing Jane's mother – Lynne Doran – and her discovery that Lynne was the latest in a long line of hosts for her ancestress. When André and Katrin Dalcaşcu's parents had kidnapped Annette from under her mother's nose, Gran had agreed to help them hide the girl until Hasina finally died. Unfortunately, Jane hadn't received the diary until after she had already undone all her grandmother's careful work.

'I couldn't stop her,' she blurted out. 'Hasina switched into Annette's body.'

The Gran-like figure blinked rapidly a couple of times. To Jane it looked like a robot assimilating new information, not a human being reacting in surprise; which oddly enough made her feel more comfortable opening up about the events of the last few weeks. She explained about Malcolm's return, their meetings with Annette, the plan to intercept Hasina during her spell, and the disaster that had unfolded in the atrium. 'Annette's young – twenty-seven, I think,' she finished, an edge of frustration creeping into her voice. 'She can have a whole pack of children of her own.'

'That's true,' not-Gran confirmed sternly, but somehow serenely. 'And even if she never finds a new body, this

178

transfer has provided her with many more years of life. Witches will die as long as she lives; I fear that you are in even more danger than you were before.'

'Maybe she'll have to stop, now that more of us know about her,' Jane suggested halfheartedly, knowing before the words were fully out how ridiculous that hope was.

'She won't,' un-Gran replied, and Jane wondered if she were imagining the hint of surprise in her familiar voice. 'It is necessary in order to maintain her power.'

'I don't understand,' Jane said as she frowned. 'Are other witches some kind of threat to her?' It was hard to imagine, given how Hasina had grown over the millennia.

'It's far more than that.' Gran's image went on to explain that Hasina's magic had stopped behaving normally after her first body's life had ended. Magic replenished itself on life, she reminded Jane: it needed organic energy for fuel. No matter how drained of magic Jane might feel — and she had felt pretty empty after the battle in the atrium — her power always rose back to its natural levels with a little rest (*and a lot of food,* Jane amended silently). When magic was sent to inhabit something that wasn't alive, however — as when it was stored in silver, for example — it wouldn't just remain inert and waiting. It slowly leeched back into the world, dissipating year by year until it was gone.

While Hasina wasn't an inanimate object, of course, she wasn't quite alive, either. The thing that animated her, the life force, didn't belong to the body it inhabited. The spirit that did belong there had no control over its own body, and quickly grew weaker and more confused until it couldn't really be called a 'person' at all. So the body had a harder and harder time maintaining its magic the longer Hasina was in control . . . and Hasina wasn't partial to being short on power.

'So she *has* to kill other witches, to take their magic,' Jane finished slowly, and the Gran-like image nodded gravely. Something clicked in Jane's brain: she had been so focused on the present that she had almost forgotten the reason why Gran had investigated Lynne Doran's secrets in the first place. 'Is that why – do you think that's what happened to my parents? She killed them for my mother's magic?'

The image hesitated ever so slightly, then nodded. 'I believe that Hasina killed your mother in order to steal her magic.'

There was something odd and stilted about her speech, and Jane frowned. '"My mother,"' she repeated pointedly. She had pictured the car accident hundreds of times growing up, piecing it together from the scraps of information that Gran had occasionally let fall. The specific details shifted and changed in her mind, but she knew that there had been a narrow, winding mountain road in North Carolina, a flash flood, and a brutal crash. She knew that a kindly neighbour had insisted on babysitting for the young couple, or else ten-month-old Jane would have died as well. And she knew that both of her parents had been in the car.

'Hasina could have killed her alone,' un–Gran admitted finally. 'But she had an old, old grudge against your father as well, and I imagine that the opportunity to avenge herself on him while also gaining magic from your mother was especially appealing to her. In fact, a theory that Lynne Doran might have acted on her family's bad blood with his was what led me to discover Hasina's existence in the first place.'

Jane felt her breathing speed up and grow shallow. The real Gran had never been willing to tell Jane much of anything about her father. He had evidently changed his last name to 'Boyle' after marrying Angeline, making it impossible for Jane to learn even basic information about his life. Gran's stubborn silence on that topic had been one of the many things that had sent teenaged Jane into helpless fits of rage, but no matter whether she shouted or reasoned or went on a hunger strike, Gran refused to budge. *But her memory is answering all my questions,* she realized. It must have been created without Gran's own stubborn reservations. Jane sucked in a deep breath and forged ahead. 'Tell me about the grudge. Who was my father to Hasina?'

'It goes back to long before his birth,' the memory cautioned. 'Hasina's memory is as long as her life, and she can carry a vendetta through many generations. It began with the famous witch trials in Salem – you'll remember them, of course.' Jane didn't bother to answer. Gran herself had homeschooled her, so she knew perfectly well

181

that Jane knew all about them. 'What you most likely do *not* know is that the accusers and judges were merely the tools of actual witches. For some time the New World had been home to the last surviving descendants of Anila, one of Ambika's daughters. They had lived in relative peace and obscurity for some time, but to their dismay Hasina's daughters crossed over, invading the territory that had been theirs alone. They managed to discover her secret and realized that she was an even greater threat than they had realized: it was imperative to their continued survival that she be killed.'

'So they tried to use regular nonwitches to do the job?' Jane was appalled; it was like trying to smother a forest fire by throwing fluffy bunnies at it. Then again, she thought, maybe it was clever. Hasina was deeply dedicated to fitting in with the rest of society and would go to extraordinary lengths to seem socially 'correct' – maybe even far enough to get ensnared in a well-laid trap.

'They used the locals as camouflage,' the diary confirmed, 'or at least they tried. Some of Hasina's more minor relatives were actually caught up in the executions, but of course Hasina herself wasn't touched. When she discovered that Anila's family was behind the hunt, she killed every last witch in their line.'

Jane exhaled slowly. 'Malcolm said that a couple of the witch families were extinct.'

Gran's memory nodded, but Jane knew her well enough to understand that her agreement was qualified. 'The witches in them, at least. Hasina continued to seek out Anila's children for several generations, until there was no real hope that magic would ever resurface in their line. But there were a few children — distant relatives, mostly males — whom she was willing to ignore.'

'Until one of them married a witch,' Jane finished for her. Even if her father had been generations removed from any of his family's actual magic, the attraction of one magical being to another might have been there; faint, but there. Gran would have known who her daughter's suitor really was — even if he had no idea himself — and knowing that the marriage would draw unwelcome attention, she had opposed it. But Angeline had married Jane's father anyway, leaving Gran with no choice but to hide the couple with all her fierce strength, including convincing him to change his name. As a daughter of not one but two magical lines, the infant Jane inherited more power than any other infant in her generation — maybe even more than Annette. Hasina would never stop until she had found the child and taken her magic . . . and her life.

But Angeline had insisted on raising her daughter as a 'normal' girl, free of the magical world and the danger that came with it. She moved her family to North Carolina, hoping to leave her past behind, and Gran had tried to respect her wishes. *And that's how my parents died,* Jane realized. 'Tell me everything,' she told the image. 'Please. Start from the beginning.'

The image exhaled with a touch of loving exasperation.

Jane longed to throw her arms around her, but she knew she would have to settle for listening. Around them, the darkness spun, shimmered, and resolved. Jane saw a sandy-haired young man in a well-tailored but well-worn suit. He sat in a one-piece plastic chair in front of a massive window, and Jane saw a line of bullet-nosed airplanes waiting on the other side. The young man held a boarding pass in his hand, and he kept flexing open its paper sheath to read the numbers on it again and again. 'Your father's name was Matthew Vincent,' Gran's voice began, and Jane listened raptly.

Chapter Twenty

THE SUN WAS low on the horizon by the time Jane emerged from Gran's diary. She was exhausted, and her mind was reeling from the massive volume of new information she had taken in during the afternoon. She felt like there was too much in her now to be contained in her one bedroom, or even in the entire sprawling house. She needed the open sky around her rather than walls pressing in, so she pulled a soft wool wrap around her shoulders and slipped outside.

She crossed the lawn quickly, and without even thinking found herself face-to-face with Dee's little stone marker, nestled carefully into a flat space between the dunes. She had no idea where Emer had gotten it on such short notice, but then she supposed that the Montagues specialized in putting troubled souls to rest, so of course they must have some rather macabre supplies on hand. The narrow stone stood just under a foot high, and although it was brand-new, its edges already looked a little weathered and worn. A pentacle was carved into its smooth front surface; its other sides had been left rough and unfinished. Dee would have said that it was perfect, Jane knew, and her eyes filled with tears.

'I miss you,' she whispered, dropping down to kneel on the grass before the marker. It was springy and damp, and she felt moisture seeping into the ballerina-like chiffon layers of her skirt. But it wasn't really hers, and she didn't care, anyway. Her entire heart was swollen with longing, so full it felt like it might burst.

Dee, Gran, Maman, Papa . . . even Malcolm, or who I thought Malcolm could be. Harris, whom I used to think might become more than a friend, and now he's even less. 'I miss you,' she said again, brushing Dee's marker with her fingertips but speaking at least a little bit to all of them. The stone was still warm from the heat of the day, although the sun had disappeared behind the house and a few stars were peeking out of the sky over the water. *It has life,* Jane thought irrationally; *it has some of her fierce kinetic energy in it.*

'I found out why Hasina is so dangerous,' she told the

stone softly, dropping her gaze to her lap and twisting her fingers together. 'She's like a vampire, only with magic instead of blood. She can't produce it herself anymore, so she has to keep taking it. She tried to get Gran's, and she probably took my mother's after she ran her car off the road.'

Saying the words out loud made them feel more real and frightening, but it also calmed some of the chaotic whirlwind of her thoughts. So she kept talking, pouring out every detail of what Gran's diary had told her, using as many of the exact words as she could remember. She added in her own conclusions, as well as the questions that still remained. In the end she just talked, telling Dee everything that had crossed her mind in the days since her friend's violent death.

By the time she had finished, nearly the entire sky was covered in a thick carpet of stars, and the fat white moon had cast a trail across the water. It ended on the beach just on the other side of the dunes, and Jane felt as though she could cross the sand, step out onto the gleaming ocean, and walk across to the other side.

'You would know what to do now,' she said, sighing. 'I wish I had taken your advice from the very start. Remember when I accidentally showed Lynne that I knew about my magic, and she sent Yuri to your place to bring me back? You told me to run then, but you never blamed me for a second when I insisted that I knew better. I could have gotten out of the city, and you could have kept working at Hattie's bakery, and Annette could still be an anonymous barmaid in London. But I thought I was outsmarting Lynne, playing on her weaknesses. I knew she wouldn't take any risks with me before that insane wedding, and I thought that meant the same thing as being safe. I thought Malcolm knew his family best, and he would be able to keep us hidden from them, and that on my own I couldn't do anything. And I should have listened to you instead, because you were the one who taught me how to do so many amazing things, and you knew I'd be fine as long as I didn't get cocky enough to actually try to take on Lynne Doran.'

And time went on, and I listened even less. She hadn't so much as called Dee during the first few miserable weeks after the wedding. Instead, she had stubbornly waited until she had figured things out on her own before contacting the one person who could help. *The one person who was always happy to.* Dee had been a perfect, loyal friend, yet Jane had let them drift apart, never imagining how little time they had left.

'I was jealous,' she whispered, glancing over her shoulder instinctively to make sure that no one had come out from the house after her. The moonlight shone on the perfectly manicured lawn, green and glossy and completely empty. 'I had that silly crush on Harris, and I didn't want to see you two getting closer, building something real between you. I let a stupid infatuation come between our friendship. And I thought if I ignored the problem, things would eventually go back to normal.' She laughed a little, regretfully. 'Okay, I thought you would break up and he'd throw himself at me and you would get used to it. Either way, I thought we would have years, decades even, to get back to the kind of friends we started as.'

Dee would have made sure that they did, Jane knew. Their talk on the Montagues' roof just a couple of weeks earlier was proof of that. But Jane would have known it even without any evidence. Real friendship created real faith, and her relationship with Dee was one of the realest she had ever known.

'I wish I'd been a better friend,' Jane told her sincerely. 'If I was, you'd be here to tell me what to do next. And I'd do it.' She hesitated, plucking at layers of her skirt. 'I can't run away from this anymore. I should never have tried to save Annette — and I'm so, so sorry. It seemed like the right, noble thing to do, but if I'd really understood what I was risking, that I was putting more on the line than just myself, I would never have done it. But I'm not concerned about protecting her anymore. I'm just sorry that I didn't see it that way before, when you were still here.' She bit her lip, feeling Annette's magic slice through her throat again. The pain had been icy for a moment, then Dee's blood had flowed hotly out onto her skin. By the time Jane was thrown clear, it felt as if her skin were on fire. 'I have to fight. I can't just hide, hoping that Hasina takes someone else for fuel, and die alone in my bed after sixty years of looking over my shoulder every minute.'

But what could she do? Even with the help of the Montagues, which was no sure thing anymore, another face-to-face confrontation was out of the question. *What do you do when you can't fight and you can't walk away?* Gran might have known, and Dee might have had an idea, but Jane was alone.

The little marker seemed to almost glow in the moonlight, and Jane reached out and touched it again on impulse. It was still warm, and she wondered if it really was just leftover heat absorbed from the sun. *Maybe Emer did something special to it,* she guessed, pleased at the thought. Perhaps she had some magic like the witch who had given Malcolm the spirit box, and she had made the stone reflect Dee's substance somehow. It was a relief to know that someone was out there shepherding the dead, when so many of the people in Jane's life had died. *I should ask her, and I should ask her to teach me what she does.*

A little part of her hoped that the warmth in the stone wasn't Emer's magic at all, but Dee herself, letting Jane know that she had heard. The crazy swirl of noise in her head had stilled, and although she was still tired, she felt somehow refreshed. *She's helping me, even now. After everything.* 'I'll come back,' she offered tentatively, absurdly afraid of being rejected by the inanimate object in the grass. 'I'd like to, I mean. I wish I could make up for what happened to you.' The tears she had blinked back earlier welled up again, and this time they rolled down her cheeks to fall silently to the ground.

By the time she stood up to return to the house, her thigh and calf muscles had gone stiff and wooden. She made a futile attempt to smooth her skirt with her hands, gave up, and trudged back across the moonlit lawn to the darkened house. She looked up once, and for a moment she caught sight of a face, and a flash of reddish hair, in one of the black upper windows. Red hair didn't narrow it down much on the Montagues' farm, but Jane knew instinctively that the watching face belonged to Harris. She had nothing to say to him, though, so she pretended not to notice and made her way back to her room alone.

Chapter Twenty-one

A GHOSTLY LIGHT GLOWED in the middle of Jane's darkened room, only to disappear almost as soon as she walked in and saw it. *What the—?* It blinked again, and this time she recognized it as the screen of Ella's cell phone. She had dropped it onto her bedspread earlier that day when she dumped out the contents of her purse in a frustrated hunt for lipstick. She kept her hands out searchingly in front of her as she crossed the pitch-black room, bumped into her bed with her thighs, and mumbled a curse as she started to feel around on the bedspread. Just as she found the cool metal edges of the phone it lit up again. '*2 Missed Calls.*'

Jane flipped it open curiously, and an odd abortive beep was followed by the sound of an open line. The call timer had ticked up to five seconds before she realized that someone must have called at that exact moment. 'Hello?'

'Thank God,' André growled, although he didn't sound especially thankful. 'Where the hell have you been?'

Jane glared at the phone, aware as she did how pointless the gesture was. 'Burying a friend,' she growled back. Who the hell did he think he was? She hadn't been at his beck and call as Ella, and she certainly wasn't about to start now.

But André didn't seem surprised or cowed by her anger; his tone remained just as harsh as before. 'At least you got to bury her,' he snapped. 'I don't even know what *happened* to my sister's body.'

Jane sat down heavily on the bed. *Katrin?* She hadn't liked Katrin at all, and was sure that the feeling had been mutual, but Jane couldn't help feeling a grudging respect for the tough Romanian witch. She may not have had much magic, but she had been clever, ruthless, and relentlessly devoted to her family. Not to mention almost brilliantly devious.

To her horror, when André spoke again it sounded distinctly like he was crying. 'That crazy bitch killed her. Her hotel room is basically a crater. Jane, I know you were going after Hasina. What the fuck did you *do*?'

'*Nothing,*' Jane half shouted, half wailed. She hadn't even been able to keep her own allies safe.

'You didn't even try?' André prodded viciously, and Jane closed her eyes.

'Of *course* I tried,' she snapped into the phone. 'I even got into the house, but Annette turned on me, okay? Maybe with some more help, we could have . . . that is . . . she beat us. She killed my friend, knocked me out, and became Hasina.' It hadn't happened in quite that order, but the timeline wasn't exactly a huge issue right now. 'And for the record,' she added bravely, testing the edges of her grief, 'I never got my friend's body back, either.'

'I'm sorry.' André's tone was perfunctory, but the fact that he had bothered to offer a condolence at all was a little surprising.

'I'm sorry about Katrin,' she offered in return, and a short silence crackled along the line between them.

Finally André cleared his throat hoarsely. 'It doesn't make any sense.'

Death never does, Jane thought grimly. 'Annette's really, really strong,' she pointed out. 'I know your sister was smart, but if Annette wanted to kill her, there isn't much she could have done to protect herself.'

'That's just my point.' André's voice crackled with impatience. 'Annette – *Hasina* – is strong right now. She had a ton of magic already; their family has always been savvy about breeding magic with magic. She shouldn't have needed to kill another witch for years. Decades, even.'

Jane's mind spun. It was true: Hasina's magic would

seep out of her new body, but slowly. *When he demanded to know what I'd done, he assumed I'd drained her magic off somehow, like when I made Lynne give up hers. He thought I'd created Hasina's motive for killing his sister. No wonder he was so angry.* But less than a second later, another thought crowded that one out. 'You said you didn't know why Hasina killed witches,' she said accusingly. 'But you do. You have all along.'

There was another silence, substantially less sympathetic than the last one had been. 'My darling Jane,' he said at last, 'you and I hardly have an expectation of openness and honesty. It was never that sort of relationship between us.'

'I expect you to act intelligently, at least,' she snapped back. 'Maybe if you'd told me about Hasina's little magical storage problem—'

'Nothing,' André hissed. 'If I had told you, then nothing. I told you she kills witches, and that was all you needed to know. Katrin said that even that was telling you too much; that if you didn't know you might be careless, and she would catch you first and buy more time for the rest of us. My family comes first, Jane, and I put them at risk by telling you *anything*.'

Jane sucked in a breath to retort, but the fairer part of her brain had to admit that he had a point. Would she have proceeded differently if she had known *why* Hasina was a murderer? Probably not – she would have been just as determined to keep the ancient witch from changing bodies, and she wouldn't have had any better ideas of how to do it. 'Okay,' she agreed finally. 'I do *not* forgive you, but I agree that knowing the whole truth wouldn't have changed what I did.'

'You would have still charged in to save the day.' He was mocking now, but at least he sounded a little less furious. 'Ever give any thought to retiring from public service? The public would probably appreciate it.'

Jane closed her eyes and leaned back onto her pillow, eliciting a startled cry from Maki, whose tail she narrowly had missed. Her pillow was warm and indented from the cat's huge body, and she knew that she was probably getting fur mixed in with her hair, but it was impossible to care about that sort of thing right now. 'Staying out of harm's way apparently isn't all it's cracked up to be,' she pointed out tartly.

To her relief, he took her gibe in stride. 'New York City is harm's way,' he countered. 'This entire godforsaken country, in fact, has been nothing but a death trap for witches since Hasina first set foot on its shores. Our parents had a stroke of luck here, finding little Annette, but it was a terrible mistake to think that that meant we would enjoy the same good fortune.' He snorted. '"The American Dream," indeed – if that nonsense applies to anyone, it most certainly isn't witches.'

He's right, Jane realized somewhere down in the pit of her stomach. *Hasina came here and wiped out the witches in my father's family, kept the Montagues living in fear of her, drove my gran out of the country, and killed my mother when she came back*. Back in Paris, Jane used to have a firm policy of never dating American men – a policy she had broken for Malcolm – which may have been even smarter than she realized at the time. 'You're leaving,' she said – a statement, not a question. Making a stand wasn't in André's nature, and at this point it was hard for Jane to completely blame him. She had known that being a witch was dangerous, but she hadn't truly appreciated what 'dangerous' meant until now.

'I have nieces,' he replied crisply, his accent skewing the last word so that it took her an extra moment to decode it. 'Without Katrin to protect them, without even the magic that she could have left them, they are a pair of helpless little rabbits. Normally I would say that they don't have enough power for Hasina to even bother with, but obviously I don't understand her as well as I thought.'

She shouldn't have needed to kill another witch for years, Jane thought glumly. Hasina's blood sacrifices had until now been so few and far between that most witches hadn't even known for sure that they were going on, much less why. What had changed? Only her body . . . and the spirit she had crowded to the back of it. 'Do you think it could actually be *Annette* who wants to kill more?'

André's silence lasted so long that if it weren't for the faint static on the line Jane would have assumed the call had been cut off. 'I told you she was unstable,' he remarked finally.

Jane nodded silently, forgetting for the moment that

André couldn't see her. It was hard to deny the evidence in front of them. Hasina had plenty of magic, enough to keep her going strong until André and Jane were old and grey, yet she had still killed a witch – and not even one of the group who had recently attacked her. She had killed a witch guilty of nothing more than being in the neighbourhood. It was a vicious, senseless murder, and the only motive Jane could think of was Annette's, not Hasina's. Katrin had taken care of Annette when she first arrived, frightened and amnesiac, at the London orphanage. Katrin had been the little girl's first friend and confidante, and later the only constant in her life as she was shuffled from foster home to foster home. Annette had nearly killed André when she discovered the truth to their relationship – and now she had completed the job with Katrin. 'Annette's instability is influencing her.' Saying the words out loud made them sound even more obvious. 'She's even more dangerous now than she was before.'

André chuckled, but there was no humor in it, only bitterness. 'You could come back to Europe with me,' he offered offhandedly. 'My nieces could use a teacher, someone to help them use what power they have.'

Someone to cast protection spells around all of you and maybe share your bed on colder nights, Jane translated cynically. But it didn't matter what he'd really meant, so she didn't bother to contradict him. 'I can't do that,' she said instead, and she heard him sigh heavily into his phone. 'I may

not have a knack for – what did you call it? – public service, but I don't seem to be any good at avoiding trouble,
either. Sooner or later it's going to come down to Hasina
or me, and I can't spend the rest of my life looking over
my shoulder. I certainly couldn't do it knowing that I was
attracting even more danger to you and your nieces at the
same time. With my luck, while I'm contorting myself to
watch all those backs, I would walk straight into Hasina's
trap.'

André's laugh was a little warmer this time, more
sincere. 'I hope that you succeed, Jane – for what it's
worth, I really do. If it weren't for Katrin's little girls, I
honestly think you might have been able to talk me into
your next suicide mission. You're so adorably sincere.'

'We're not that different,' Jane answered, realizing
as she said it that it was actually true. 'We both put our
family absolutely first. We just have different definitions
of "family."'

'You flatter me,' he murmured, almost a purr. 'Are you
sure I can't persuade you to leave town? This is just an
awful time to be a known witch, and I would be quite sad
if anything fatal were to happen to you.'

'Thank you,' she temporized. There was no point
in arguing for either of them, she knew. André had to
return to Romania, and Jane had to stay in New York.
He had nieces to hide, and it was up to her to make it so
that they could one day come out of hiding. That, or she
would die trying.

'Goodbye, Jane,' he told her sadly.

She closed her eyes for a moment, then said her own goodbye and flipped the phone closed. Suddenly it felt even darker in her room than before, but she didn't have the energy to even get up and pull the curtains aside. She fell asleep instantly, still in her clothes and with the phone clutched tightly in one hand.

Chapter Twenty-two

JANE BLINKED AT the short, dark-skinned woman on the farmhouse's doorstep, taking in her chunky jewellrey, thick kohl eyeliner, and slick black topknot. The woman's eyes were an incongruent ice-pale blue, like little chips of paint. 'I'm sorry,' Jane repeated stupidly, wishing that she'd had a more restful night's sleep. 'You say you know Emer?'

'But I'm here for *you*,' the little woman repeated in a thick accent that Jane didn't recognize. She suspected that it came from half a dozen countries at least.

'Well, um, I'm sure she'll be awake soon, so . . .' Jane hesitated, hoping that the odd woman would make things easier by offering to come back. After everything that had happened and the news about Katrin Dalcaşcu, letting a complete stranger waltz into their home could be beyond impolite – it could be dangerous.

Jane quickly spun a thread of magic, directing it at the woman, wanting to find out who she was and what she was doing here. But the woman's mind was a blank wall, and from the way her blue eyes glared up through her thick-lensed glasses, she seemed to know that Jane had just tried to read it.

Feeling rather at a loss, Jane blurted out the first thing that came into her head. 'Are you a good witch, or a bad witch?'

The woman chuckled rustily and ran a thick, calloused finger down Jane's cheek. 'You're new here, Blondie,' she replied. 'I'm not. I know my way to the kitchen, thank you. If you want to be useful, maybe boil some water for tea?'

Fortunately, at that moment there was a flurry of activity in the vestibule behind her, and Jane fell back gratefully. To her surprise, Emer Montague all but threw herself into the arms of the stranger. Stepping back, she breathed, 'Jane, sweetheart, it's my profound honour to introduce you to Penelope Lotuma.'

'It's a paying gig, Emer love,' Penelope cautioned, though Jane didn't follow enough of what was going on to understand the look of shock on Emer's lined face.

'I'm sorry.' She wasn't, but it seemed like a good idea

to try to be diplomatic. 'I didn't know who she was.' *Who is she?* The name didn't sound familiar to her at all, but Emer had pronounced it as if it were synonymous with a royal title.

'Pen, you're welcome for as long as you like, but I'm afraid we can't afford your services at the moment,' Emer continued. 'There must have been a mix-up.'

'I'm prepaid,' Penelope assured her, swinging a massive rolling suitcase through the door and pulling a printed silk scarf from around her neck. 'Blondie's young man put up my fee – he sends his best, by the way,' she added, turning to catch Jane's hands and press them between her own. 'He said he couldn't come himself, though – something about respecting your wishes.'

She swished past Jane and Emer in a swirl of multicoloured silk. Jane stared after her with her mouth hanging open. *Malcolm.* Of course. Somehow, Malcolm had convinced a witch – and apparently a rather well-known one – to help them. *But how?* Emer and the strange woman were obviously on good terms, but if she was an ally, then her arrival wouldn't have been so obviously unlooked for. 'Who *are* you?' she blurted.

Penelope paused on the sage-and-sand area rug in the centre of the great room. 'Don't be slow, girl. It's the second time our paths have crossed – mine, and that lovely young man's, and yours as well. You've got something I created in this very house; I can see its shadows through the ceiling.'

Jane looked upward, though she couldn't see what Penelope saw. Comprehension finally washed over her. *The spirit box. A witch who deals with the dead – like Emer – whom Malcolm had traded with once before.* Nodding crisply as if Jane had spoken her thoughts aloud, the little witch resumed her progress across the room.

'She stayed with us for a while in the seventies,' Emer told Jane quietly as Penelope's back vanished into the kitchen. 'She taught us . . . a great deal, really. Though I know it was only the tiniest fraction of what she knows. She would never say, but I'm almost certain she's one of Jyoti's descendants, like your Romanian friends. Rogues and tricksters, all of them, and nearly impossible to find, much less hire. I can't imagine . . .' She trailed off, then shivered and forced a smile. 'We're beyond lucky to have her help,' she finished. 'I can't think of a more useful person who could have shown up on my doorstep.'

'We're in rather desperate need, Pen,' Emer admitted frankly as they crossed together into the kitchen, where Penelope was already perched on a stool like an exotic bird. Her short fingers were wrapped around an ivy-patterned mug, and thick steam rose from it even though she hadn't been in the room for more than a minute. 'Hasina has found a fresh body after all this time, and though our Jane here led a valiant attempt to prevent her, she has switched. It's likely that she'll hold a grudge, and anyway, she'll keep killing for much longer now.'

'She has to,' Jane piped up, forcing herself to stop staring at the mug. The other two turned curiously toward her, and she quickly explained what she had learned from Gran's diary. After a brief hesitation, she added a synopsis of André's phone call as well. If Penelope really was here to help, then she needed all the information they had to offer. And strangely, Jane already trusted her. Penelope's obviously mercenary motives felt a bit reassuring after Annette's double cross; it was easier to trust a stranger who was bought and paid for than to try to guess about her possible hidden motives. At this new information, Emer's emerald-green eyes widened in shock, but Penelope's wood-block face remained closed, thoughtful.

'I could teach you to buy time,' she offered finally. Her thick fingernails gestured absently toward her necklace, a thin, dark chain with at least fifteen little glass bubbles hanging from it. 'But the pretty young man made it sound as though that wasn't what you would want.'

'No,' Jane agreed. In the corner, a teakettle whistled shrilly, and Emer moved to remove it from the heat.

Jane frowned at it, then at Penelope, who raised her steaming cup in a cheery toast. 'For you,' she explained, nodding her topknot toward the kettle smugly.

'Rooibos and Penelope,' a voice chimed from the stairway door. 'What on earth have I done to deserve this little paradise?'

Jane swung to see Charlotte, her reddish-gold hair piled on top of her head and some carefully applied fawn-colored eye shadow artfully accentuating her creases. 'She says Malcolm sent her,' Jane explained. Then she frowned and turned to Penelope. 'That *is* what you said, isn't it?'

'Malcolm is the tanned young man with the psycho for a sister, yes?' Penelope blew delicately on the surface of her tea, her blue eyes wide and innocent.

'That's the one.' Emer grinned.

'How did he possibly convince you to come here?' Jane asked. He must have jumped on a plane the very night she threw him out in order to track down the elusive witch so quickly. And it meant something, she knew, that he understood her enough to still stay away, even after providing this invaluable help.

Emer and her daughter fixed Penelope with matching stares. The little witch sipped at her tea, seemingly oblivious to the sudden silence that filled the kitchen.

'Transactional details are confidential,' she said slyly. 'I will tell you, though, that my services don't come cheap. You're one lucky girl.'

'Oh.' Jane realized that the glittering eyes of all three witches were fixed curiously on her face. She blushed. 'Okay,' she said instead. 'So what do you know about evicting a witch who doesn't want to die?'

'"Evicting,"' Penelope repeated, rolling the syllables around her mouth as if she were tasting them. 'How humane. Much nicer than what she deserves, after thousands of years of possession and murder.' She glanced significantly at Emer. 'The young man who hired me did indicate that she was *moral*.'

Jane sucked in a breath, but Charlotte cut in. 'She's not being squeamish about Hasina,' she assured the black-haired witch. 'Painful eviction would, in fact, be ideal, and killing the host body to accomplish it is certainly not out of the question. But the main goal is to get rid of Hasina for good. Any side effects of her banishment are strictly that: side effects.'

Penelope nodded briskly. 'Easier to just kill her now, then, don't you think?'

'Not enough firepower,' Emer murmured. 'Last time we took her on, we failed the mission and lost a sister.' Jane nodded, touched by the choice of wording. Even though she didn't share their genetics, Dee had been one of them.

'Well, Blondie's friend bought the full package,' Penelope informed them, seemingly unconcerned. 'I'll help plan, help train, or help fight. Just point where you need me.' She turned to Jane. 'He loves you madly, you know. Or at least, he certainly acted like someone in love, like a knight on some quest to redeem his lady's honour. So few people love the way they used to anymore; it's really quite a shame.'

Jane's heart suddenly felt as though it would burst out of her chest. *It doesn't matter,* she tried to remind herself. *I can't let him win me over with shallow grand gestures; I have to focus on the big picture.* But if Malcolm hadn't returned to claim his credit, what kind of shallow gesture was that?

Penelope was watching her with shrewd blue eyes. 'It's not easy to find me, you know, much less to find me twice. I was in Caracas this time,' she continued idly, and as she said it her accent grew somehow thicker. 'We had met already in Ecuador last month. Your knight had crossed the path of a self-proclaimed "witch hunter," and very thoughtfully warned me. That bought him your trinket – an excellent bargain for him – and then we were done. Apparently, though, the coven I crossed the border with wasn't quite as discreet as I would have preferred. I wouldn't have stayed in the area nearly so long if I had known what gossips they were, and not enough power to turn on a lightbulb between the four of them.'

'Well, four,' Emer scoffed, and Charlotte and Penelope chuckled appreciatively. Jane, who didn't get the joke, folded her arms across her chest and waited.

'It's much harder to do magic in even numbers,' Charlotte explained unhelpfully. 'Three, five, seven are the best . . . twelve works because it's divisible by three . . . eleven is unlucky and will cause your spell to rebound . . . there are a lot more rules to magic once you're in a group.'

She shrugged in a sort of apology, and Jane felt a sudden pang of missing Dee. She had always been Jane's magical translator. *Besides, we were an odd number when we went into the mansion, and I don't think it helped a bit.*

'It's complicated,' Emer chimed in gently, covering Jane's hand with her own, 'but only if you need to complicate it. Your power is your power, and its only limit is itself. But combine it with a coven, or a specific spell, and the structure can hinder just as much as it can help.'

'But what does that even *mean*?' Jane complained, unable to keep quiet any longer. Jane half expected them to giggle at her confusion again, but Penelope just fixed her eyes on Jane's, and Jane felt her entire body still. Even her pulse seemed to slow. 'It's like building an engine around the raw power that is combustion,' she explained. 'With that clear, can we begin now? I see the dead all over you, Blondie, and I'll need to know everything you've learned from them.'

Chapter Twenty-three

BY THE TIME Jane finished telling Penelope about her last vision of Dee, her conversation with Gran's diary, and everything André had told her, the kitchen's population had changed several times. First Maeve had come down, yawning and wearing fuzzy slippers. She had managed to sit at the little wooden table quietly enough, but Leah's entrance had caused more of a disturbance. Her mother had quickly taken her out, then returned through the great-room door just as Harris had descended by the stairs on the other side. Then Leah had returned, only to be herded sternly away again by her mother, and in the end Jane was alone with Penelope, repeating every detail she could remember from the last week.

'Hasina,' Penelope breathed when she had finally finished. 'It may surprise you, but until your knight came to find me I wasn't sure that her unlikely life was anything more than a myth.'

Jane's mouth twisted into a frown; that was hardly encouraging news.

'You know, of course, about Ambika and her seven daughters,' Penelope went on.

'I know the basics,' Jane agreed. 'But something tells me that you know a lot more than that.'

Penelope's smile revealed an even row of tiny white teeth. 'Ambika was the first witch,' she began agreeably. 'She inherited her kingdom from her warlord father, but his followers wanted nothing to do with a woman ruler. Their head priests took Ambika into a hut and filled it with perfumed smoke, trying to make their gods show them who her father's true heir should be. But when the smoke cleared, there stood Ambika. And she had changed.'

'The priests made her a witch?' Could witches be 'made,' somehow? It didn't fit with anything that Jane knew.

'Of course not,' Penelope scoffed. 'It was their gods who made her, who appointed her their ruler, and the people knew that it was good for them and knelt in the mud and worshipped her from that day forward.'

'Oh. Well, that sounds a little better, then. And from

what I hear, in addition to being touched by those gods she was incredibly fertile.'

'Seven sons, seven daughters,' Penelope confirmed. 'She remembered the lessons of her own ascension to the throne and, in an attempt to prevent the same from happening to her children, divided up her lands among her sons, for all the good it did them. History doesn't even remember their names. Those of us who still carry her magic know the names of her daughters, though. It was to them that she left her true inheritance, split into seven equal parts.'

'Jyoti,' Jane remembered, the common ancestress of both Penelope and the Dalcaşcus. 'Hasina, and Anila – she was the one whose descendants Hasina wiped out after Salem.' She frowned, trying to remember any of the other four names she had read in Rosalie Goddard's journals. 'Anulet?'

'Amunet,' Penelope corrected. 'A nasty piece of work, that one. Maya, of course, but hers are all gone now. There was Sumitra, who is oh-so-indirectly responsible for this lovely kitchen we're sitting in now. And the youngest was Aditi. She's the one your people came from, Blondie. A little slip of a thing; all eyes, really. And conscience, more's the pity.'

Jane pitched forward on her stool. 'You know them?' she whispered. 'You've spoken with them?'

Penelope smiled and leaned back a little in her small wooden chair. Jane was, she realized belatedly, looming over the other woman, but she didn't seem to care or even especially notice. 'I speak with the dead,' she explained. 'Nearly all the day long, in fact. I live with them. I breathe their air, walk in their footsteps, wear their fates like jewels. I know them all by reputation at the very least. Even those who lived at the dawn of humanity itself.'

A million questions popped into Jane's head at once, but Penelope was there for a specific reason and she felt honour bound to try to focus on that. 'I've been thinking,' she began slowly. 'No one in generations has been able to stop Hasina, even when they've known who she is and what she's doing to stay alive. But her sisters were just as strong as she is, and her mother would have been even stronger. I bet if they'd known what she was going to do, they would have been able to keep her from ever moving into her first new body.'

Penelope's mouth twisted thoughtfully. 'Probably,' she agreed. 'They might even be able to give you some pointers – or they could, anyway, if we could talk to them.'

Jane's mouth opened and then closed again. When she managed to make it form words, she heard a faint pleading tone in her voice. 'Isn't that what you do, though?'

Penelope didn't seem ruffled in the slightest by Jane's skepticism. She pushed her thick glasses a little higher on her nose and sighed. 'Even experts in their fields have limits. Or were you going to tell me that you know where Ambika and her daughters are buried? And that you have some previously unknown spell to reconstitute their

213

skeletons, since I doubt any of them was in a hermetically sealed tomb. They have truly returned to the dust by now, and no one even knows which dust.'

'*Having the body, though — the bones, really — makes up for just about any other lack,*' Emer had said once. And what was the rest? '*If you're truly adept and you have someone's bones, you can call them back for real.*' But they didn't have any bones, and they didn't have anything else, either. The first witches' belongings were long gone, and everyone who had known them was long dead. Even if Penelope was every bit as good as her remarkable reputation, she couldn't be expected to work miracles out of thin air.

'Even an heirloom would be a long shot anyway, wouldn't it?' Jane asked, finishing her train of thought out loud. 'Anything but a skeleton would, when the person has been dead so incredibly long. Even if we found something that one of them owned, it wouldn't be enough.'

'It wouldn't.' Penelope's accented voice was crisp and calm.

It's not an urgent problem to her, Jane realized darkly. *It's just a job. If we all die in some futile attempt to take out Hasina, she'll take her payment and just disappear.*

Before she could voice her annoyance, however, Penelope spoke again. 'You may well be correct that one of those original witches could help us. But without their bones we could never raise them, not even a fleeting shadow of what they left on the world. So we will have to pursue other avenues.'

'I don't suppose you have any in mind.'

'Of course I do,' Penelope replied, unperturbed. 'Hasina transfers bodies using a spell. It's a difficult one that requires tremendous power focused through impossibly convoluted conduits, but still, a spell. Something like that doesn't just end once the body switch is complete – it takes effort to maintain her presence there for the rest of that body's life. It's performed the one time, but it continues indefinitely.'

Jane took a moment to process that information. The orb she had used to become Ella Medeiros had sort of worked that way, she realized. It had functioned on a strict time limit, fueling her disguise for exactly twenty-eight days. After that it had vanished – burned up or collapsed on itself or just winked out of existence, perhaps. Jane wasn't sure. She had been on the street when the spell ended, far from the orb, watching André's handsome face grow increasingly murderous as he realized who she was. But Hasina's spell would not self-destruct that way; it must provide a different sort of energy, so that casting it once would continue releasing that energy until the spell was cast again. 'Okay,' she agreed. 'But we tried to stop her from finishing the spell, and we got beaten. Now it'll keep her in Annette's body until the next time she needs to perform it, and once she has new heirs she can do that whenever she wants. We won't be able to predict it, and we know from experience that we won't be able to interrupt it, so—'

215

'Do you need me here for this?' Penelope interrupted. When she seemed convinced that Jane would be quiet, she continued. 'The spell is cast, but it's still working,' she explained slowly. 'If we learn enough about the spell, then we may be able to disrupt its effects, to change the way it works on Hasina's soul.'

'We could break the connection,' Jane said, realizing what Penelope meant.

Penelope held up a warning hand. 'Maybe. But it would be best if we knew every last detail of the spell in question, and only Hasina knows all that. You'll have to tell me everything you know about it, and then Emer and her family need to do the same. Don't leave anything out. If you can't remember the exact words that your grandmother's diary used on the subject, then I'll need to interview it, as well.'

'I remember.' She knew Gran's words by heart, and of course she had seen the spell under way, hadn't she? Abruptly, the smell of smoke filled Jane's nostrils, and she felt an angry heat licking at her skin. She closed her eyes against the remembered flames. *Snap out of it,* her brain urged frantically, but she couldn't. *Then at least use it,* she told herself. *See what you saw.* There were shapes in the darkness, and she needed to know what they were. Lynne's tall, trim form was outlined against the atrium's windows, and next to her something glowed with an unearthly light.

But I didn't see; I didn't see. Annette's dark, predatory

eyes kept getting in her way, and attacks had come from every side. Jane was confused and disoriented, her lungs on fire.

Then a door banged open and Dee was there, her face as fierce as any Amazon's. Dee saw, Jane thought with relief, and her world jolted and shifted and realigned until she reached the moments when she had looked out through Dee's amber eyes. Something bubbled in between Annette and her twin crones, giving off the same unearthly glow that Jane had seen earlier. Somewhere far away, as though in a different world, she felt her lips trying to form words to describe the odd substance. But her real self was trapped here with Dee, hearing the terrible rising rushing noise, watching as Belinda and Cora withered and collapsed, and turning away as the light began to pour from Annette's suspended body.

Then the blood was back, flowing freely down her shirt just as it had on almost a nightly basis since Dee had been murdered. Jane choked on it, gagging as she tried to speak. The darkness rushed at her like an angry tide. She tried to swim against it, choking and struggling, but it came faster and deeper until she was buried.

From a great distance she heard more shouting, another door slamming open, running feet. Then something soft and warm was pressed against her forehead, and her body remembered how to open its eyes. When she did, Emer's green ones were peering back into them, and her tiny, fine-boned hand held a damp washcloth to Jane's head.

'I don't know what kind of a ship you're running here, Emer,' Penelope said, looking thoroughly unconcerned, 'but this one seems to have a touch of that posttraumatic stress thingy that the young people are always going on about these days. You can go upstairs and lie down for a bit, Blondie,' she added, her tone more gentle. 'I'll start with the other interviews while you pull yourself together.'

Jane stood unsteadily and was mortified to see Maeve and Charlotte and even Harris and Leah peering into the kitchen through both of its doors. Her head throbbed painfully, but she managed a weak smile and even a little wave before dragging herself up the stairs toward her bed.

Behind her, she heard Penelope's voice again. It was softer now, but she could still make out the chiding words. 'You should have told me that the girl has experienced death, Emer,' she scolded. 'Even if it was only by proxy. You know that sort of thing leaves a mark.' Jane couldn't make out the reply, but she held herself perfectly still at the top of the stairs, holding her breath until Penelope's next words floated up to her. 'You're lucky I came when I did. I can't even imagine the mess that you might have made of things without my help.'

Chapter Twenty-four

WHEN JANE CAME downstairs the following morning, the atmosphere in the farmhouse had changed perceptibly. Penelope was the only one missing from the kitchen. At first Jane assumed that she was off doing some strange ritual or research – but none of the Montagues would meet Jane's eyes, and she realized the reason behind Penelope's absence. *They sent her away,* she thought with uncanny certainty. *This is a family meeting, and she wasn't welcome.*

'Sorry,' she blurted lamely, and some of the pale faces in the kitchen turned her way. 'I can just—' She waved vaguely toward the stairway's other outlet toward the formal dining room. *Sit outside until you're done. Walk into town and get a muffin. Disappear.*

'Thank you, Jane,' Charlotte said stiffly, and Jane felt her own cheeks flush a mortified shade of red. She spun to leave, but Maeve's voice caught her before she could go more than a step.

'Wait,' her friend snapped. Her voice was raw with frustration, and Jane wondered how long the five of them had been arguing already. 'This concerns her as much as any of us.'

'Not quite as much,' Harris mumbled, but he was staring into his coffee so fixedly that Jane had trouble making out the words.

'That's not fair, and you know it,' Maeve began, but Charlotte clicked her tongue and her niece and nephew quieted down, though petulantly.

'Annette Doran, or Hasina rather, contacted us this morning,' the redheaded woman explained, straightening her silk Carine Gilson robe conscientiously. 'It's set off quite a stir, as you can see.'

Jane shot her a strained smile. '"Contacted us,"' she repeated, putting a question into the word. But the guilty, awkward looks on the faces around her told a different story. *Oh. Not 'us,' then. 'Them.'* Whatever Annette's message had been, it separated her from the group as neatly as a knife.

'She had an offer,' Harris explained. Maeve opened her

mouth to protest, but before she could speak, he cut her off. 'What? That's what it was.'

'So says Mr. Everything-Is-a-Trap,' Leah muttered under her breath, picking a paper napkin into smaller and smaller shreds with her YSL-logoed fingernails.

'Will someone just tell me what's going on?' Jane felt guilty pushing them on what was clearly a sensitive subject, but she didn't think she could stand any more oblique and unhelpful bickering.

'Annette has offered us a trade,' Charlotte finished crisply. 'She claims that, if you meet her tomorrow evening, she will leave the rest of us alone.'

Emer looked at her sadly. 'She's offered my family one hundred years of amnesty.'

Jane considered that for a moment. André had insisted that it was impossible to make any kind of truce or deal with Hasina, because she had lived far too long to consider a human deal permanent. But even with Annette's instability, as long as Hasina was in charge they should be able to stick to a bargain that lasted a mere hundred years. There might be fewer witches in the world than there used to be – thanks to Hasina's own hunting practices as much as natural attrition – but there were assuredly enough to keep her powered for a hundred years without even touching the Montagues. If there wasn't too much of Annette's angry, vengeful influence hovering around the body that used to be hers, then this could be the deal of a lifetime for Jane's closest friends. *I wanted to keep them safe,*

221

a little voice reminded her. *That was always the point of this.* 'That sounds like a good deal,' she said, then cleared her throat; there was something strange about the sound of her voice. 'I hope you told her I would go.'

'Obviously we told her to go to hell,' Maeve said sarcastically. 'Oh, no, wait. We said we'd think about it. Talk it over with you. Because Carrie – that's our cousin, Jane, she's in medical research – has invented this operation called a "sanity-ectomy," and this morning we all went out and had one.' She glared around the kitchen, but from the conspicuous lack of reaction Jane guessed that this wasn't her first hostile outburst of the morning.

'Oh. Well, it's okay you didn't give her an answer,' Jane reassured all of them, trying to avoid Maeve's furious glare. 'Like Maeve said before, this concerns me, too. I appreciate you waiting to talk it over with me,' she added, ignoring the fact that they hadn't especially welcomed her into their discussion with open arms.

'You're fine with volunteering to stick your head into the lion's mouth?' Leah finished for her, perking up and looking genuinely interested. 'Because that would have saved us a whole lot of moral ambiguity if you'd popped in and said so, like, two hours ago.'

'We were holding a *secret* family conference,' Maeve pointed out hotly. 'Which, for the record, I said was totally pointless – two hours ago. We could have just told Annette to go to hell and then woken Jane up for brunch.' In spite of her indignation, Maeve couldn't seem to resist a glare and then a shudder at the plate of greyish eggs that sat, untouched, in front of her.

'This "meeting" with Annette is a trap,' Charlotte pointed out in a neutral tone that made it clear that she knew how very obvious that was.

'Everything is a trap,' Harris muttered.

'Yes, everything *is* a trap,' Jane agreed with a shrug. 'But in this case it's a trap for me, and a bargain for you.'

'You *would* see it that way,' Maeve glowered. 'So the decent people among us thought we shouldn't tell you about the offer at all.' She turned her ferocious glare on Harris, who looked fixedly at his thumbs.

'Maeve, berating people is not the way to convince anyone of your point of view,' her grandmother corrected sternly. 'Don't tempt me to recommend charm school for you the next time your father checks in; it's never too late.' Jane felt a sudden pang; she would have really loved to belong to a whole, living family, and especially to this family.

'I know you're worried about me,' she told Maeve softly, 'but I'm worried about you, too. I brought this craziness into all your lives, and now I have a chance to end it.' The two final words rang in her ears over and over again, and she tried to suppress a shudder. *Am I really worth one hundred years?* she wondered in the most private part of her mind. It couldn't just be Annette's anger driving such a generous offer; Hasina must really want Jane. *Two magical parents,* she mused, *and one of them part of her old blood vendetta. I guess I do have family, after all*. She didn't know what attracted Hasina more – Jane's own substantial magic, or the fact that a living witch had popped up from Anila's line after all this time – but the combination must be irresistible.

'I did think that you had a right to know, Jane, but I . . .' Emer trailed off, handing Jane a mug of steaming tea and pressing her hands gently to her mouth as if to search for her missing words.

Jane wrapped her hands around the warm mug and gratefully took a sip. *She doesn't want me sacrificed, but she's also responsible for all of them, and the rest of her family as well.* It was an impossible position; no wonder Emer had been so quiet. 'Annette intends to kill me,' Jane conceded. 'That doesn't mean that she'll succeed.'

Charlotte pursed her lips skeptically, but refrained from reminding Jane that they had already learned otherwise the hard way. Annette had been born powerful and had only grown more so. Serving up Jane's magic to her on a silver platter was hardly the best course of action, even if she vowed not to use it against the Montagues. Something about the thought nagged at the edges of Jane's mind, but with so much attention on her she couldn't focus on what it was.

'This is my life we're talking about here, so it's my choice,' she said flatly, making eye contact with Emer in particular. 'I know I'm a guest in your home, so you can kick me out onto the street if you really don't approve of my decisions. I guess you could even knock me out and tie me up to keep me from going – or you could try, at least.' She raised an eyebrow at Maeve, mimicking the exact angle that Lynne Doran had always used to make her feel about three inches tall.

Maeve half stood as Jane crossed the kitchen toward the door to the back lawn, but Jane flicked her eyes in warning, and her friend froze in place. Jane imagined her stuck there as she crossed the dewy grass toward an ivy-covered gazebo that overlooked the ocean. To her surprise and relief, Maeve didn't follow her.

Ignoring the stone benches that ringed the gazebo's lattice walls, Jane stretched out lengthwise along its cool slate paving stones, spinning the plain silver ring on her right hand as she struggled to catch hold of the thought that had half formed in the kitchen. It came to her in a flash. The deal that Annette had offered was for Jane, but Jane was just a person. She had been born with magic and inherited even more, but the magic wasn't an inseparable part of her. Gran had poured her own into the ring that was currently on Jane's finger – and Lynne had given hers to Jane inside an ancient, rune-covered athame.

There was no reason why Jane had to walk into Annette's trap and provide her with even more ammunition. She could give up being a witch and leave her magic with her friends. *Then, when the truce runs out a hundred years from now, maybe Maeve's and Leah's granddaughters will have inherited enough power to fend off Hasina on their own.*

She could feel the earth turning, she thought, ever so slowly to her left and down. There were noises, too, and more of them the longer she was still. It was just the wind through the ivy at first, and then she could separate out the sound of the waves in the distance. A lawnmower grumbled somewhere even farther away, and a little bird trilled happily from the wooden lattice of the gazebo's walls. When it changed its mind and flew away, Jane could hear the beating of its tiny wings against the air. There were sounds inside the earth as well, she realized after a while: worms tunnelling, mice burrowing, ants carrying morsels of food along long, blind hallways.

Jane lay for a while, and turned with the earth, and listened. Her magic had come from this world somehow; it was a part of the sounds and the life stirring around her. If she released what she had and then destroyed both the ring and the double-edged knife, the tremendous magic they contained would flow back into the world, harmless and unharnessed. Would it make some kind of difference? Might the earth spin a tiny bit faster, or its rivers run with a little more energy? Or would the magic that she had freed just work its way into newly born witches, encouraging them to envy and covet and kill in perpetuity? She had tried so hard to do the right thing, but it seemed like there was always some vital piece of information that she didn't know.

I'm going to die. The thought seemed unreal, as though it surely belonged to someone else, but she knew that she needed to face the possibility. *Tomorrow night.* The sun would set, then it would rise over the water that she was

226

listening to right now. And that would be the last time that her heart would beat while it rose.

She would fight, of course. It just wasn't in her nature to placidly accept something so permanent and final. Even now a small, angry part of her brain was tossing out possibilities: she could use Lynne's magic herself, set a trap of her own, strike first and strike hard. She *would* try, but she would fail, and her failure would have to count to the rest of the world nearly as much as her success would have. *I'll be okay with it if it buys them safety. I don't want to die, but I know that I can.* This was the first and most important difference, she realized, between herself and Hasina.

She turned her attention away from the ocean, bringing it in closer to her own body until she could feel her pulse thump steadily against her eardrums. She wondered whether she would notice the last beat, or if there would be so many distractions that she would miss it entirely. That possibility seemed unbearably sad. *I'll make myself notice,* she decided dreamily. *I'm sure that I will remember to do that.* Her heart beat a tiny bit faster for a moment, as if in acknowledgment, then returned to its normal, slow march.

Finally, she slipped her old iPhone out of her pocket, unlocked it, and opened up her email. *'Malcolm,'* she typed when a blank email screen winked open.

I have no idea what you did to get Penelope to come here, but she's been a godsend. We've been working really hard together, and I think that we might have a breakthrough soon.

227

So thank you, for doing whatever it was. I'm sorry about the way that things happened that night at the farm; I wish that we had talked a little more so that I could have explained better. I hope you know that I still care deeply about you, and I hope that wherever you are you are continuing to become the man I know that you've always wanted to be. Most of all I hope I get to meet him someday.

Jane stopped typing for a moment and frowned at the screen. It looked okay, she decided: almost upbeat. But the next part of what she had to say would be harder to disguise.

I want to thank you for always trying. I should have known when you left so quietly that you would immediately turn around and make something good come of it. It means a lot to me that your first instinct was to help. It's enough to make me wonder if I had been too quick to judge the things you said that night, and I hope that I was. Whatever you do, please keep proving me wrong.

Jane

After a moment she erased the last line, and replaced it with 'Love, Jane.' She almost typed 'Love always,' but it was too risky. No matter what she wished she could say to Malcolm now, the most important thing was that he not realize she was saying goodbye.

Chapter Twenty-five

'THEY'RE A BUNCH of cowards,' Maeve snarled, storming into the gazebo and throwing herself onto one of the stone benches.

Suddenly Jane thought that she looked almost exactly like her cousin Leah, but she politely refrained from saying so. For a moment she was disoriented, watching the play of dappled light through Maeve's wild mop of red curls. Then the explanation came to her: it looked wrong because the sun had shifted. 'How long have I been out here?' she asked, stretching her arms out to the sides experimentally. There were a bunch of angry new knots in the muscles of her back and neck, and she thought that she could guess at the answer before her friend said it out loud.

'It's just past three,' Maeve answered nonchalantly, then frowned. 'You've been here since you walked out? Like, right there in the middle of nowhere just *sitting*?'

'Lying down, mostly,' Jane pointed out, although it did nothing to relieve her self-consciousness. 'I've been napping. Or meditating. Or something like that.' The truth was that she might have slept for a while, but she was pretty sure that she hadn't. And there had been nothing as intentional as meditation on her mind, either: she had just lain there, drifting on the slate stones, not moving or particularly wanting to move. *It isn't time to go yet. And when it is, I will.*

'I figured you'd skipped town,' Maeve said with a grimace, crossing her delicate ankles and swinging them gently back and forth. 'I hoped, anyway, that you would have had the good sense not to stick around a bunch of losers who would turn you over to some evil arch-bitch just to save their own skins for a few years.'

'A hundred,' Jane corrected primly. The gazebo's floor suddenly felt cold and unyielding beneath her, and she moved awkwardly to a bench one away from Maeve's. It was made of stone as well, but something about being able to stretch her legs downward actually did help her to feel a tiny bit more comfortable, so she stayed put. 'And I can't help but notice that you came looking for me here, anyway.'

'I said I hoped you would show some basic sense, not

that I completely gave up my own. Whatever the most bullheadedly stupid thing is that could possibly, remotely be construed as 'noble,' there you are. Doing it.'

Jane grinned, and Maeve's bow mouth tugged up a little at the corners as if by reflex. Her brown eyes, though, stayed hard and angry. 'They're not "turning me over," Mae,' Jane reminded her gently. 'I know you'd rather pretend Annette's call never came. But it did, so I had to know about it, so I have to meet her. That's not your family's fault at all.'

Maeve snorted delicately, but shifted the topic. 'Jane,' she pleaded earnestly, 'just let us help you hide. We could smuggle you through our place in Chamonix to anywhere you wanted to go.'

'Tell me more about this phone call,' Jane asked, ignoring Maeve's suggestion even though it tugged at her heart. *I'll never get to go to Chamonix. I always meant to.* But something about Maeve's anger was beginning to sound evasive, and Jane had too much to deal with in the present to let her mind dwell on some nonexistent future. 'What was the exact wording?'

'You can't read my mind,' Maeve argued defensively. 'Not anymore, anyway.' She frowned suddenly, then cocked her head to the side in a curious gesture so familiar that Jane wanted to cry. 'Did you ever read my mind before?' she asked suddenly. 'Did you see any of the stuff I thought about that assistant curator in Drawings, for example?'

Jane smiled at her and shook her head definitively. 'No, but you're going to have to tell me all about him sometime soon. Just make it after tomorrow night. I think I'll have a little trouble focusing on things between now and then, but it would be nice to have something to look forward to when it's all done.'

Maeve stuck her tongue out childishly. 'Skip town,' she urged, growing serious again. 'Did you see how many extra cars Harris keeps just sitting in the barn here? He's a total freak about lending them out, but between the two of us we could totally swipe his keys.'

'You know I won't do that. And it's just as well, I think, since Hasina threatened you all if I don't show up. Right?'

Maeve jumped up off the bench and stormed out of the gazebo, her face a furious scowl. After a moment she returned and sat again, as Jane had guessed she would. 'Her *existence* is a threat to us,' she pointed out angrily. 'It has been for pretty much forever; knowing about it doesn't suddenly make it true.'

'There's a difference,' Jane told her gently. 'There's a difference between her picking off witches at random to rebuild her magic, and targeting your family specifically because she's pissed off.'

'No, there isn't,' Maeve countered, but Jane could see that she didn't really have an argument beyond that.

'There really is,' she said firmly. 'But it's a moot point, because I'd decided to go before I even knew about that little bit of blackmail.'

Maeve bit at her lip, twisting it. 'I figured you'd say something like that,' she admitted. 'But I don't really get it. This whole time you've been all gung-ho to take on Lynne. You stayed in New York way, way longer than you had to, and then you rallied Grandma and even Harris and convinced them to go face off against someone they've been afraid of their entire lives. We got so used to being Manhattan's *weaker* witch family — scrappy second place — and you came in and treated us like—' She hesitated, weaving her fingers together: one over, one under. 'Equals,' she said finally, her voice barely louder than the breeze off the dunes.

Jane said nothing. Everything she could think of would only come across as patronizing, and she had no intention of sounding like that. From the moment she learned about her power, she had seen herself as an underdog. All the other witches she knew had gotten a massive head start in terms of training. But deep down, Jane knew she had always thought of that as a temporary status, something that she would grow out of once she understood more. She couldn't imagine how it must feel to face an entire lifetime of always having less power, of always depending on the goodwill of stronger witches.

Maeve finally finished her thought, breaking the silence between them. 'I just don't get why you're suddenly so willing to walk right into that horrible house. Straight to your own death.'

'I don't think that that's what I'm doing,' Jane argued.

233

Not necessarily; not exactly. It felt reckless somehow, to say it out loud, but in a way it was true.

Maeve tossed her hair back, her eyes suddenly fierce. 'You're going to fight, then.'

Jane heard a ringing note of satisfaction in her friend's voice, and she smiled. 'Well, I certainly don't plan to just walk in and shout up the stairs for someone to come down and kill me.'

Maeve's coppery-brown eyes searched her face more closely than she would have liked, especially since the girl didn't seem satisfied with whatever she saw there. 'You know that Hasina doesn't feel all that bound by her word,' she pointed out. 'You think that if you somehow manage to get out of this meeting alive, she'll stick to the hundred years' offer? Trust me, she won't. No matter how she phrased the deal, she won't agree that she got her end of it unless she kills you.'

Jane frowned; was that true? She had hoped that a time-limited deal would be binding somehow, but maybe that was hoping for too much from an offer of Hasina's. Not to mention that the unstable mind she had taken over was a wild card in itself. How much of her reaction would be ruled by Annette's impulsive fury? 'On the bright side,' Jane offered carefully, 'I probably *won't* make it out alive. So.'

Maeve heaved an exasperated sigh and reached into an inside pocket of her shrunken Polo blazer. She pulled out something lumpy and grey and tossed it to Jane, who didn't know whether she would be better off trying to catch it or dodge it, and ended up splitting the difference. The object bounced off her stiff-fingered hands and fell onto her knees. 'Don't drop that!' Maeve cautioned, a bit too late, but at least it hadn't hit the slate floor. Jane peered at it; it seemed unharmed, but how was she supposed to tell? 'It's a smoke bomb,' Maeve explained once she seemed satisfied that it wouldn't roll away. 'Leah made a few of them. Actually, she said she was trying to make an invisibility charm, but I'm pretty sure that if you swallowed that, it would kill you.'

Jane ran a finger across the fabric surface of the smoke bomb, surprised at how touched she was by the gift. 'Thank you. And thank Leah.'

'Come back inside and thank her yourself,' Maeve snapped impatiently. 'Jane, she's been sitting in the sunroom building an arsenal all morning long. Do you have any idea how badly that's cut into her usual texting schedule?'

Jane chuckled and shook her head. She leaned back to slip the little grey pouch into the pocket of her jeans, but its roundness was too unyielding to fit. For lack of other options, she ended up holding the bomb loosely in her hand, its dusty surface scratching against her skin.

'I'm serious,' Maeve pressed, standing up pointedly. 'If you plan to fight, at least plan. To fight. And let us help. Penelope's been working frantically on figuring out Hasina's body-snatching spell, but she doesn't think there's any way she'll be ready to interrupt it by tomorrow night. I'd bet that Annette knows that, and doesn't want to give us the time to figure it out, so let's use our resources more wisely. Go into the house, pull Penelope off her fool's errand, and tell her you need weapons instead. She's got some scary-good ones,' she added in an almost confessional tone. 'Aunt Charlotte says she makes this powder out of human skulls, then distills it into a liqueur with a little orange flower, and it doubles the range of her spells. More than doubles, maybe; if you drink enough of it you could probably knock Annette on her ass without ever leaving the farm. They're all in there working on *something,* even if it's a stupid something, while you've just been sitting out here "meditating."'

Finally, Jane nodded. Although she highly doubted that these last thirty hours would matter too much in the battle to come, she stood and linked her arm through Maeve's. She held the small gray pouch carefully away on the other side of her body, wrinkling her nose as a strange odor wafted up from it as she moved.

'Really don't drop it,' Maeve cautioned, her eyes wide and round with sincerity. 'They all make smoke, but some of them double as stink bombs.'

Jane smiled in spite of herself, turning the pouch over a few times between her fingers as she let Maeve steer her back toward the house. 'Leah seems to have a real gift for driving you crazy,' she observed almost cheerfully. 'If she can get under Annette's skin half as well, I may actually have a shot.'

Maeve kicked at her ankle. It wasn't much of a kick; more of a tap, really, but it still snagged Jane's foot and made her stumble a little. 'You'll have more than "a shot" if you start cooperating,' she pointed out tartly. 'We're all in there making sure you go to the mansion as prepared as you can be, and you're lying out here like you're practising being dead.'

Is that what I've been doing? Jane wondered, even as she made the appropriate denials out loud. She had certainly said goodbye to Malcolm, and it had felt at times like she was doing the same with the rest of the world. But she had felt very much alive the entire time – or, at least, for as much of the time as she could remember. She put on her most resolute face as they approached the herb garden.

Emer was clipping some purplish leaves; Jane noticed that she was wearing gloves and being unusually careful not to let them touch her bare skin. Although she was the only person whom Jane could see, she could somehow sense a sort of magical shadow of Penelope's activity from inside the house. *I'm here to make plans,* Jane reminded herself, tilting her chin up and trying to look confident. *I'm here because everyone in this house is trying to help me live past tomorrow night.*

Chapter Twenty-six

J ANE STOOD IN front of her bedroom's closet, one hand
    on her hip, feeling hopelessly indecisive. *What do you wear
on the day you're supposed to die?* The first time, it had been
a one-of-a-kind haute-couture wedding gown. Then a
flimsy cocktail dress with crystal-studded sandals, and then
a soft black sweater and a knit cap. The difference, of course,
was that on those occasions, the prospect of an untimely
death had come on her unexpectedly. This time, she was
determined to dress the part.

She had spent the morning in an old violet-and-lime
silk robe of Charlotte's, delaying this decision for as long

as she could. But there had come a point when the sun was inching higher, Leah was starting to dig through the kitchen looking for something to heat up for lunch, and Jane had no choice but to try to get dressed.

Maki curled around her ankles – or, rather, just below her knees. His long gray bottle-brush of a tail reached nearly to her waist, and Jane swayed a little from the force of his affection.

'What do you think, kitty?' she mused. 'It's a serious occasion, so probably nothing too bright. And sequins are just plain out. But if I'm going to give myself any chance at fighting, I'll need to feel confident.' She pulled a pair of shea-butter-soft leather pants out of the closet full of hand-me-downs and held it up against her hips, turning this way and that thoughtfully. 'Then again, if I go in looking all combat-ready, I'll lose the element of surprise.'

Maki hopped heavily onto her bed and blinked at her with unfathomable green eyes. 'You're right,' she agreed. 'I won't have the element of surprise anyway, no matter what I wear. Still, leather pants just don't feel right. I'm still me, not Ella.' The oversized cat turned his back on her very deliberately and curled himself into a ball. 'You're no help,' she complained, but his only response was to twitch his tail a little more closely around his body. She sighed. 'It's okay. I think I know.'

She reached to the far right of the front rack, where a blue-and-white Carolina Herrera dress had caught her eye over and over again. The V-neckline plunged a little farther – okay, a lot farther – than seemed appropriate, and the overlapping iris pattern was more 'garden party' than 'battle to the death.' But she felt perversely delighted at the prospect of irritating Hasina with a slightly out-of-season dress, and anyway, it felt perfect. She pulled it over her head, the soft fabric sliding across her face, arms, breasts, stomach, thighs. It looked even more flirtatious on her curvy body than it had been on the hanger. There was no doubt about it: this was the dress.

'Can I zip that for you?'

Jane jumped nearly a foot in the air, twisting as she did and banging her wrist sharply against the mirrored door. It shuddered and swung, showing a blue-and-white blur of her dress and her bedroom before filling with a million perfect shades of gold. *Malcolm.*

She blinked a few times, focusing one by one on his familiar, perfect features. 'What are you doing here?' she gasped.

He held up his phone almost sheepishly, switching on its glowing screen as he did. It was too small for her to read it at that distance, but she already knew what was there anyway. 'I got your email,' he explained, confirming her guess.

And here I was thinking I'd been so clever and vague. Of course he had seen right through her message; he knew her better than she gave him credit for. 'You sure do hop around the globe with lightning speed,' she muttered darkly. She'd never met anyone with such a penchant for dropping everything and skipping halfway across the world at a moment's notice. 'First down to Venezuela to send reinforcements, then right back here.'

'I know I said I wouldn't,' he apologized. 'And I'll leave as soon as we talk this out. But I want to know why you apparently think you're going to die, and what I can do to help.'

'You've helped,' she started earnestly. 'I put that in the email, because I needed you to know. You've already helped. A lot.'

'But?'

But. There always has to be one of those, doesn't there? She reluctantly told him about Annette's phone call the morning before, and the decision that she had reached, glossing over the part about how Harris, for one, seemed to prefer things that way. *Maybe more of them do,* she had to acknowledge to herself. *Maybe the others are just better at hiding their relief.* Emer, Charlotte, Maeve, and Leah had been working more or less nonstop on ways to help Jane survive her meeting with Annette, but even Maeve had stopped trying to talk her out of it. Penelope, who had never bothered with that to begin with, had spent all night outside on the lawn, dangling prisms from her fingers and occasionally moving them in unfathomable arcs. Jane didn't ask questions.

'But we ran out of time sooner than I'd expected,' she admitted. She tried to ignore the way his face darkened as she explained why she had accepted the meeting, but by the time she finished it felt as though his anger had pulled nearly all the light out of the room. 'We're putting together some spells – some weapons,' she finished appeasingly, 'and Penelope is making me some kind of . . . well, I don't actually know. But she's helping as much as she can, and it might make all the difference.'

' "The difference," ' he repeated flatly, and she flinched from his cold, fatalistic tone. 'You mean there's an outside chance that you might not die in a few hours.'

'I can't argue about this anymore,' she told him honestly, hearing her own fatigue in the way her voice had worn thin. 'I've already had to work it out with myself, then I had to convince Maeve and the rest of them.'

'Did they put up much of a fight?' Malcolm asked sarcastically. But she knew he was just afraid for her, and she smiled wearily.

'Maeve has been a trouper,' she assured him. 'And I don't think that any of them is actually *happy* about the way things have turned out.'

'I know I'm not,' he said simply.

His hands clenched and unclenched by his sides, and she instinctively covered one with one of hers. 'But you get it,' she prompted. 'You don't like it, but you understand why I'm choosing this. And you're going to give me your blessing to go, instead of sending me off into this thing that is, by the way, actually pretty scary, with more arguing rattling around in my brain.'

He pulled away and turned abruptly toward the door, only to pause there, a half step away. Jane could see the muscles of his back working against one another through the fine woven cotton of his shirt. 'I could go with you,' he said quietly, his voice tight with emotion. 'I could sneak into the house while she's focused on waiting for you. I could come in right behind you with a gun, or I could –'

'Isn't it enough for one of us to be stupidly brave?' she interrupted. 'You really want me to risk my life *and* feel the same way about you that you're feeling right now about me?'

His shoulders flinched, but he still didn't turn around. 'I want you to have the best chance that I can give you.'

She crossed to him and reached out a hand tentatively toward his back. It was warm, almost radiating heat. 'We're past all this now,' she told him, knowing that it was true. 'Hasina wants my power, and somewhere deep inside of her your sister hates me. If I can't drive Hasina out, then I'll either have to kill her or die. But I'm done trying to strategize the perfect battle plan where we all come out alive and happy and skip off into the sunset together. Dee was enough collateral damage; I won't let Hasina have any more of you. She just gets me – whatever I am, whatever I can do, whatever force I can call up to fight her.'

Malcolm turned suddenly and gripped her arm. There was a desperate light in his eyes, so she wasn't surprised by his next attempt to change her mind. 'If you lose,' he warned, 'she'll still be at large. She could come after

243

any one of us next, and I'm sure she'll get to all of us eventually.'

Jane smiled sadly. 'You're her brother,' she reminded him, 'and even though you meant exactly the opposite, you did her a favour the last time we tried to attack. If you don't cross her again, she'll probably forgive you, or at least make a show of getting along with you. And the rest of them get one hundred years: that's more than enough.' She poked him playfully in the ribs, smiling more broadly when he jumped a little. 'Not to mention the fact that none of you ever bothers to mention: *I might win.*'

He opened his mouth, closed it sharply, then opened it again. 'You might,' he agreed finally. 'When we were trying to find you, my mother talked all the time about how powerful you would be. You came from two magical lines – which is rare enough, considering how much the magical families distrust each other now – but there's more to it even than that. It's something about being a direct descendant of Ambika, through an unbroken line of practicing witches. Being a true heiress of her legacy, however distant, makes you stronger.'

Jane pictured the marble wall of Lynne's parlour, with its thousands of years of tiny branching names. They hadn't bothered to keep track of the male lines; sons were a dead end as far as the family tree went. But there was a steady line down the middle, one woman's name followed by another, and at its end was Annette Doran. 'Annette is Ambika's direct descendant, too,' Jane mused, 'and probably through about as many generations as I am. Hasina's stolen and hoarded magic along the way, of course, but she also bleeds it out over the years. There's every chance that we're evenly matched.' *Except for how Hasina has had thousands of years to learn the intricacies of magic and ways to use it, while I've had just a few months,* she thought but didn't say.

Jane could all too vividly remember the sensation of the air burning out of her lungs, smothering her from the inside out. Her magic hadn't stood up to Annette's assault: How much worse would it be now that Hasina was occupying her body? From Malcolm's worried eyebrows, she could tell that he was thinking the same thing. 'At least let Penelope help you prepare,' he offered, as a compromise. 'She knows a thing or twelve about survival.'

'Of course I will,' Jane agreed, though being the object of Penelope's creepy gaze wasn't her first choice of how to spend what were probably her last few hours of life. It made her feel like a dead thing that the woman planned to dissect. *She might help,* Jane reminded herself dutifully. *I said I'd try.*

'And take this,' Malcolm continued relentlessly, as if she hadn't spoken. He shoved a silk-wrapped bundle into her hands, and she recognized the long, cold shape beneath the fabric immediately. 'You've seen nothing your whole life but proof that hiding doesn't work. Not for witches, and not for power. Magic was meant to be used, and there's no one I'd rather see use it than you.'

Before Jane could say anything else, Malcolm bent down and kissed her softly, gently, on the lips. His mouth lingered on hers, and she felt the fine hairs on her arms stand up from her suddenly charged skin. The magic in her blood hummed and sang, racing its way to her heart and then returning, full again, to carry the news of Malcolm's nearness through every inch of her body. She felt her skin flush from head to toe, and leaned a little closer, letting his arms wrap around her. His kiss became deeper then, a little more passionate. But before she could tell where it might go, he let go of her and stepped back. 'Fight,' he told her roughly. 'I can't stand the thought of a world without at least the possibility of you in it. That's my north star; that's what keeps me on the path to be a better man than I was raised to be.'

You are better, she thought, but she couldn't say it out loud. If she told him, he might insist on coming with her no matter what she did to stop him, and she couldn't bear the thought of it. *He was right about killing Annette, but even when I threw him out anyway, he acted with such nobility.* The thought reminded her of another lingering question, and she knew that she had to ask. She tilted her chin up at him, taking in the square jaw, the warm skin, the dark, shining eyes. 'What did you do?' she whispered. 'Emer made it sound like hardly anyone can afford Penelope, like she only takes awful things in payment. How did you manage to convince her to come here?'

She held her breath as she waited for his reply, hoping

that she had misunderstood and that Penelope in fact accepted MasterCard. A tiny, awful part of her, though, somehow hoped for the worst. *Tell me that you threw a baby down a well or gave some poor soul bad directions to Emer's Summerlands. Tell me that you're not really everything that I hope you have become. It would make it so much easier to leave you behind.*

But he just smiled, one corner of his mouth curling up in the way that she knew and loved so well. 'Silly Jane,' he said lightly. 'Don't you understand? There's not one single thing I wouldn't give to help you. Absolutely all of it is yours.'

Then, before she could demand that he answer her more fully, he kissed her once on the forehead, turned, and left the room. From the bed, Maki lifted his tufted grey head to watch him go, and his flat green eyes looked almost wistful. Jane turned over the bundle that Malcolm had thrust into her hands, not sure whether she should unwrap it yet or not. *He went to Venezuela to send me Penelope, then to the Financial District to bring me Lynne's athame.* His tireless devotion to arming her for her battles touched her beyond anything that she could express in words. When Jane finally stepped forward into the place that Malcolm had been standing a moment before, the air around her still felt warm.

Chapter Twenty-seven

'IT IS A circle, from your third eye to your head to your heart to the very pit of your stomach down into the earth and back again,' Penelope lectured, and Jane closed her eyes, trying frantically to figure out just what the hell that meant.

Dee might have been a relentless tutor, but at least I had a vague idea of what she was trying to explain to me, she remembered with a sharp pang of loss. *And I could tell that she was actually rooting for me.* Penelope, by contrast, had grown increasingly frustrated by their attempts to marshal Jane's magical focus in preparation for the battle ahead. After nearly two hours of false starts and crossed signals, Jane half wished that it could be night-time already.

Malcolm sent her, she reminded herself for the hundredth time. And whatever price he had paid, she had a feeling that it hadn't been cheap. 'Draw it for me again?' she asked humbly, pretending not to notice Penelope's exaggerated eye roll behind the thick distortion of her glasses.

Penelope whipped out her pencil and a piece of paper with 'Messages' printed in optimistic blue ink at the top. The paper was already divided into dozens of tiny sections, each of which was crammed with diagrams, words, and, in some cases, mathematical equations. There was at least one that Jane could swear she had learned during her Advanced Physics lessons with Gran, although unfortunately that didn't make it any easier to remember now. 'It goes like this,' Penelope told her in short, staccato tones, her brown hand tracing a design on the paper that didn't look anything like a circle, or a human body, or anything that Jane could recognize.

She sighed. 'Maybe I could just, you know, meditate?' *If only Dee were around to hear me ask* that! Meditation and the slower, more controlled aspects of magic had never been Jane's forte, and as a result she found them annoying and usually boring. But even that was better than feeling useless, and she knew from experience that her ability to control her magic grew as she learned to focus her mind.

'This *is* meditating,' Penelope insisted, tapping the paper a few times with the point of her pencil for emphasis. Its dulled tip broke sideways with a loud snap, and Penelope stared at it in evident surprise.

'My brain feels like the pencil.' Jane raised her eyebrows for emphasis of her own.

'Fine.' Her exasperated tutor stuck the pencil into her slick topknot of hair so roughly that Jane was sure that she would stab her scalp with it. 'We start with the agate again. Tell me what you feel . . . here.' She slid a thin sliver of stone toward Jane. It was rough and gray on the outside, with a glasslike layer of blue that shaded from midnight to almost white in its centre. Penelope's thick fingernail pointed firmly to a spot just inside the dusty-looking crust, where the blue reminded Jane of a pair of Baccarat studs that Malcolm had given her for their three-month anniversary. Against Jane's pale skin and hair, the crystals had glowed almost black.

Jane stared at it, willing it to speak to her somehow. In spite of their best efforts, it hadn't yet. And just as she had during her first few attempts, she found her mind wandering almost immediately, completely unresponsive to her struggle to keep it on-task. *I wonder what Lynne did with those earrings – with all my things that I had to leave behind.* She had picked up her little red flight bag, pulled a trench coat over her wedding dress, and left every other remnant of her life up until that point in the room that she had shared with Malcolm. *And since then I've kept losing possessions at a rather unsettling rate.* 'It feels lonely,' she murmured, barely aware that she was speaking out loud.

Penelope's eyes, which matched one of the agate's innermost rings, widened appreciatively. 'And here?'

Of course praise would be out of the question. But Jane knew she didn't need to be coddled at the moment; she needed to be prepared. The spot on the outer crust of the stone that Penelope had indicated had the same dusty, light-sucking quality as Leah's smoke bombs, four of which were tucked neatly into Jane's satchel. 'It's loyal,' she replied, certain that she was right. 'An unlikely ally, maybe, but a faithful one.'

A ray of real sunlight pierced the thick clouds overhead, lancing through the glass of the sunroom's ceiling to strike directly on the stone in between the two witches. Jane felt her heart jump in her chest.

'It feels happy,' Penelope told her, glancing slyly up through her thick-lensed glasses. 'Novices think that crystals focus the witch's thoughts and power, but they have minds of their own. Like everything else, they have a purpose and an intention. A soul, almost.'

'Does that mean that you can talk to them, or make them do what you tell them to?' Jane asked curiously, but it was obviously the wrong thing to say. Penelope's purple-red lips curled down disapprovingly, and she turned her gaze back to her cluttered piece of paper.

'You'll be carrying jasper tonight.' The bespectacled woman cleared her throat and set a stone on the floor between them. It was a beautiful blood-red colour, marbled with smoky threads of black and a single narrow stream of white near one end. Jane was already wearing earrings set with smaller matching stones, and Emer had found her a bracelet made of unpolished ones on a thin silver chain, like tiny bits of brick.

She stared at the glossy stone that almost glowed on the pale carpet, waiting for it to speak to her. *Blood and bricks,* she thought. *And black smoke, forked with lightning.* But that was just what it looked like, not what it felt. Or was her edginess, her unease when she concentrated on it, a sign of that very thing after all?

'Its yellow form is more useful for most,' Penelope told her clinically, 'but not so many people go to real war anymore.' Her undefinable accent made each word sound foreign and exotic, and Jane strained to pick each one out correctly. 'Yellow is for struggle; it is for obstacles. Red is for when you have to build giant pyramids, or cut your way through swaths of enemies with a sword. You will carry this and as many other like it as the boy can dig up in this house before you go.'

Blood and bricks, Jane thought with satisfaction, though part of her was distracted with wondering how Harris had liked being assigned to jewellery-sorting duty. As hard as it was for her to picture, though, he must be used to doing grunt work for witches by now. He'd probably been accustomed to it all his life, really; the fad of patriarchy had never caught on in magical families. Jane inhaled, then exhaled in a rush. 'Okay. I feel it. We can try to go back to the circle thing now, if you want.'

Penelope nodded in sharp satisfaction and held up her paper again. 'The jasper enhances the lower way stations of your magic's path through your body. Its material is of the earth, and so is its spirit, so there is no balance. You will have to provide the power for the upper way stations only: like a carnival ride with the people all waving their hands up in the air.'

Jane frowned. She had hoped that her little breakthrough with the crystals would somehow make this part suddenly, wonderfully obvious, but apparently that wasn't how it worked. 'The circle carnival ride?' she asked hopelessly, trying to adjust her vocabulary to Penelope's rather eclectic one. 'The one like a big wheel?'

The older witch snorted in disgust. 'You don't listen,' she complained. 'No, not that. Just because I say 'circle' doesn't mean that it happens like a circle in the world. You think this is about shape, with magic?'

'Of course not,' Jane assured her, although even in her own mind she couldn't say for sure how sarcastic she was being. 'A circle, but not a circle like a circle is.'

'Better,' Penelope grunted, peering up through her lenses suspiciously. 'Are you ready to try it, or just being funny again?'

'Funny again,' she had to admit. 'Tell me about my ancestress. You said her name was Aditi, and something about her having too much conscience.'

'Did I?' Penelope asked, her blue eyes maddeningly vague now that the topic was one that interested her pupil. 'Well. Before courts of law, before police, before the idea of hell or even the threat of damnation by history, because of course there was no such thing as history yet . . .' She shrugged. 'Back then, it wasn't so important to be a good person, especially when no one was watching. Or at least, it wasn't so important to everyone.'

'Hasina,' Jane remarked, although it was probably too obvious to require saying out loud.

But Penelope nodded amiably, her lips pursed and her eyes far away. 'At first, she wanted to live forever because she thought that the last sister living would inherit their mother's full power and have it all to herself. They didn't know back then that magic was a part of the air and the earth and the fire in the human heart. It goes back into those things when a witch's flesh ceases to hold it, and from those things it is born into every new witch. Fewer witches now, so more in the air. You pull it down like a string into your head, then down past your throat to your mouth, and move it into the earth below where it becomes air again.'

She raised one pencilled black eyebrow hopefully, but even though that had actually made a little bit of sense to Jane, she shook her head stubbornly. 'Aditi.'

Penelope sighed. 'When their first children were born, Hasina began to realize that she had misunderstood the nature of their gift. Their daughters were just as strong as they were, but they grew no weaker. Ambika's power had been too great to be contained even in seven powerful vessels, or perhaps there had been power beyond Ambika's in the world even after she had claimed hers. Either way, her grandchildren had magic, too, and Hasina realized that she could not simply wait for more to spontaneously come to her. Her inheritance was all that she had a right to, unless she staked a claim to more.'

'By killing a witch.' Jane's own soul recoiled from such a horrible thought – as if killing weren't bad enough, the only witches in the world back then had been Hasina's closest relatives.

'Jyoti.' Penelope picked up the chunk of jasper, idly passing it from hand to hand. Her gaze followed it closely, but Jane knew that her mind was thousands of years away. She remembered that Emer had guessed Jyoti was Penelope's and the Dalcaşcus' common ancestress. *Does she take it personally, since the dead are so real for her? Do old crimes feel recent?* But it felt too intrusive to ask, so Jane just waited.

'She was a troublemaker, and at first the others believed that she had come to some sort of bad end on her own. But there were rumors and whispers and suspicions, and finally Sumitra performed a powerful magic that allowed her to walk in the land of the dead. She found her sister and spoke with her, and then Hasina could no longer hide in plain sight. Amunet joined her happily; she loved any opportunity to have something that the others didn't. But when she discovered that Hasina still only had what the rest of them had, the two quarreled.'

'Wait,' Jane interrupted. 'What do you mean about not having anything else? She had killed a witch, hadn't she?'

'Yes,' Penelope admitted, 'but Jyoti was only the second witch ever to die. Her power flowed back into the air, and Hasina gained nothing. It was only after, as she battled with Amunet, that she remembered the way that their mother had breathed her last bequest into seven silver knives, one of which Hasina kept with her always. It was her most prized possession, and when she stabbed her sister with it she quickly pulled the blade back out and pressed it to Amunet's lips while she died.'

'And from then on, witches could steal each other's magic,' Jane recited dully; how much simpler would life have been if that accidental knowledge had died with Ambika's daughters.

'From then on, they have done so. Hasina more than any of them, of course, but do not think of the others as innocent lambs. In fact, their next move was to take Hasina's daughter as hostage. Most of them wanted to use her as a lure, so that Hasina would meet with them to discuss terms and the four remaining sisters would kill her. But your Aditi refused. She said that magic was too new to the world for everyone to understand how to use it wisely, and she insisted that Hasina should be allowed the chance to mend her ways. She spoke for three days, and at the end they sent a messenger to Hasina saying that they would slit the little girl's throat if Hasina did not return her stolen power and go into exile.'

Jane sighed; it was an almost depressingly familiar scenario. 'But it didn't work.'

Penelope snorted. 'Of course not. Too much conscience, Blondie, and everyone you love dies screaming.'

Dee didn't get a chance to scream. Neither did Gran. Did my parents, or Katrin? But Penelope had made her point all the same. 'I have to break the cycle. I have to finally reject Aditi's legacy and be ruthless.'

The words sounded powerful when she said them, but Penelope's laughter was immediate and sincere. 'That "cycle" has been broken thousands of times over the years. You think that just because you were related to someone hundreds of generations back, you are the same person? Our families are all full of good and bad witches; Hasina is the only one who never changes. After all, if you take just one more step backward, we all come from the same person. Just as much as you are Aditi's, you are Ambika's. And so am I: we are her own flesh and bone.'

'Flesh and blood,' Jane corrected absently, echoing Malcolm's words from earlier, then flushed as Penelope glowered at her. 'Your way is fine; it's just a common expression, is all.'

There was a long, tense silence, and in it Jane's mind replayed the two phrases over and over, gaining speed until they jumbled together in a cascade of meaningless syllables. *Flesh and blood. Flesh and bone.*

257

'We will go back to the circle now,' Penelope told her stiffly. Her dignity was clearly wounded, but suddenly Jane's brain was far too full for her to care.

'We won't,' she corrected abruptly, her heart starting to race. Was it possible that magic could flow through loopholes? *Of course it is,* her magic hummed in her ears, pulsing like a second heartbeat. *The spell is just a shape; the power is the power. The only thing that matters is having it.*

Penelope cocked her head, her eyes nothing but frosty blue slits behind her glasses. But she seemed to sense some of the revolution going on inside of Jane, because she said nothing, waiting.

'Get everyone,' Jane said finally, when she was sure. 'Get everyone in the kitchen now, and start getting yourself ready. We're going to do some magic. All of us.'

Chapter Twenty-eight

JANE COUNTED SIX pairs of eyes riveted on her face and searched herself for any sense of nervousness or stage fright. But there was nothing but a cold, hard certainty. The Montagues stood in the kitchen, ranged like a rather peculiar army on the far side of the countertop, with Penelope hovering between them and Jane. 'We're going to raise the dead,' she told the waiting assembly flatly, not bothering to try to decipher the various expressions that crossed their faces. 'We're going to raise Ambika, and she is going to come and take her daughter back to the grave where she belongs.'

259

There was a murmur of sound at that: a rush of whispers and mumbles that never quite blossomed into outright protests, although their intent was clear enough.

'We can't do that, Jane,' Maeve said finally, so quietly that Jane wondered if her friend feared for her sanity. 'You know we'd need something of hers, or people who knew her, or—'

'I know.' Penelope was looking at her a little too shrewdly now, so Jane kept her focus on the rest of them instead. 'Emer, I think everything else that we need should already be in the house, right? And we still have a couple of hours. I was thinking you could set up in the sunroom once we're done here; if you move the furniture, we should be able to make a respectable circle.' Jane looked pointedly at Harris, who flinched a little under her intensity. 'You too, please. I'm going to need everyone on this; it'll take all our power and concentration together. She's been dead a long time; it wouldn't be easy no matter what we had of hers.'

'But we don't *have* anything of hers,' Leah half whined. For a moment Jane thought that the girl might actually stomp her foot, but somehow she restrained herself. 'You can't just wave away the main ingredient like it doesn't matter.'

'Jane,' Charlotte said in a more conciliatory tone, 'I'll be happy to help you try whatever you'd like, but with all the power between us we couldn't call up so much as a shade of Ambika. Not enough to speak to us, even, or tell us what to do. I'd hate to see you rest your hopes on a séance that won't even have its guest of honor present.

Surely there's something else we can do to help you better.'

'This is it,' Jane insisted, 'and I'm not talking about a séance. Your mother told me that, with a person's bones, someone like Penelope – a real adept – could call someone back into this world almost as fully as before they left it. Nothing less than that will help us, so that's what we're going to do.'

Harris bit his lip and dropped his eyes toward the floor, but he didn't have to say anything for Jane to guess that he assumed the worst. He thought that she had cracked under the pressure and lost her mind, or that this was some elaborate plot for her to escape her fatal appointment with Annette. She could certainly imagine how incoherent she must sound at the moment, but the idea of explaining in explicit detail might literally make her sick.

'With the bones,' Penelope repeated, her voice like an icy gust rattling the windows. 'With enough magic you can do anything, but even you don't have *that* much, Blondie.'

Jane inhaled, then forced all the air out of her lungs. This was the hard part, but she knew it would only get harder if she stalled. She half raised a hand and then lowered it, resting it on the handle of an eight-inch chef's knife of the type that Dee had especially favoured. Still sheathed in its butcher block, the knife felt awkward and unwieldy, but she knew how sharp it must be.

'Penelope very kindly reminded me that all of us here are part of the shadow that Ambika cast across the world. We are a part of her, and she is still a part of us. We are'— she drew the knife—'her flesh and bone.'

261

Maeve started forward, but her cousin was between her and the end of the counter and there was a confused pileup as she tried to get by. In those few seconds, Jane spread her left hand out on the cool granite countertop, the knife still held loosely in her right. *Pinky, ring, middle, pinky, middle, pinky* – but there was only one option that wouldn't require her to contort her hand and maybe miss her strike, and if she waited another second she would lose her nerve. With a flash and a chorus of screams that she was only pretty sure weren't her own, Jane brought the blade of the knife down in a shining arc onto the counter. When she lifted her hands again, the knife and one finger – her own left index finger – remained on the stone.

It felt cold at first, but not quite numb: more of an angry cold, like frozen steel against her bare skin. Then came the heat, searing up her hand and into her arm, and black spots flowered in her vision. She could feel herself beginning to sway a little, blood and red hair swimming in a confusing sea around her, but she couldn't afford to go under; not now.

One, two, three, four. Four fingers, four corners, four directions. Four, three, two, one. The black spots receded a little, and Jane counted her breaths, from one to four and back again, and concentrated on not crying. She set her jaw and held her body poker straight, and when some of the shapes around her resolved, she saw that Maeve was pressing a crimson tea towel to her maimed hand.

With her good hand she picked up the finger from

the counter, trying not to see it too clearly. It had been sliced cleanly off just above the knuckle, leaving three progressively smaller pieces of priceless finger bone in an unfortunately gruesome sheath of flesh. 'Harris,' she called hoarsely, and the commotion around her froze solid.

It was only five pairs of eyes on hers now – Maeve's head was bent attentively over her injured hand – and the faces they stared out from were definitely paler than they had been before. Even Penelope looked shaken behind her thick glasses: she clutched at a few of the chunky necklaces hanging across her impressive bosom as if they might ward off Jane's sudden madness.

Careful not to show the slightest sign of her absolute revulsion, Jane casually tossed the severed finger at Harris. He blanched even more and flinched again, but to his credit he caught it out of the air and didn't let it drop. 'Boil that,' she told him in a reasonable approximation of her own normal tone of voice. 'Boil it until it's only bones; I don't want to look at it. Penelope, tell everyone else how to set up whatever we need to call on Ambika. And, everyone else . . . do it. Right the hell now.'

She pressed her own right hand against the tea towel, pulling it gently away from Maeve so that she would know that Jane's orders applied to her as well. It was warm and a little sticky, and bile rose in Jane's throat. But there was nothing to do but keep it pressed to her bleeding knuckle and wait, while her six allies scattered in every direction to raise the dead.

Chapter Twenty-nine

J ANE COULD TELL as soon as she entered the mansion that Annette had prepared it for battle. There was no one in the gold-and-marble entryway, and the elevator stood open, waiting, as it had never been that she could remember. Since Annette could have tried to kill her on the street or just inside the front door, Jane understood that Hasina's need for correctness and propriety had forced her hand once again: there would be a real fight.

She stepped into the elevator, and its doors slid silently closed behind her. There was a strange tingling in her limbs, and especially in her wounded hand, where it became confused with the painful throbbing that lingered despite Leah's best healing efforts. *Ambika,* she thought, bouncing on the balls of her toes, although of course it wasn't quite. Even with their combined power and Jane's sacrificed bones, Penelope had warned her that they wouldn't be able to bind their common ancestress to the mortal plane for long. It would do her no good if Ambika returned to her final rest too soon, so Jane had to risk calling her too late. She slipped her right hand around the bulky silver amulet that Penelope had given her, fingering the strange dark stone at its centre, counting the floors as the elevator rose.

When its doors slid open again, Jane was thoroughly unsurprised to see the blackened floor and soot-stained windows of the eighth–floor atrium. At the far end, where Lynne had lurked before, she could clearly make out Annette's silhouette against the mingled light from the streetlamps below and the full moon above. Partway along the side wall between them hovered a huge, indecisive shape that could only be her brother Charles. Jane stepped forward, pulling her magic around her like a shroud.

It was only then that she saw the third shape beside Charles, against the windows where Dee had been bound during her last moments of life. Her magic was so primed and ready that as soon as she wished to see it better, light flared through the atrium: cool, steady, and without any apparent source. What it showed her made her heart sink.

Annette stood at the far side of the huge room,

immaculately dressed in vintage white Chanel with her hair pulled back so that only a few dark-gold waves framed her face. Charles stood vigilantly about halfway between them, looking much the same as Jane remembered him: unkempt, his slack face wearing a permanent expression of confusion and resentment. And behind him was the third Doran sibling, apparently unconscious and bound by something glowing and greenish to a splintered window frame.

Of course he didn't just leave. By refusing Malcolm's offer of help, Jane realized now, she had practically guaranteed that he would try some kind of doomed attack on his own. In the cool light of her magic it looked as though his attempt on his sister's life had ended painfully: his mouth and one eye were swollen grotesquely, and she could only guess at the injuries she couldn't see. She couldn't bear to think about what he must have been through – and there was more to come. His well-intentioned but hopeless attack had put him in the middle of what was about to be an ugly battle. Her nails bit into her palms at the thought that he could be a casualty of the coming fight. *I'll fix this,* she thought at him, willing him to hear her somehow. *Just hold on, and I'll send her where she can never hurt you again.*

'Perhaps we could keep this between the two of us,' Jane suggested out loud, projecting her voice as clearly as she could across the burned floor. She gestured toward Annette's two brothers; Malcolm stirred a little and

Charles waved shyly at her. 'This is no place for either of them.'

'That's what *I* said,' Annette snapped, her hands clenching and unclenching as if she weren't even aware of the motion. 'I told you to come alone. I made it very clear.'

Jane bit her lip, feeling the pulse of the amulet against her breastbone. 'I did,' she argued, and it was true. Technically, her dead ancestress hadn't arrived yet.

Annette took a couple of short, angry strides forward, until Jane could clearly make out the rage that twisted her features. 'Then what,' she practically shrieked, 'is *he* doing here?'

She whipped one hand toward Malcolm, her manicured nail pointing straight for his heart. Jane opened her mouth to explain the mistake: she hadn't known a thing about his plan and would have stopped him if she had. But before she could make a sound, Annette's nail made a strange back-and-forth slashing motion in the air, and the words died in Jane's throat as crimson blood began to seep from fresh wounds across Malcolm's throat and chest.

He woke up then, and for a brief, strange moment their eyes met. 'Jane,' he mouthed, and his battered face relaxed into a smile before his eyes closed again.

No. She wanted to scream, to run to him, to throw her body across his and weep for days. But he was already gone; she could see him leaving. Something in him glowed against the sourceless light that filled the atrium: a white flash that moved through it. It flowed from his limp body

267

to seep through the cracked windowpane and out into the night air beyond. She could actually see the light of his soul as it left, and even through her pain and shock and regret, it filled her with wonder.

'You can't imagine how boring this sort of pettiness has become,' Hasina sneered. To Jane, her voice sounded like it was coming from the end of a long tunnel. 'Love, betrayal, loss. It's all terrifically shocking – the first three hundred times. Now it's utterly dull. You, on the other hand, are a considerably rarer find. Generations of magic passed down through an unbroken bloodline, and magic on the other side. My dear, you're one of a kind.'

'Just me and Annette,' Jane guessed. Was the girl even in there? It had seemed that way when she had allowed herself to show emotion over Malcolm, but now Hasina's lens-like eyes betrayed no sign of her. *She's already forgotten him.* Jane stole a quick glance toward the empty, slumped body still bound to the window frame, but she couldn't bear to look at it for long.

'Your child with my line would have been a miracle,' Hasina went on. 'A child from the lines of Anila, Aditi, and me . . . The entire world would have been at my feet, once I was in a body like that.'

'The world is better off.' Jane raised her right hand to her chest in a convulsive movement, finding the silver amulet and closing her fingers around it. *Come to me,* she thought: it was nearly a prayer. *Come now.*

The tingling in her limbs grew stronger, and in a moment

it was matched by a humming from the floor beneath her feet and the air itself. Charles backed instinctively toward the wall until his body almost touched his brother's lifeless one, but Hasina didn't seem to feel the shift of the world around them yet. 'Take that out of here,' she ordered crisply, waving her hand again so that the glowing bonds holding Malcolm to the wall evaporated.

His body slumped forward, and Charles half caught it across one meaty arm. He stared into Malcolm's beaten face uncertainly, examining each feature with, Jane thought, an expression of hope. *My lover; his brother. His friend, when he had so few.* 'Take him out of here,' she echoed gently, and Charles's muddy brown eyes swung toward hers. 'Take him and yourself out of this house, and don't come back.'

Hasina made an angry retort, Jane knew from watching her face, but she couldn't hear a word over the magic that had grown to a roar in her ears. Charles didn't seem to hear it, either, because without a backward glance he lifted Malcolm's bulk carefully in his arms and shambled toward the elevator.

Go quickly, Jane thought after him. *Something else is coming.*

Annette finally seemed to sense it, too, and Jane was mildly surprised to see tongues of living flame arc across the space between them, seeking Jane's flesh with their angry heat. But each one died out before it reached her, drowning in the cool light that filled the room before they could even reach the shield of her magic.

Then Jane blinked, and when she opened her eyes again Annette wasn't alone. Inside her somehow, but much larger, was the shape of another woman. It was hard to make out her features, because the light wasn't quite right and she was, technically, invisible, but Jane got the impression of a long, flat nose, high, proud cheekbones, and a floodlike spill of coarse dark hair. *Hasina*.

Annette's dark pools of eyes widened in sudden fear, and Jane knew without looking that a similar apparition must now be surrounding and emanating from her own body.

'Ambika,' she whispered, feeling the first witch's phenomenal energy flowing through and around her own, 'please. Take your daughter home.'

She felt the answer deep in her bones, the ones that she shared with Ambika. The ghostly presence of Hasina was a shock, a profound wrongness, a tear across the fabric of the world. She did not belong there, and the first witch's mind joined with Jane's in wholehearted agreement. It was long past time for Hasina to die.

Annette's flames ripped through the floor this time, throwing up splinters of already-burnt wood as they raced toward Jane's feet. She dove toward the windows, feeling the heat against her legs but narrowly missing being burned. 'What the hell do you think you're doing, Jane?' the girl cried, and this time when she spoke Jane could hear two distinct voices blended into one.

Jane lashed out in return before she had even formed a

clear idea in her mind of what form her magic should take
– sloppy, Dee would have called it. But Ambika's ghostly
fingers trailed through the magic just as it left Jane's own,
turning it into a river of crackling electricity that made
her hair stand on end. Hasina blocked the unnatural flood
of lightning with a hastily constructed wall of darkness,
but Jane felt a grim sort of satisfaction when it fell again
and she saw that her enemy's face-framing tendrils had
gone flat and frizzy. 'You don't belong here,' she told the
shadow behind, above, within Annette. 'You know it, I
know it, and the woman who gave you life and magic
knows it, too. Your descendants may have welcomed you
in, but the rest of us want you gone.'

Then something glowed between Hasina's shadowy
hands, and Jane had no time to think about anything
anymore except for parrying and returning violent volleys
of magic. Snakes boiled out of the ground around her feet,
and a sudden tornado slammed Annette back against the
windows behind her, shattering one of them into a huge
spiderweb of crystalline cracks. Ambika's magic flowed
through the jasper stone in one of the hidden pockets
of Jane's full skirt, and then with a pulse that threatened
to tear her apart, every last one of the floor-to-ceiling
windows around the room exploded outward. Annette's
body was thrown to the floor by the blast, but as she
turned to stand back up Jane saw Hasina's arm curl out,
stretching impossibly far out into the empty night air. Jane
ducked instinctively as the arm whipped back toward her,

realizing only after she had that the air where her head had just been was now filled with hundreds of flying shards of broken window glass.

'My mother's been in the ground a long time,' Hasina hissed as the glass sliced through the air. 'I've used that time to learn a few tricks.'

A few of the razor-sharp edges caught the back of Jane's arm and shoulder, and for the second time that day she felt her own warm blood flowing freely across her skin. *I should soak the dress right away,* she thought absurdly, her head spinning for a moment even after the motion of her body had stopped. In the silence that followed, she heard Ambika's voice murmuring in her ear. She couldn't understand the words – the language Ambika spoke had been dead for thousands of years. But the message seemed to be flowing into Jane's own mind, and she pressed her palms flat against the charred floor, blocking her missing finger out of her vision as she pooled her magic into the remaining nine.

Ripples ran away across the floor as if it had suddenly been made into water. Above Jane's head, Ambika countered some attack of Hasina's; whatever it was scorched the hairs on the back of Jane's neck. Then the ripples reached Annette, and she sank up – or down – to her rib cage in the liquefied floorboards before Ambika signaled to Jane to lift her hands away and stop the magic.

The floor resolidified instantly, trapping Annette with her arms at her sides and nothing below her chest visible at all. *Gotcha,* Jane thought wildly, struggling to her feet and pressing her hand experimentally against the sliced skin behind her shoulder. Both responses came simultaneously: along with Ambika's warning whisper, the entire house began to shake beneath her.

Annette's eyes had gone wide and round, two deep pools of panic. Jane tried to focus her magic into the shape of a net, or chains like the glowing ones that had held Malcolm against the window. But she wasn't entirely sure how that was supposed to work, and Ambika's will was pulling her spell in a different direction that she didn't understand at all, and then the floor around Annette was breaking apart like a frozen pond at the end of winter. Jane's magic went wide and wild, careening through the atrium like the wind that had begun to twist through the blown-out windows and stirring Annette's limp tendrils of hair. A wickedly proud smile turned the trapped witch's full lips upward, and in an instant she was no longer trapped.

Jane screamed out in frustration, but it did nothing to change the gaping, empty hole in the floor where Annette had worked her way free to the level below. Ambika knew of something that might, though, and Jane obediently lifted her arms to the sky, calling on the guardian of the Watchtower of the West, just as Dee had once taught her, to summon their element to find her enemy. Water flowed from nowhere into the hole in the floor, first a lively stream and then a raging river of it. It funnelled

273

through the floorboards, spinning into a whirlpool before vanishing downward to flood the room below.

As Jane watched, a prickling in the back of her neck informed her that her half-present ancestress expected to see the water returning back up through the splintered hole, but more and more of it just kept pouring in. *It's not working*, she realized. *Hasina is getting rid of it somehow.*

The strip of sky outside the broken windows tipped and swayed sickeningly, and Jane struggled to remain standing. Aside from the attic, she was at the highest point of the looming mansion, with a possessed and furious witch somewhere out of sight below her – not an ideal position. With the house shuddering all the way down to its foundation, the elevator was out; so she turned toward the door to the back staircase. But the floor pitched and rolled like the deck of a ship, and Jane fell hard to her knees. The broken place where Annette had dropped to the floor below widened, and a crack ran across the boards, pointing toward Jane with a rapidly growing finger of blackness. She froze for a moment, stuck between her instinct to roll away and Ambika's transmitted instruction to stand and run. In that moment of hesitation, the floor opened up the rest of the way and swallowed her.

Darkness tumbled end over end with faint, distant lights, and then there was a shower of stars as Jane landed, back-first, on a pile of burnt wood on top of an embroidered bedspread. A cloud of dust and soot exploded up into the air around her, making it impossible to see if Annette was nearby. *No water, though.* She had no earthly idea where it had all gone, and her back ached.

The four-poster bed caught fire all at once, the splinters around her wicking it closer like kindling. Through the mounting flames Jane could see Hasina's face, but not Annette's. Was that even possible? She threw a bolt of crackling energy at Hasina, but it passed through her without causing her to even blink. Then something heavy and hard struck Jane across her back, and she fell forward, her hair tumbling down on either side of her face to get singed at its ends.

Hasina was in front of her, she realized slowly, but Annette was behind her.

Jane twisted herself backward off the bed, pushing her magic out before her to form a shield. Like a wrenching in a phantom limb, she felt Ambika spin the other way, toward her wayward daughter. Annette was waiting for Jane, a board in her hands and a strange, broken vacancy in her eyes.

'You took her.' Her voice was a shocked rasp, and her chest heaved massively under her stained white jacket. 'My family, my inheritance – Hasina was *all* of it. How could you make her leave me now?'

Jane reached instinctively into the plunging neckline of her dress and felt for the rune-covered handle of Lynne's athame. She tugged at it and it slid free immediately, springing into the dusty, dry air with a life of its own. The mirrorlike surface of its slim blade reflected the strange light of the ghosts and flames with an enthusiasm all its own.

Then the floor shook beneath them again, and both women turned instinctively toward the ghosts on the far side of the burning bed. Any semblance of humanity was gone from the two unearthly figures, who had somehow wrapped themselves around and even through each other, twisting and distorting their features until they were thoroughly unrecognizable.

Jane heard a clatter from Annette's direction and spun back just in time. The girl had finally noticed Lynne's athame. She had dropped her splintered board and was advancing warily, her dark eyes fixed on the humming blade.

'That's mine,' she warned, her voice rough.

'It's mine,' Jane corrected sharply. She felt nearly as battered as Annette sounded, but there was no way she would show it now. 'I won it fair and square.'

At that, Annette lunged at Jane, raking the arm that held the athame with her sharp fingernails and the four fiery trails of magic that followed them. Jane spun away, pressing her other hand to her stinging arm.

When she turned back, Jane felt a fury she had never experienced in her entire life. It consumed her like Annette's flames. She had tried so hard to save Annette, to see past her damaged exterior to some kind of salvageable core, but it wasn't there. She was empty inside. She wanted to be possessed by some immortal lunatic – and she had killed Malcolm. *No more. Not another* second *more.* Jane whispered a word that she had heard in Ambika's mind, focusing her power through it. It felt something like a verbal prism, breaking her magic into pieces that were each still whole, living lines. Some of them arced up, and some shot down through the floor that was shaking and rocking more than ever now. But most of them surrounded Annette, binding her arms to her sides and cramming her magic back below the surface of her skin.

With her magic otherwise occupied and the walls starting to crumble around her ears, Jane did the first thing that came to mind: she dropped the athame to the floor, clenched her five right fingers into a tight fist, and smashed it into Annette's nose. The witch's dark-blond head snapped back, blood spurted over her once-white suit, and there was a wrenching scream that seemed to come from all around Jane at once. Then Hasina and Ambika disappeared, and then the entire house did the same.

Chapter Thirty

WHEN JANE'S EYELIDS fluttered open, she was confused to find herself staring at the sky. There were no stars – there was far too much glare from the city's billions of lights for that – but the slim icicle of the moon hung in the dark-blue haze almost directly above her. The otherwise-empty blue was bounded on three sides by the tall outlines of buildings, looming a little too far above her head to match her last memories. *I think I fell,* she thought cautiously. *How far did I fall?*

She tentatively felt the dusty, broken surface around her, noticing the absence of her left forefinger with an unpleasant flicker of surprise. For a moment she remembered the way she had pushed her tongue into the spaces left by her baby teeth, when she was a child. There was another gaping loss that she would need to face, she knew, but the pain from that would hurt far worse than her finger, so she forced it aside.

Walls rose on three sides of her: two stone and one brick with marble trim at its edges. On the fourth side, inexplicably, was a wide city street, divided down the centre by a line of green-clad trees. A yellow cab glided silently by, flanked by a couple of nondescript black sedans and followed a moment later by a dingy white van. It was Park Avenue; she was sure of it. But then where was the house she had just been standing in?

She heaved herself up to a sitting position with her hands, breathing shallowly and trying to take in each new piece of information at once. The air around her was swimming with particles of dust and soot; eddies of them caught the orange light from the streetlamps and glowed like schools of tiny tropical fish. The street and the smooth white sidewalk were at least a story below her — ten feet, she estimated, or maybe a little more. But the uneven and shifting surface below her was the most indecipherable thing of all.

Then her head began to clear a little, and all those little details spun like one of the dust currents until it made an entire picture. *We knocked the house down. I'm still in it; it's just not here.* The strange new surface around her looked like all the photos she had ever seen of demolished buildings. It had just been hard to recognize it at first from her unusual perspective: she was sitting right on top of a pile of rubble, which was all that remained of 665 Park Avenue.

It's not '665' anymore, she realized with a peculiar stab of pride. With the brass number plate gone, along with the entire façade that had contained it, this was nothing but the heap of stone and wood occupying Lot 666. Gone with the structure of the mansion was any pretence that it had been something other than what it was.

Jane patted various parts of her body experimentally, but other than a few bruises, scrapes, and burns, she seemed largely unhurt. Filthy, of course – the once-blue irises on her dress were no longer distinguishable from the once-white background – but no more injured than she had been before falling five stories. It was either a miracle, or magic.

She looked around again, this time focusing on the rubble itself. There was no sign of either of the prehistoric witches who had battled there earlier in the evening, and Jane's hand went half consciously to the amulet around her neck. It was cold and still; whatever had been humming inside of it was thoroughly gone now. But she knew, even before she tried to re-create the events from the bedroom in her mind, that Ambika had won. How else could it have gone? The fact that Jane was more or less still standing and the mansion was, well, *not* seemed like all the proof she needed.

Ambika is gone, and she took Hasina with her, but I'm still here. That must mean that Annette was somewhere in the chaotic pile, too. Jane scanned the moonscape around her, but between its broken, pitted surface and the flat, unhelpful light from the streetlamps, she couldn't make out any sign of where the other witch might be. *Crushed, probably,* she thought, but uncertainty lingered in her mind. If Annette *had* somehow managed to survive the collapse of her house, it was highly unlikely that making amends would be her present goal. Jane may have banished Hasina, but she had left behind another enemy who was nearly as dangerous. No matter how much Jane would rather walk away right now, the safest plan was to find Annette.

She inhaled slowly, reaching inward to seek out the magic in her blood. It was there — she could hear it, feel it inside — but it was discouragingly faint. She hadn't made any effort to hold some in reserve while she fought Annette, and now she had almost none left. *It'll come back,* she reminded herself, wiggling her toes idly. *As long as I'm alive, it will always come back.*

She clambered stiffly to her feet, discovering new soreness in her muscles with every movement. After a quick glance, she decided to start with the back of the house, so that no one could sneak up on her while she searched. As she moved, the thing underneath her (a largish piece of some interior wall, she guessed), shifted, slanting dangerously, and her foot slipped and wedged between it and something that looked like it had once been an armoire. She hissed her breath out between her teeth, pried her foot loose, and started again, this time more cautiously.

She stayed mainly in a low crouch or on her knees for better stability, testing each ruined piece of the house gently before trying to move it. Some were too heavy to lift at all, but she was unwilling to use the remaining dregs of her magic in her search. There was too much of a risk that she might need it all once she found what she was looking for. Still, she made decent enough progress to feel that she really was looking, working her way from one back corner of the lot to the other, then back again in a tight zigzagging pattern. She tried to pay some attention to the rest of the rubble as she went, too, in particular training her ears toward the street in case something started to shift in that direction.

But nothing did. *How has no one noticed this yet?* she wondered, grunting a little as she pushed aside three wooden stairs, still attached by their risers. Surely the fall of the mansion had made a massive clamour, and no matter how late it was, plenty of people would still be awake to hear it. But every time she raised her head from her work, the street remained oddly empty, with nothing more than the occasional car passing incuriously by. *Some kind of spell?* she guessed, recalling that the street had been empty the night they had broken in to interrupt Hasina, as well. There was a good chance the spell wouldn't last much longer than the house itself. She tried to hurry her search a little, nearly slipped again, and decided that she would just have to deal with one problem at a time.

A faint scratching noise came from somewhere behind her, and she froze in place. The sound came again, and Jane began to make her way carefully toward it.

It seemed to take forever to crawl the twenty-five metres, and in the back of her mind she wondered nervously how long she had already been clambering around the wrecked mansion. When she reached the place where she thought the noise had come from, she noticed that a rectangular stone she hadn't been able to move earlier was, on closer inspection, leaning at a bit of an angle. She braced herself against a section of drywall and, taking a deep breath, managed to tip it over to the side.

In the space that it left, Jane saw something that, if it hadn't been so covered in dust and plaster, looked like it would have been a rich, deep red. *She was wearing a bracelet that color,* Jane was almost certain. *Her shoes would have matched.*

She began clearing away bits and pieces, following Annette's leg up to the hem of her skirt, then guessing at where her head might be and starting again there. A heavily massive headboard had been blocking it, but once Jane managed to shift it aside she saw that it had been resting on a few skewed posts from the same bed, creating a small protected shelter for Annette's head.

When the light struck her face, Annette's dark eyes flew open.

'Stay down,' Jane snapped.

The witch's eyes narrowed, but she did as she was told. Jane brushed away a little more of the plaster and splinters, wondering what her next step should be. She couldn't bring herself to kill someone in cold blood, even someone who so thoroughly deserved it. But walking away from Annette would be like turning her back on a wounded boar. Then, along the length of Annette's right arm, Jane's fingers brushed warm metal, and she knew what to do.

'I'm not going to dig you all the way out,' she told Annette in a conversational tone, brushing away the rest of the dust from the object that had caught her attention. 'You might be hurt, and I could just make things worse. Besides, I don't really like you all that much anymore. But I'll tell you what I *will* do: I'll call 911 and tell them exactly where to find you. And then I'll go away. But that will make twice that I've knocked you out and then spared your life, so this time you'll have to do something for me.'

She pried the object loose, shaking the last bits of debris from it and rocking back on her heels. Its mirrorlike blade glittered wickedly in the moonlight, and the ancient carvings on its handle seemed to writhe a little against her skin. *I wonder if it's the same one. I wonder if it's the one Ambika used to give Hasina her inheritance, and the same one Hasina used to steal her sister's.*

Annette's eyes fixated on the athame, following its every slight movement. 'Let me guess,' she whispered, and Jane could tell that it took some effort.

'I think you can,' she agreed pleasantly. 'You're going to take your last breath as a witch right here and now, and then I'm going to take this pretty little knife. And then you and I are done, for good.' She switched the athame over in her hand so that its blade pointed downward toward the thin skin of Annette's throat where the girl's pulse beat visibly. 'There are alternatives, but I'd prefer to dwell on the positive. We don't even need to talk about how I'll put you down like a rabid lapdog if you don't agree right the hell now.'

Annette took a fraction of a second longer than Jane would have preferred, but when she managed a half nod, it was a definite *yes*. 'Hold it for me,' she rasped, setting her square jaw stubbornly.

Jane moved the blade of the athame to Annette's dusty lips. The girl closed her eyes, and Jane felt the same pressure of magic that she had once felt while standing with Lynne in Central Park. She was ready for it this time, and she listened attentively to the almost inaudible sound of it rushing into the athame. When it was done, Annette opened her eyes again. They were bright and alive with hatred.

'I know you're already planning your revenge,' Jane said to the trapped girl, turning the athame idly in her hands. It whispered darkly to her, the power in it pulling at hers like a magnet. Jane stood, gathering her own magic into the hand that held the athame. She still didn't have much, but it was already more than she'd had when she had first woken up. It would be enough. 'But before you do, please listen carefully. I'm not going to hide from you. I'm not going to run away or gather an army to fight you or hoard my power against the day when you come after me. Because if you're smart, you'll stay as far away from me and mine as you possibly can. I promise you now that if you ever lift a finger to hurt me or anyone I love again – hell, anyone I even kind of like – I'll find you and finish you. There's a world of difference between a rich girl and a witch. Remember that no matter what money and connections you may have inherited, all of your *real* power is gone. For good.'

Her magic flared, and the silver in her hand began to glow red. Malcolm had told her how to destroy silver that held magic once, and she whispered a silent thank-you to him as she performed the necessary alchemy. The athame held its shape for a long moment, then the blade began to sag unnaturally. Its luster faded as the entire thing dissolved into a stream of liquid mercury. It ran from Jane's hand to splatter on the rubble beside Annette's pinned form, finding the cracks until most of it had disappeared entirely into the debris. Jane held her hand up, showing that it was still unburned, and gave Annette a little wave.

Then she turned on her heel and walked toward the street.

Chapter Thirty-one

MALCOLM DORAN'S FUNERAL was nearly the state occasion that his mother's had been. Even without Hasina's well-honed sense of propriety, Annette had made good use of her BlackBerry. St. Paul's had been packed to the gills, and now the cemetery was covered in a sea of black couture stretching as far as the eye could see. Jane spotted Madison Avery, a striking brunette whom Malcolm had briefly dated, in a hat that wouldn't have been out of place at the British royal wedding.

She leaned her head against a maple tree and watched from a distance, afraid of the media frenzy that would erupt if Malcolm's mysterious wife of less than two months were spotted. She had decided from the moment she heard about the services that she would keep her distance. She believed that Annette would take her threats seriously, but there was no need to test their truce if she didn't need to. It was enough for Jane just to be there – she didn't need to be centre stage or turn it into some kind of face-off with Malcolm's sister.

Jane reached half consciously into her purse, her fingertips finding the little wooden box with the ease of practice. She had hoped that being closer to Malcolm's remains might encourage it to pick up more traces of his spirit, but none of the love and warmth that the box radiated felt like him. *Still too soon,* she sighed to herself. Apparently it wasn't the kind of magic that could be rushed.

'Is this where the persona-non-grata picnic is being held?' a voice chirped from behind her, and Jane jumped a little. 'I brought the caviar.' Maeve's elfin features and black Issa dress were appropriately somber, but she really was holding a wicker picnic basket. In spite of her own sadness at the occasion, Jane smiled warmly at the sight of her.

'Harris is parking the car,' Leah added, picking her way around another maple tree on perilously high heels. The rest of her family was straggling behind her.

'You guys didn't have to come,' Jane told them, her throat swelling with gratitude.

'That's what makes it a gesture, love,' Charlotte reproved

mildly, but with a twinkle in her brown eyes. 'That basket of my niece's contains a bottle or two of rather nice champagne, and we thought that it would be appropriate to toast Malcolm's memory with you, if you're willing.'

Jane glanced back toward the crowded gravesite; the parade of eulogies showed no sign of slowing down. 'We should have plenty of time before anyone comes back this way,' she guessed, and Maeve slid a green bottle of Salon 1997 from her basket to pop its cork in one fluid, practised motion.

Harris arrived with a large, plaid blanket in hand and shook it out across the grass. 'I had a dream last night,' he told Jane softly when the champagne was poured and they were all settled on the blanket in a companionable little group. Jane startled a little, but waited for him to go on. 'Dee was in it. I hadn't – she hadn't – since—' He stumbled over the words, and Jane reflexively placed a soothing hand on his shoulder. He covered it with his own after a moment and squeezed it lightly. 'I'm trying to apologize,' he explained eventually. 'I don't remember most of what she said, but she set me straight and then some. Maybe I should have been more open-minded when you wanted to talk to her the first time – it would have saved me a lot of needless grudge holding.'

Jane smiled fondly. 'No, I think you were right about that. It's better that she got to choose her own time to stop in.' She raised her champagne flute to her lips, then hesitated self-consciously, the bubbles tingling her skin.

After a moment she set the full glass back down again on the blanket.

There was a small silence, and then Harris spoke again, more hesitantly this time. 'It might not have *actually* been her,' he admitted. 'It looked like her, but I've been pissed off at you and Malcolm and the world in general for a while now, and maybe I've been thinking it was about time to stop.'

Jane considered that. 'I think Dee would be really happy to be a part of that moment. Whether it was her own idea or yours.'

'I think so, too,' Harris agreed mildly, a sad smile brightening his freckle-dusted face. There were some faint new lines around his brilliant green eyes – stress, Jane thought, and pain as well – but when he smiled he looked like his old, optimistic self. 'I'm sorry you lost him,' he finished.

'I'm sorry you lost her,' Jane answered, and she leaned her upper body over to fold him into a half hug. There was the faintest hint of an electrical tingle, a tiny throb of her magic that would, she knew, always respond to the magic in his blood. But it felt different now, more like recognition than need. He was, in a way, a part of her family, and it was only right that family should get along.

'I was worried that it was too early for peaches, but try this,' Maeve ordered, pulling herself across the blanket to sit on Jane's other side and thrusting a little bowl of fruit salad into her hands.

Jane obediently scooped some into her mouth, though she was too overwhelmed by the day to taste much of anything. 'They're great,' she agreed absently, and Maeve's eyes narrowed.

'There aren't any peaches in it,' she said, sighing, and rested her curly head on Jane's shoulder affectionately. 'How are you holding up?'

Jane craned her neck for a minute, trying to get a sense of how the funeral was progressing. Although the gravesite was thronged with people, Annette looked alone and somehow frail. Hasina hadn't occupied her body for very long, but Jane wondered if her presence hadn't done some lasting damage to her hostess all the same. *It would serve her right.* 'I'm okay,' she replied honestly. 'The hardest part is the regret. I know you never get a chance to correct mistakes, but usually you at least get a chance to make amends.'

Harris glanced up at her as if he had heard his name spoken, then returned quickly to bickering good-naturedly with his cousin about the proper size of a scoop of caviar. Maeve picked a grape from Jane's fruit salad and popped it into her mouth with her fingers. 'I can see how that would be hard,' she agreed. 'And Malcolm was absolutely, madly, head over heels in love with you. But, Jane. Do you really think he would have done half of what he did for you if he didn't also know how you felt about him?'

Jane opened her mouth to reply, but found herself needing more time to really think about Maeve's question.

291

Her friend took the opportunity to shove a strawberry into it and gently pressed Jane's chin to close her mouth around the fruit. It had a little more flavour than the first bites she had taken.

'Thank you,' she said when she had swallowed. 'I guess I know he *knew*,' she conceded. 'But he still deserved to hear it from me. More often, and without all the drama and qualifications and reversals. He kept fighting on my side until it killed him, and I never got to . . .' She shrugged helplessly.

'The specific events, the details, won't matter to him wherever he is now,' Emer assured her, and Jane blushed to realize that she had been speaking loudly enough to be overheard.

'Souls don't keep score,' Charlotte agreed, patting her loose bun absentmindedly. 'That's a part of what made Hasina such an abomination – she never had to lay down her arms between lives and let her grudges go.'

'But Malcolm will have by now,' Emer finished for her, sipping delicately at her champagne. 'So there's no need to fret. He'll remember the love, and he'll feel it, even now.'

'A *lot* of love, apparently,' Leah added, her voice dripping with irony as she gestured toward the mass of mourners across the cemetery. 'We should all find out we're so popular after we're dead.' Her mother clucked her tongue reprovingly, but Jane had to chuckle a little.

'I'm thinking of not going back to MoMA,' Maeve whispered to Jane when the conversation had moved on around them. 'I don't think it's fair to stretch out my "medical leave" any longer; Archie's going crazy. And all the other witches in this city have gotten back to work – Harris and I noticed the other day that Dee's friend's bookstore was open for business again. So I definitely should be doing something, but it seems like I should be doing something a little . . . witchier. Now that I am one.'

'Well, *this* witch is thinking of becoming an architect again,' Jane suggested, 'but you'd need a whole new degree for that.' Maeve pulled a face.

'I was thinking more like a wedding planner,' she countered. 'Aren't most of them witches? Wouldn't you almost have to be?'

'It would probably help,' Jane agreed, recalling the hundreds of angry phone calls that Lynne Doran had managed to cram into each day of planning Jane's own wedding.

'Or maybe I'll travel for a while, first,' Maeve mused on. 'I could come stay with you in Paris for a while, or I could rent a place in Florence and make you come hang out with me.'

'That sounds nice.' It was true, Jane realized: Paris sounded nice, and so did Florence, and so did New York. They all sounded perfectly fine . . . even if none of them sounded like home. *I guess I'll have to start from scratch,* she thought.

After a while, the funeral began to break up, and the Montagues took that as their cue to do the same with their picnic. 'I'll stay for a bit,' Jane insisted, kissing each of them on the cheek and resisting the multitude of invitations that they seemed to be inventing on the spot to keep her occupied. 'I'd like a little time to say goodbye once the crowd is gone.'

But her friends were much more efficient about their departure than the more 'official' mourners seemed inclined to be. A good ten minutes after Emer had blown one last kiss over her shoulder, Jane was still standing under the tree, watching Annette accept condolences from a seemingly endless line of well-dressed strangers. It must have felt so strange, Jane reflected, to someone who had grown up believing that she didn't belong to anyone's family.

'And now she has all of Manhattan clamouring to be part of hers,' she muttered to herself. It was only to be expected, of course: one of the city's richest and most powerful families had been decimated almost overnight, and its heiress was a virtual unknown. Nothing in Annette's childhood had prepared her for the coming onslaught, and Jane wondered how she would fare. *Malcolm would have stepped in to help her, even after everything,* Jane thought wistfully. *He would have cared more about what she needed than about what she had earned.*

'Part of her what?' a strangely accented voice asked curiously from the other side of her maple tree, and Jane jumped for the second time that afternoon.

She crooked her head around the grey-brown bark to see Penelope Lotuma, dressed all in black, with chunky jewellery dripping from every part of her body in honour of the occasion. 'I was just thinking out loud,' Jane told her, reluctant to share the specifics of her thoughts. Although Penelope had more than come through, Jane would never feel as comfortable and open with her as she did with the Montagues. Something about Penelope's appraising, ice-chip eyes kept her instinctively at a distance. 'I thought you'd be gone by now.'

Penelope gave her a sidelong glance from around the tree, her light blue eyes unfathomable. 'I find myself in a very unusual position, Blondie. I've got a flight in a few hours, but I did want to come talk to you, first.'

'I really appreciate the help you gave us,' Jane temporized. 'It made all the difference, having you here. I know Malcolm didn't get a chance to see that before he . . . well. I hope that he knows, anyway.' Something caught in her throat, and she swallowed hard.

Penelope's fingers moved absently to the necklace of hers that had always piqued Jane's curiosity: a thin, dark chain studded with clear glass bubbles. Her hands travelled to it at times that Jane felt fairly sure were significant, but she hadn't been able to sort out a pattern yet. 'You could ask him,' the little witch pointed out archly. 'I think you know how, by now.'

'Power makes a lot of things easier,' Jane agreed, but she knew she didn't need to add that she wouldn't be raising Malcolm from the dead. He deserved peace, and she would be strong enough to give it to him.

Penelope, however, clicked her tongue disapprovingly. 'I did expect you to try, especially once that pretty toy he gave you failed to pick up his scent. I never do get used to the moral ones. So I suppose I must tell you, then: if you had gone looking for your dead man, you would never have found him. He's one of mine now.' She spun one of the little glass bubbles around on its chain, and Jane felt her eyes go wide in horror.

'Malcolm,' she gasped. 'He's . . . in there? That's what he offered you?'

'They keep me safe,' Penelope said lovingly, stroking the dark chain. 'They come to no harm here, although they can't move on, of course, either. They keep unfriendly eyes from me and can fuel my power far beyond what I was born with, if I need it. Your man was willing to make that trade just to gamble on you having a better chance.'

Jane's breath caught in her throat. *His life really is over, then — he doesn't even get to start again in the next one.* Emer and Charlotte had been wrong: Malcolm wasn't a free soul, basking in the memory of Jane's love. He had traded that future away. Her eyes flickered to the massive polished-wood coffin, barely visible beneath a mountain of roses in all colours. *They'll lower it and he'll be . . .* She shuddered violently, suddenly freezing even in the early-summer warmth.

'I'm getting to the nicer part,' Penelope said dryly. 'I have all these souls, you see, because for my entire lifetime it has been rather dangerous to be a witch. In addition to all the normal squabbling and backstabbing that you might expect, there was something, someone out there killing us off one by one, decade after decade. And now there isn't.'

'Now there isn't,' Jane agreed mindlessly. Penelope shot her an exasperated look.

'So I find myself feeling something that I have never felt before, not once. I think you might call it "indebted."'

'Or "grateful"?' Jane guessed, raising an inquisitive eyebrow. Whatever she had been expecting from Penelope, that wasn't it.

The strange woman laughed. 'Gratitude is foolishness. However, the fact remains that I obtained your lover's soul to protect myself from the very thing you used my services to go out and kill. Maybe it turns out now that I don't need *quite* so many souls to stay safe.'

Belatedly, Jane remembered the strange glowing thing that had left Malcolm's body after Annette had cut him down. She hadn't thought about it until now, but it was clear: she had watched his soul fly toward Penelope's bauble. 'Not *quite*?'

Penelope smiled, twisting the glass between her short, dark fingers. 'I could spare one. If you want it.'

'If I—' Was she supposed to start a necklace of her own? Keep Malcolm's soul on a shelf somewhere? The thought made her stomach churn sickly; a soul was no ornament. And even Penelope – who wore them herself – must know that. 'You mean, if I want him to move on, into the afterlife. If I want you to let him go.'

'That's not what happens if I break the glass.' Penelope fell silent again, but this time Jane was determined to wait her out. After a few moments, the strange witch went on. 'He died, and he left his body. A place was waiting in the Summerlands, a path laid out for him, but he signed a contract and so he turned a different way. That path is only offered once in a lifetime, so to see it again he'll have to die again.'

Jane couldn't contain her impatience anymore. 'To die again he'd have to live again, and souls are born into new bodies from the Summerlands, Emer says. So what, exactly, are you offering me?'

'The most that I can, Blondie. I open this, and your man finds a body. Not a new one, mind you: one that's on the verge of losing its own soul. One that fits him, more or less; one that suits his soul. But I can't guarantee that he'll be half as handsome as he was the first time around. I don't know if that makes a difference to you.'

'Of course it doesn't,' Jane snapped. 'But he'll be . . . him?'

'I doubt he'll remember much – at least at first.' Penelope shrugged. 'Bits of his last mortal self may still be attached to the soul, though. Some things might come back with time, or you could tell him if you want. I don't do this often enough to say for sure.'

'I could tell him,' Jane whispered, her gaze drifting to some point far away as her hand lifted to her stomach of its own accord. Annette had gotten yet another chance to turn her life around; didn't Malcolm deserve at least as much? If he could be the person he might have been all along, without his mother's malevolent influence . . . and if Jane could be there to see it . . . 'But how would I know who he was, then? If he's in some different body?'

Penelope smiled and twisted the glass bubble in an odd motion that Jane couldn't quite follow. As it came loose from the chain, Jane saw that it was set into an octagon of the same kind of dark metal that the chain was made of. It almost looked like a miniature crystal ball. Before she could ask anything else, Penelope's brown fingers closed over the glass, and it shattered between them.

In spite of herself, Jane cried out, drawing some curious looks from the nearest cluster of mourners. She quickly pulled a tissue out of her purse and held it over her face, trying to look funeral appropriate, and they turned back to their hushed conversation. When she peered out from behind her tissue again, Penelope was holding the little octagon out to her around the tree trunk.

'This will help,' the witch told her, dropping it into the hand that Jane numbly extended. 'It will miss its former occupant, and it will pull toward him like a magnet. If you want to find him, then hold it in your hand and let it lead you. Good luck, Blondie.'

Penelope stalked away across the grass, hitching her black skirts up a little to keep them from the dew. Jane stared after the peculiar woman for a moment, then let her eyes return to the metal octagon in her hand.

A lively debate raged in her head, but her heart knew that it was all just noise. Her free hand hovered protectively over her stomach again, telling her everything that she needed to know about what had to happen next. The trinket was pulling ever so slightly west, and so west she would go. She would find Malcolm and tell him about their past, and then they would tell each other about their future.